DN -A95   lot 2002

W9-AVZ-395

Seductive Surrender

She lay naked against the darkness of his cloak. For a breathless moment the Falcon's shimmering silver gaze roamed freely over her, taking in the golden length of curls that fanned out over the cloak and twined about her lovely shoulders.

"From the first moment I looked upon you, my heart, I have thought of little besides this moment." He drew a ragged breath. "You are all that any man could desire."

Kellie felt her body melting from within. This man who had risked so much to save her, these strong arms holding her, and his lips so teasing and tempting—these were all that mattered. She was beyond the point of turning back. All that mattered was the Falcon.

His lips captured hers, the kiss so deep it seemed to touch their very souls.

THE BEST IN HISTORICAL ROMANCES

TIME-KEPT PROMISES   (2422, $3.95)
by Constance O'Day Flannery

Sean O'Mara froze when he saw his wife Christina standing before him. She had vanished and the news had been written about in all of the papers—he had even been charged with her murder! But now he had living proof of his innocence, and Sean was not about to let her get away. No matter that the woman was claiming to be someone named Kristine; she still caused his blood to boil.

PASSION'S PRISONER   (2573, $3.95)
by Casey Stewart

When Cassandra Lansing put on men's clothing and entered the Rawlings saloon she didn't expect to lose anything—in fact she was sure that she would win back her prized horse Rapscallion that her grandfather lost in a card game. She almost got a smug satisfaction at the thought of fooling the gamblers into believing that she was a man. But once she caught a glimpse of the virile Josh Rawlings, Cassandra wanted to be the woman in his embrace!

ANGEL HEART   (2426, $3.95)
by Victoria Thompson

Ever since Angelica's father died, Harlan Snyder had been angling to get his hands on her ranch, the Diamond R. And now, just when she had an important government contract to fulfill, she couldn't find a single cowhand to hire—all because of Snyder's threats. It was only a matter of time before the legendary gunfighter Kid Collins turned up on her doorstep, badly wounded. Angelica assessed his firmly muscled physique and stared into his startling blue eyes. Beneath all that blood and dirt he was the handsomest man she had ever seen, and the one person who could help beat Snyder at his own game.

Available wherever paperbacks are sold, or order direct from the Publisher. Send cover price plus 50¢ per copy for mailing and handling to Zebra Books, Dept. 3265, 475 Park Avenue South, New York, N.Y. 10016. Residents of New York, New Jersey and Pennsylvania must include sales tax. DO NOT SEND CASH.

MIDNIGHT BRIDE

KATHLEEN DRYMON

ZEBRA BOOKS
KENSINGTON PUBLISHING CORP.

To the ladies of romance's very own
Falcon—Ron Hickman—
and his beautiful Rose, Alice Mydock.
Love you both,
Kathleen

ZEBRA BOOKS

are published by

Kensington Publishing Corp.
475 Park Avenue South
New York, NY 10016

First printing: January, 1991

Printed in the United States of America

Prologue

"Pursue them!" Captain Sutterfield's voice boomed out, and the *Golden Rover,* a British naval vessel under full sail, set out after its prey.

"We cannot go too close to the coastline, Captain. The tide is out; we could run aground!" The first lieutenant addressed the captain, not wishing to provoke his anger, but feeling it his duty to advise him of the danger of approaching the South Carolina coast.

"We British are not a cowardly lot, man. I gave an order, and even if that brigand sails that rebel tub into the bowels of hell, we shall be close behind. We may not have another chance like this!" Captain Burgess Sutterfield was not to be reasoned with. His one thought was to capture the band of smugglers and their blackguard leader known as the Falcon, no matter the cost.

"Yes, sir," Lieutenant Bishop responded, giving the orders to head straight for the coastline and ready the cannons to fire.

As the *Golden Rover* drew closer to land, the full

outline of the Falcon's ship could be seen through the haze of fog that had settled over the sea. "They thought to lose us by going toward land," Captain Sutterfield shouted to his officers, who were at the ready to obey his command. "By God, their plan will not stop us! We'll give these smugglers something every traitor among them will not soon be forgetting!"

Anticipating the fulfillment of their captain's oath, the soldiers standing at attention along the deck of the *Golden Rover* stared across the sea in amazement as the rebel ship appeared suddenly to stop in the midst of the fog. "They think we cannot see them," said Captain Sutterfield. "Get closer, by God, and we shall blow their mangy hides and their ship full of smuggled goods from the sea once and for all!" Burgess Sutterfield looked toward the Falcon's ship with a feral gleam in his eyes. The Falcon had outwitted him on more than one occasion, but this day, he swore to himself, he would see the brigand and his followers hanging from the tallest mast of the *Golden Rover*. He had them now in the palm of his hand—he could almost taste the victory that would be his and his alone for capturing the crafty foe of the Crown.

"We cannot go much farther, Captain!" the helmsman shouted across the deck, bringing Captain Sutterfield out of his reflections. "The sea here is too shallow."

"Lieutenant Bishop, have that man taken below at

6

once! He shall be flogged at sunrise for his insubordination!"

All those aboard the *Golden Rover* heard the captain's orders and witnessed the helmsman being led below ship and another officer appointed to take his place—a man determined not to share his mate's fate. If the captain issued an order to ground the ship, that was exactly what he would do.

"We have that cunning traitor now, Lieutenant Bishop. We have him right in our grasp." The Captain chuckled confidently at the success of his pursuit.

The *Golden Rover* moved at full speed, rapidly narrowing the distance between it and the rebel ship, but then, with a jolt that sent all of the officers toppling to the deck, the British ship ran aground.

Still in the depths of his insane reverie, Captain Sutterfield held tightly to the railing and cursed aloud. He frantically addressed the helmsman. "Push her forward, man! It cannot be so shallow here that we cannot force our way through this sand. That damn rebel ship made it, we can, too!"

"Sir, the rebel ship carries no cannons. We outweigh it by more than double!" the helmsman shouted, trying his best to somehow force the *Golden Rover* out of the thick sand.

"I want no excuses!" Captain Sutterfield shouted loudly in his fit of temper. "I want that damn rebel ship boarded and those traitors brought to justice!"

As everyone on the *Golden Rover* watched, the

7

smuggler's ship began to move slowly away from the Charleston coastline, and for the first time since the British ship's approach, the vessel seemed to come alive with activity. Shouting could be heard as the rebels began to stir about, and suddenly a dark figure appeared on deck. He was clad entirely in black, a cloaked giant of a man, and with a deep-throated laugh and a smart salute toward the captain of the *Golden Rover,* he captained his own ship off into the looming fog.

"You will pay, Falcon," Captain Sutterfield snarled under his breath. "And you will pay dearly. You can run this night, but one day soon you will have no place to flee to." He punctuated his words by beating his fists against the wood railing of the *Golden Rover.*

Chapter One

Charleston, 1766.

"Miss Kellie, Miss Kellie! You had best come, and be quick! The master done got himself into one of his fits!" A large black woman burst through the door of the small cabin, her dark eyes peering around the single room until they set upon the slim, blond young woman sitting next to a small boy on a quilted pallet.

"What is it now, Honey? What is wrong with Father?" The young woman lowered the boy's head back upon the pallet after she finished spooning the amber medicine between his lips. She handed the small bottle and spoon to a young black woman who sat against the wall of the cabin waiting patiently for any sign that she could be of help.

"Jerome done come from town with the news that young master Vern got hisself thrown into the guardhouse!" The black woman was panting, her bosom heaving with exertion. She had run all the way from the main house of Moss Rose to the cabins behind the stables.

"In the *guardhouse?*" the young woman exclaimed shrilly, at once on her feet and starting for the door. "What did Jerome say Vern had done to be thrown into such a place?" The first thing that passed through Kellie's mind was that her hotheaded cousin had gotten into a fight with one of the British soldiers, who seemed to be everywhere nowadays.

"I don't reckon I heard. As soon as Jerome told master Charles that young master Vern had been arrested, he called for me to come and fetch you quick. I be fearing that the master be having another one of his collapsing fits. He just be sitting there on the front porch and beating his cane on the floor."

As the young woman rushed out of the cabin, she remembered the little boy she had been attending to. "Lucy, see to it that Adam gets another spoon of medicine before dark. His fever should break soon, and I will come back and see him as soon as I am able."

"Yes, ma'am, I do just as you be saying."

With Honey following, Kellie hurried to the large estate-house. Her thoughts were in an uproar as she pictured her cousin behind bars. *As if she did not have enough to contend with here at Moss Rose!* she thought. Now she had to confront the reality of her cousin being imprisoned.

Charles McBride was sitting in his wheelchair on the front veranda of the large, two-story brick house when Kellie came around from the back. His gray hair was in disarray and his face a beet red. He held his oak cane in nervous irritation, beating a rapid tattoo upon the wood flooring of the porch.

"What has happened, Father?" Kellie rushed up the front steps, her hands clutching the folds of her skirts.

"Those damn British have confiscated your cousin's ship and placed him in the guardhouse. This is an *outrage* to our family and our name. I will have someone's head for such an injustice!"

"But why on earth would the British arrest Vern?" In her rush to the house, wisps of her blond hair had escaped its ribbon, and with her emerald eyes flashing, the young girl looked for all the world as though she, too, were ready for vengeance.

"That is why I sent for you, girl. You know that Jerome is good for nothing more than running errands and posting a letter at the tavern. He did not wait to find out any details about your cousin's arrest. As soon as he heard that John Vern had been arrested, he hightailed it back to Moss Rose with the news."

"I am sure that it is a simple mistake. We all know that Vern would never do anything that would result in his arrest." The young woman patted her father's hand. "I will only take a minute to change and then I'll go to town and find out what is going on." Kellie glanced down at the somber gown she had donned that morning.

11

"Damn these useless legs," Charles McBride ranted. "If I could go instead of you, my girl, I would, in a minute. But I fear that all I can do is send Jerome with you."

"Things will work out fine, Father. I will handle everything." *As I have for some time,* she added privately—Kellie had been somewhat in charge at Moss Rose ever since a riding accident had left her father wheelchair-bound. Kellie turned toward Honey and told her to lay out a gown, and without another word, she started through the house and up the stairs, her hands already moving to the long row of buttons at her back. With the countryside in a state of turmoil and everyone taking sides over the British Crown, she knew deep down that it might not be easy to rescue her cousin.

"Hurry, Honey, the green velvet will do." She turned her back to the black house servant who finished with the buttons. "No, Honey, I will not have time to change my petticoats. What I have on now will just have to do." She pulled off the gown and, as the servant began to pull out the pale green petticoats that went with the gown, she brushed her aside.

"Now, Miss Kellie, ye can't be a'traipsing about the whole of Charleston without the proper clothes on." The black woman scolded, but helped her to pull the green velvet over her head and settle it properly about her hips. She knew that it would do little good to argue with her young mistress. Kellie

Dawn McBride was in fact much like her father, given to her own thoughts and bound to get her way no matter the circumstances.

"No one is going to be seeing what is under my gown, Honey. Now please get my shoes." Kellie went to her dressing table and began brushing out her long, golden curls. She pulled the mass of tresses back with a matching green velvet ribbon.

Placing the shoes near the dressing table, Honey moved to the bedchamber door. "I be only a few minutes, Miss Kellie," she said. "I got's to fetch a clean apron and a hat and I be ready to go along."

Kellie heaved a sigh as she pulled on the slippers. "I am only taking Jerome with me, Honey. I do not have time to wait for you." The girl knew that the elder house servant would only be in her way. She had no idea what she would have to do to see her cousin free.

Stopping in her tracks, Honey spun about, her dark eyes widening and her large head shaking in the negative. "No, ma'am, no, ma'am. Ya ain't about to go to town without me at yer side. I done heard all the stories of what's been goin' on nowadays in Charleston. Mabel, the Stuarts' cook told me. Why, she be saying that Charleston ain't a fitting place for a lady these days. The redcoats are carousing openly with the ladies of the streets and there ain't none to put a stop to their actions."

Kellie did not point out that she often went into Charleston without a chaperon at her side. And she had also heard the stories about the British soldiers. They did indulge, with the women of Charleston who were accustomed to giving their favors away. She had not heard of any decent women being set upon. "I do not have time to argue with you now, Honey. If I am to help Vern, I must hurry. There is no telling what conditions exist in that guardhouse."

"Yes, ma'am, I be knowing all of that, but I can't be allowing you to be going alone."

"Oh, drat, Honey. I am *not* going to town on a social call. I can take care of myself!" With this the young woman stepped past her servant and hurried down the stairs.

"I done told yer pappy over and over that he should keep a tighter rein on you. Yer gonna find yerself in trouble one of these days," Honey called after her young mistress.

With a quick kiss on her father's forehead and the reassurance that he was not to worry, she would handle everything, Kellie was helped into the McBride carriage and driven down the long drive of Moss Rose.

Moss Rose was only a few miles out of town, and in a fevered state of agitation Kellie willed Jerome to drive at a quicker pace. She and her cousin had always been the closest of friends. Even in early childhood they had shared their thoughts and secrets. When Vern had come to live at Moss Rose when her father became disabled, they had grown even closer; though these days Vern spent little time on the estate, claiming that his ship and business matters kept him away. Still, they kept in constant touch. All Kellie could think of now was the fact that her cousin was alone and in the guardhouse.

Barely waiting for the carriage to come to a halt upon their arrival, Kellie climbed down from the carriage without the aid of Jerome and stepped to the wooden sidewalk in front of the brick guardhouse. She kept her head high as several of the townspeople looked her way.

With a mounting rage at the high-handedness with which the British had dared incarcerate her cousin, Kellie marched through the front door. As she slammed the door behind her, a middle-aged, thin, bespectacled man rose to his feet from behind his desk. Glimpsing the visitor, a small, slanted smile settled about his thin lips. "Why, Mistress McBride, what brings you to such lowly surroundings?" His tone was haughty and his manner full of disdain as he swept his arms wide to indicate the dim interior of the front room of the guardhouse.

Bracing herself for the inevitable confrontation, Kellie looked the man straight in the eye. "I have come for my cousin, Mr. Beeking. I demand his release this very moment!" Kellie McBride was not one to beat around the bush and her mind was no different now as she stood before the pompous, lackluster moneygrubber, who had somehow found himself in a position of power.

"Then I am afraid that you have embarked upon

15

a useless mission, mistress." Elroy Beeking still wore the same smile, but now his red, watery eyes went over the attractive figure and beautiful features of the woman before him. "Your cousin has been accused of smuggling and, as everyone knows, this is no small offense."

"Smuggling!" Kellie was aghast at such an accusation. "Why, this charge is outrageous! My cousin is no more a smuggler than you or I."

"Well, I have no say in the matter one way or the other. He was accused. Until Governor Mansfield arrives in a few days, I, as acting governor, had no alternative except to send out officers to arrest your cousin and to confiscate his ship."

"You dared to take his ship?" She remembered her father had mentioned this fact but at the time it had not fully penetrated her mind. As she looked at Elroy Beeking, she began to glimpse the full scope of her kin's position.

"Throughout all of the colonies, everyone knows that violators of the British commercial laws have to answer for their crimes," the man spouted out in one breath that caused his thin chest to swell.

"Then you have indeed made a most serious mistake, sir. My father has many friends in Charleston and they will not take kindly to such treatment of his sister's son. If I were you, I would seriously reconsider this arrest."

Thinking over her words very carefully, Elroy Beeking saw some truth to what she was saying. He knew full well that the planters in Charleston did indeed hold much power about the countryside these days, and Charles McBride was well known throughout the colonies. But he held his duty dear, for he had gained many added coins for his purse with this simple job of controlling the harbor and collecting the taxes from the colonists. He had come from London to the colonies with the express purpose of refurbishing his fortune. Now that he was to be replaced by the new governor, he could return to the mother country. His only desire was for smooth sailing. But as he looked at the headstrong, beautiful young woman before him, his mind began to seize upon an ingenious scheme. "And what if you are right, mistress? What gain could there be for me in looking the other way in your kin's dubious affairs?"

At last, Kellie thought. Everyone in Charleston knew of Elroy Beeking's love of gold. She now saw her chance to gain her cousin's release. Her father certainly would not object if she were to offer gold for Vern's freedom. "Set your price, Mr. Beeking," she stated quietly.

"I leave for London at the end of the month." His smile vanished and a new light filled his eyes. "I would take with me a wife," he stated boldly.

Kellie stared at the man, uncomprehending. Did he mean that he wished her to play matchmaker for him, perhaps with one of Charleston's eligible young ladies?

17

"My price is you, mistress. Agree to wed me and sail with me to England and your cousin will be released and his ship returned to him. I will have all charges dropped."

Kellie looked at the man with disbelief.

"As you say, mistress, your family has many friends, and with your wealth we could settle quite comfortably at my family's home in England." The more Elroy talked, the better he liked the scheme. He knew well that the planters were all condemning the Crown for their high taxes, but he also knew that Charles McBride was a shrewd businessman who had avoided the financial troubles that many of the other planters in the colonies were experiencing. There would be a sizable dowry to go with Kellie McBride when she married, and at this moment he was determined that he would be the one to gain it. The whole of London would be envious of him when he stepped off the ship with such a beauty upon his arm, and with all that she would bring to him, he could perhaps even purchase himself a title from the Crown. He believed this to be possible, given the shortage of money in London, and the Crown loudly demanding more gold. With Kellie McBride at his side, no one would ever again look down their noses at the second son of Lawrence Beeking.

Kellie tried to maintain her composure. Squaring her shoulders and looking the man straight in the eye, she stated, "No! I am afraid that I will have to refuse you, Mr. Beeking. I am not ready to wed *anyone,* nor do I have any desire to go to England. My home is here in Charleston, at Moss Rose."

Elroy Beeking assumed a businesslike demeanor. "Of course you shall have a short time before we wed. I am a patient man and will be willing to postpone my leave-taking for a short while. I know of your father's condition and realize that there will be much that will have to be arranged." He had met Charles McBride on occasion and knew that the man was a cripple and had to depend upon others for his simplest needs. He had also heard rumors that the young woman before him ran Moss Rose herself, as though she were a son and not the only daughter of a rich planter. But this, he reasoned, would change when she became his bride. He would quickly take full control of the McBride holdings and, after insuring that the old man would be taken care of by servants of his own choosing, he and his new wife would return to England.

"It is neither time nor my father's condition, Mr. Beeking, that prompts my refusal." Kellie took a deep breath, remembering that her cousin's very life depended upon this man's whim. "It is that I do not know you, sir, nor do I love you. I am not ready to marry any man at this time of my life." She kept a soft edge to her voice as she remembered her genteel upbringing, and tried to put him off in the most civil manner she could. After all, she did have experience with the subject. She had been proposed to by half a dozen young men already, but none had stirred the deep inner passions of her heart. Most, she had admitted, had been more eager for her family's wealth than for herself, and being a woman of strong convictions, she was adamant about his one subject: She would marry only for love, and if this love never came to her, she would be satisfied with her lot, taking care of her father and Moss Rose.

"Love has little to do with marriage, my dear. We shall call our union a . . . *merger* of sorts." Yes indeed, Elroy Beeking liked the sound of that. As he looked at her petal-soft lips and flashing emerald eyes he knew that there would be more advantages to marrying this woman than the fact that she would bring with her the McBride wealth.

"There shall be no *mergers,* of any fashion, between you and me, Mr. Beeking. I desire only the release of my cousin. If your price is in gold, I shall see that you get the required amount before the day is through; anything else, I cannot grant you." Her tone became chilling as she glared at the odious man.

"Then there is little that I can do for you, Mistress McBride. As a servant to the Crown, unlike much of the rabble hereabouts in the colonies, I have my duty to uphold!" Elroy Beeking restrained himself from shouting by speaking through clenched teeth. His pride and his honor were being stepped on by a bit of fluff who thought herself so much better than he. It was always thus, he fumed inwardly. These planters in their rich clothes, riding in their fine carriages and holding lavish parties that he was never invited to, thought themselves as high lords of the colonies, and this young woman and her family were the worst sort. But as he glared at her he swore to himself that he would make her rue the day she had shunned him. In the end he would have her! And on that day, she would find herself falling to her knees and begging his forgiveness for rejecting his initial proposal.

"I would see my cousin now, Mr. Beeking." Kellie knew that she dared much with such a request. But she would not be blackmailed into marriage, no matter the threat to her cousin's freedom. She would have to find another way to get Vern out of the guardhouse.

"For all the good it will do you, Mistress McBride, you may see this smuggler who is your kin." Elroy Beeking's first thought was to refuse her request, his anger was so high, but he reasoned with himself that perhaps it would suit his purpose if she were to see her precious cousin behind the guardhouse bars.

Stepping aside, Kellie held her breath as Elroy Beeking opened the door to the back of the guardhouse and motioned her to enter.

"You have only a few minutes, mistress. I have business to attend to and cannot be delayed."

With a slight nod of her head, Kellie stepped into the guardhouse, her green eyes adjusting to the dim-ness as she looked through the bars and found the relaxed form of her cousin. She gasped at the foul conditions of the place as she hurried to the bare cell. "Vern, it is I," she called, oblivious to Elroy Beeking's contemptuous glare from the door before he turned away.

"You should not have come here, my sweet pet." John Vern Fielding rose to his feet, his tall, muscular form moving quickly to the bars of the cell. He took her hands into his own and squeezed tightly.

"What on earth is happening, Vern? Why have you been arrested and your ship taken?"

"Someone has accused me of smuggling, dear cousin," was all he replied.

"But why? Who would dare accuse you of such activity?"

"It matters little now. I imagine that I will soon find myself going to Halifax to face a British judge who will set my fate."

"What can I do?" Tears sparkled in Kellie's jade eyes. "Father is beside himself with worry, and I am at a loss as to what to do." She felt desperate as she thought of what his future could hold if his case were to come to trial. *Trial;* she scorned the word inwardly. It would be no trial—a British magistrate would simply judge him guilty. The British were in need of more ships, and his would be an easy one for the Crown to gain.

A new light filled his deep blue eyes as Vern looked at his beautiful cousin. "There is one thing you can do for me, Kellie."

"Tell me. I will do whatever I can." Her own thoughts envisioned her cousin's escape. She wondered what part she would play in such an escapade.

"Go to Lord Savage and tell him of my plight." Vern again squeezed her hand.

At first Kellie thought she had misunderstood him. "You wish me to go to Lord Blakely Savage? Whatever will such a one as *he* be able to do for you? He is not interested in us, his only concerns are with clothes and fancy furnishings for that mansion of his!"

"Just do this one thing for me, sweet. Perhaps he will be able to help." Vern knew her distaste for the man in question, but still he insisted.

"But Vern, he will do no more than bemoan the fact that you have been accused of going against the Crown. Why, only the other day when I came to town with Honey, he was strutting down the sidewalk as though the town offended his delicate sensibilities! I see no reason to waste time by telling him of your troubles. Perhaps I should seek out a lawyer."

"Nay, the lawyers of this town are no better than Elroy Beeking. They are paid by the Crown and look only to England's interests. You must promise me, Kellie, that you will go to Lord Savage and tell him of my circumstances. Perhaps he can persuade our Mr. Beeking to be lenient."

"I, for one, seriously doubt that," Kellie huffed.

How could such a fop as Blakely Savage help them now? she thought.

"Go now, dear cuz. I do not wish you to be in this hellhole any longer than necessary." He released her hand. His determined manner left her little option than to do as he requested.

"I will go to Savage Hall, but, I dare say, I think the whole matter pointless. I would much rather we set about a plan of rescue. Perhaps I could bring in some of the field hands and we could *force* Mr. Beeking to release you."

"Would you have Moss Rose confiscated also?" Vern cautioned her.

Such an idea sobered Kellie. Moss Rose had belonged to her grandfather, and if the McBrides were to lose even an inch of the land, it would put her father in his grave. "You are right, as usual," she capitulated. "But I wish there were some other way . . ."

"Perhaps all is not lost yet, sweet cuz. Go to Savage and tell him that I await him here." Kellie saw no other way to dissuade her cousin, and, reasoning that anything was worth the chance, she left the guardhouse, ordering Jerome to make haste for Savage Hall.

Clutching her hands tightly in her lap, Kellie fumed inwardly that she had been forced into confronting Blakely Savage. The irksome dandy would probably sigh and then yawn as though the news of Vern's plight bored him to death.

Savage Hall lay along the coast, not far from Charleston, and was the neighboring property to Moss Rose. Rumor had it that Emory Savage, who had lived at Savage Hall a few years past, had been a recluse. It was not long after reports had circulated that he had died aboard a British ship, that Blakely Savage had taken up residence at Savage Hall.

As Jerome directed the McBride carriage toward the towering stone building, Kellie felt a chill run the length of her backbone.

The house was more like a fortress. The glint of cool gray stone rose up along the coastline, stark against the clear blue sky. A rush of turbulent waves broke repeatedly against the cliffs. Kellie swallowed nervously; she had little choice but to carry out Vern's instructions.

It was some moments after Kellie had employed the golden lion's-head knocker that a small, dark-clothed, bent figure of a man silently opened the door a crack and peered out. His dark, piercing eyes looked questioningly at the woman standing on the front step. Clearing her throat, Kellie stammered out her request to see Lord Savage.

Showing some reluctance to welcome her into the cool, dim interior of the house, the little man at last stepped aside and motioned her into the foyer. "Wait in the parlor," he instructed, and without another word disappeared down a maze of hallways.

Kellie hesitatingly entered the first room on her

right, surprised indeed by the loveliness of the front parlor. The room was large, airy, and bright. Cream, gold, and peach were artfully blended to make a charming color scheme.

Not daring to take a seat or in any way make herself at home, Kellie circled the room, admiring the ivory miniature statues on a long gleaming table. Glimpsing a collection of crystal figurines, she was hard put not to devour their beauty.

To think that one such as Lord Blakely Savage was the owner of such rare pieces of craftmanship! She would have reached out to caress the smooth-cut glass, but was brought up short by the clearing of a throat.

"You wished to see me, madam?" The high, whining voice of Blakely Savage filled her ears as the man in scarlet and yellow satin strutted into the parlor.

With distaste, Kellie took in his dress in a single glance. The tresses of his powdered and curled wig rested upon the scarlet padded shoulders of his jacket. His silk ruffled blouse was shot through with artfully stitched threads of yellow silk. The effect was overwhelming to the eyes; for a moment Kellie felt dizzy. Slowly she nodded her head as her hand held onto the back of a chair for support. "If you have a moment, my lord, I have brought a message from my cousin, John Vern Fielding." She looked at his powdered face and, wishing not to remain in his presence any longer than necessary, she prepared herself to come right to the point.

"Then, why do we not have a seat and make ourselves comfortable? Would you care for a glass of sherry, or perhaps some of my fine madeira?" Lord Savage stepped around her and sat in a wing-back chair across from the settee. He crossed his stockinged legs with great aplomb and settled himself fussingly.

Kellie crossed to the settee and sat down gingerly, making sure that she was at the opposite end of the sofa rather than directly across from him. "I am afraid that I have little time and do not wish to impose upon your graciousness, my lord," she stated. She was revolted by the gaudy colors of his garments and his pale, pasty features.

"Then perhaps you would care to tell me what has brought you to Savage Hall this fine day?" His gaze held her seekingly.

"My cousin is at this very moment being detained in the guardhouse. His ship has been taken by the British. He has been unjustly accused."

"Unjustly accused? How so, madam? What is this cousin of yours accused of?" Lord Savage seemed unable to speak without gesturing lavishly with his hands.

"Someone has claimed that my cousin is a smuggler. This is absurd, of course. He is a businessman. He ships goods from the colonies to London. He is an honest man."

The man she addressed was silent.

"In truth, sir, I hold no reasoning with my cousin's insistence that I appeal to you on his behalf. But I did promise him that I would come to you at once."

For several moments Blakely Savage did not respond. He sat back in his chair, and appeared not to have listened to her story. His pale gray eyes studied her. "Then, by all means," he said at last, "if this cousin of yours has such strong faith in my abilities, we must see what can be done for him."

Kellie was taken aback. "You mean that you will help Vern?" Perhaps her cousin had been wise, she thought, in instructing her to come to Lord Savage, as surprised as she was to admit it. Had she misjudged the man?

"Well, now, I dare say I will be able to do some good on your cousin's behalf. Though of course the Crown's interests must be upheld."

He had raised Kellie's hopes and then dashed them in the same breath. She jumped to her feet. "The Crown and all of England can go to tarnation, for all I care. My only concern is that my cousin be freed from that dreadful guardhouse!" Kellie surprised herself with her outburst—she was unaccustomed to denouncing the Crown.

Instantly Lord Savage brought his hand up to cover his mouth, as a smile came over his lips. "Let us not get in a huff, madam. We shall see what can be done for this smuggler cousin of yours." Blakely Savage slowly rose to his full height and with a hand at her elbow steered Kellie toward the parlor door.

For an instant, Kellie glimpsed Lord Savage's smile and the crazed notion passed her mind that he was rather handsome. His eyes held a strange light almost of admiration . . . but as quickly as these thoughts arose, they were quelled. With the contact of his hand upon her arm, she thought with ire of what he had called her cousin. "I will have you know this instant, Lord Savage, my cousin is *not* a smuggler. He is a law-abiding shipmaster."

"As is always the case in these situations, madam, the family members are the last to know." They reached the foyer and he awaited his manservant to fetch his gloves and a bright scarlet hat.

Kellie watched him primping before the full-length mirror in the foyer, but seeing little reason to talk with him further, she kept her thoughts to herself. Let him say whatever he wished! As long as he helped secure Vern's release, she cared little for his opinion.

"Would you care to ride with me in my carriage, madam?" he asked as they were at last able to leave the house.

With a quick shake of her head, Kellie denied his request. She was determined that none in town would see her sitting in Lord Savage's gilded carriage appearing to enjoy the company of the over-dressed popinjay. "My own carriage is waiting," she added politely. After all, if he were truly able to help her cousin, she must not appear rude.

"As you wish, my lady," he responded, as his vehicle and team of matching horses were brought around to the front of the house.

With some relief, Kellie settled her skirts about her on the comfortable seat of her father's carriage, happy for the time away from Lord Savage.

As her carriage pulled up in front of the guardhouse, Kellie saw that a small group of men had gathered outside the front door. Kellie heard shouting from within the guardhouse, and the men outside were engaged in what appeared to be a heated exchange. Alighting with the aid of Jerome, Kellie questioned one of the gentlemen.

"It be the tavern keeper, mistress. The redcoats brought him to the guardhouse for failing to pay his taxes."

Kellie was shocked. She had known the Darring family for years. In fact, Marie Darring, the tavern keeper's daughter, was one of her closest friends. Hearing the commotion inside, she could well imagine the fight that the burly Samuel Darring was putting up in the face of British attempts to restrain him. "What are they going to do with him?" she questioned the man.

"The redcoats be closing old Samuel's tavern down right this moment, mistress. Until he pays the tax for the license that is owed, they'll not release him."

At this remark, several of the men standing about the guardhouse began to grumble about the unfairness of such tyranny. One man exclaimed that the only pleasure the British had left the colonists was the right to spend their few hard-earned coins on a mug of ale, and now they were going to interfere even in this activity.

Before Kellie could express her own feelings about Samuel Darring's arrest, Blakely Savage, whose carriage had pulled up after hers, took hold of her arm. "Let us see to your cousin before you take on any more causes, madam." It took a moment for her to recognize his voice; it sounded deeper than usual as he spoke next to her ear.

Being led into the front room of the guardhouse, Kellie witnessed mass confusion there as a half dozen British soldiers held the straining form of Samuel Darring. The large, boisterous man was cursing and yelling for all he was worth at those who would dare treat him in such a highhanded manner.

"It be unfair, I say, for a poor man trying to support his family to have to pay such an *outrageous* amount of tax!" the large tavern keeper shouted at Elroy Beeking.

"I did not set the price of twenty shillings for your license, but as any loyal citizen you must conform as others and obey the Crown," Elroy Beeking rejoined, while keeping himself on the opposite side of his desk and out of reach of the bulging, straining muscles of his prisoner.

"Ye can't be keeping me here, ye bloody blackguards. Who will be running me tavern if I be locked up behind bars?"

"That is also not my problem," came the answer. "You know the law. If you do not pay your taxes, you cannot stay in business. Your tavern is to be closed until your license is renewed." Elroy Beeking himself was not bothered in the least by the closing of the tavern; he was not one to frequent places with those he considered beneath him. He prided himself on his fine wine cellar and upon occasion, when he indulged, he did so in the privacy of his own home.

"Ye damn cutthroats!" the accused shouted about the room. "Ye can't be shutting down me tavern. Me wife and family will not be able to tend to things if they be having no income."

"Then pay your taxes, my good man!" Elroy Beeking gestured to the soldiers, and they dragged the yelling Samuel Darring through the door leading to the cells.

As the door slammed shut behind the soldiers and the room quieted, Elroy Beeking's attention was drawn toward Kellie McBride and Blakely Savage. Holding Kellie in a possessive yet angry stare, he addressed her companion. "Good day to you, Lord Savage. Can I be of some help?"

"Why, I do believe so, my good man," Lord Savage answered somewhat shrilly. "I have been informed that you have detained a young man by the name of John Vern Fielding here in your fine guardhouse."

Elroy Beeking glared at Kellie. "Why, yes, he is here, sir. He was accused of smuggling. There was little to do but arrest him."

"I fully understand, Master Beeking; smuggling is a nasty business. But I believe that we have a slight problem." Lord Savage plunked himself down nonchalantly in the chair before the desk, intent thereupon to straighten out his clothing and make sure that none of his garments was wrinkled.

"What problem is that, sir?" Elroy Beeking knew full well that Blakely Savage held a title and much influence, and Beeking was always more than willing to help anyone who might in the future help him; attempting to conceal his ire, he bestowed a smile upon the man before him.

"The charges must be dropped this very moment, my good sir," Savage drawled. As Elroy Beeking started to argue the point, he held up his hand. "I can attest to young Fielding's innocence in the matter. You see, your prisoner has been working for me the last several months. His ship goes to the port of London on a regular basis with its hull full of rice and cotton. Nothing aboard is smuggled or illegal. Whoever your accuser is, I dare say, he has made a mistake."

Both Kellie and Elroy Beeking looked wide-eyed at Lord Savage, Kellie not believing her ears that such a man would manage so effortlessly to tell an outright lie. Elroy Beeking, not wishing to set himself against Lord Savage, but loath to turn John Vern Fielding free, hesitated before he spoke. "I . . . I had thought that we would let the new governor tend to this affair, my lord." He sat down behind his desk, his fingers making a dull thudding on the desktop.

"I am afraid that will not do, my good sir," Blakely Savage rejoined. As Elroy Beeking looked across the desk he glimpsed a hardness about the lips and eyes of a man to whom in the past he had given little thought.

"What would you have me do?" Elroy Beeking asked.

"Release my man at once. After all, we cannot have the Crown's interests delayed any longer than necessary, now can we, my good man?"

Elroy Beeking knew that he was deeply enmeshed in a delicate situation, and as he sat and contemplated what would best benefit himself, his bespectacled eyes went from Lord Savage to Kellie McBride. Was it only an hour or so ago that he had thought he had ensnared the lovely enchantress in a fine web of his own making? But as his eyes went back to Lord Savage, he knew that he must await another opportunity to gain the woman for his own. "What would you have me do then to the accuser, my lord? Arrest him, as is the law?"

"Nay, I am sure that this whole affair has been a terrible . . . misunderstanding. If you would but write the accuser's name down upon a slip of paper,

I shall attend to the matter personally."

Having little choice but to comply, Elroy Beeking nodded his head. "I am truly sorry about this whole affair, my lord. Of course, given your testimony, Master Fielding cannot be a smuggler, and I shall have him released immediately." Before he got to his feet, he scribbled something upon a small piece of paper and pushed it across the desk toward Lord Savage.

With a quick glance at the name upon the paper, Blakely Savage tucked the note away in the folds of his scarlet satin jacket. Elroy Beeking left the room to attend to John Vern's release, and Blakely Savage looked directly at Kellie.

For a moment Kellie caught a glimpse of laughter in the gray eyes that locked with hers, but as quickly Lord Savage looked away. "Thank you so much, my lord. But are you sure that you should have made such statements to Mr. Beeking?"

"Do not worry yourself, madam. It is indeed a fact that your cousin has held some of my cargo in the bottom of his ship."

Before Kellie could question him further about this business between her cousin and himself, Elroy Beeking stepped into the front room with Vern at his side. Kellie ran across the room and flung herself upon her cousin, her features aglow as he hugged her against his chest.

"Thanks, sweet cuz, I knew that you could do it," he whispered into her sweet-smelling curls before releasing her.

With considerable aplomb and ceremony, Blakely Savage pulled himself from his chair. "Come, you two, it has been a terribly taxing day for all of us. I, for one, wish a warm brandy and my bed."

Vern chuckled to himself, and Kellie felt the deep rumbling from within the solid chest she leaned against. "Of course you are right, my lord." He grinned widely and then, tucking Kellie's arm within the crook of his own, he led her out into the sunshine.

Blakely Savage was close behind as the small group departed the guardhouse and Elroy Beeking. "John, I shall come out to Moss Rose for a visit tomorrow," the brightly bedecked lord called as Vern handed Kellie up into the carriage. Her cousin heard Kellie's groan of annoyance at the prospect of Lord Savage visiting their home.

"That will be fine, my lord. We shall be expecting you," Vern called back.

As Savage's carriage pulled away from the guardhouse and the driver quickly set about whipping the team up, Kellie turned on her cousin. "Why on earth did you tell him that?"

Vern grinned at her. "Lord Savage has just helped me out of a most uncomfortable situation, dear one. Would you have me be rude to him now?"

Kellie did not mince words. "I, too, thank him on your behalf, Vern, but to be forced to look upon his garish dress again! And would you not think that he would find himself a more appealing wig? The one he wears is so thick with powder and so long, down to his shoulders!"

Vern chuckled and patted her hand lovingly. "Have you not ever wondered what Lord Blakely Savage would look like beneath all of that fluff and finery, dear cuz?"

Kellie looked shocked at such a question as she pictured Blakely Savage without his colorful clothes and great wig. "To be sure, he would be a balding, fat toad even then," she stated.

Laughing with glee, Vern was barely able to catch his breath as he hugged Kellie close to his side. "You are a real treasure, my sweet cousin, a treasure indeed."

Chapter Two

"It would appear that good old Christopher Gadsden has gotten the countryside stirred up once again." The shrill voice of Blakely Savage cut the air as Charles McBride, his nephew, and their guest sat at their leisure on the front veranda of Moss Rose. Lord Savage, in his usual colorful attire, sat back comfortably in a wood rocker and scanned the paper in his hand. "It states here that he has incited the rabble into terrorizing the stamp masters, even going so far as to call for them to tar and feather our good British employees and to run them out of town. Upon my word, I hate to think what our country is coming to! These outlaws are bold enough to call themselves the Sons of Liberty."

"Would you truly expect any less, man?" Charles McBride responded, with evident emotion in his voice. "Does it not cut deeply to be forced to pay a stamp duty for the simplest of pleasures? Even that paper you are reading holds one of those damnable stamps. There are few these days who can afford to sit back, as you, my Lord, and read the news that not long ago was virtually free."

"But England has her needs, Charles." Blakely Savage's gray eyes held a lively light as he sipped at the warmed brandy that Honey had served to the gentlemen.

"England wishes to force the colonies into submission and to drain us of our very substance in order to fatten her own purse," Charles McBride retaliated, his green eyes becoming hard as he looked at the overdressed, self-indulgent guest sitting across from him.

"The planters have not been as harshly affected as the rest of the colonies, though," Savage offered as he laid the paper aside, plainly enjoying the discussion with the older man. At times his gaze moved to the silent John Vern as if to gauge his response to the conversation.

"We planters have not got it so easy, I assure you, my lord. By the time our crops are sent to London, they are so heavily taxed we receive only a small percentage of the profit. What is left is lavished out to the mercantile houses in bartered goods that are neither genteel nor well fashioned. Many of my best friends are so deeply in debt to these greedy London merchants that they are thinking of leaving the land they have sweated over as their fathers did before them."

Before any further discussion could take place, Charles McBride smiled with some pleasure as he stated, "Here comes my lovely daughter, gentlemen."

His two companions looked to see the fashionably dressed Kellie McBride, sitting atop a prancing sorrel stallion making its way across the grounds of Moss Rose toward the veranda where the men were gathered.

"Lovely, indeed," Lord Savage murmured. Directing his attentions to the beauty that had drawn closer, he called, "Good day to you, Mistress McBride." He stood and stepped to the rail of the porch, his gray eyes filled with admiration as they beheld the lovely image in royal blue.

Kellie simply nodded her head in his direction, taking in the purple and fuchsia of his outfit with a single glance. With a smile at Vern and one for her father, she started to dismount. "Henry has the field hands clearing the North pasture, Father. By the end of the month we should be ready to plant as we had planned." As she started up the steps, Blakely Savage, on surprisingly light feet, moved to the end of the porch and offered her his arm.

Kellie knew she could not politely refuse him, though she was loath to place her hand upon the purple jacket. "I see that you are at your usual best this day, my lord." She looked into the lightly powdered face and glimpsed the darkly colored artificial beauty spot painted upon his right cheek. She quickly looked away.

"Why, thank you, madam. It is a pleasure to know that there are still women of good taste in the colonies."

Kellie forced a smile and took her hand from his arm to greet her father. Bending, she placed a loving kiss upon his gray head and then with a warm smile she looked at her cousin. "You look well rested this day, Vern."

"I guess I did sleep a tad late this morning. When I came down to breakfast you had already gone."

"I had to go and check on Adam, Penny's boy. He has been sick, but seems to have improved. Then of course I had to make sure that Henry had started on the North pasture."

"I do not know how Moss Rose would be able to run so smoothly without Kellie's attentions. I only fear that she is wasting away her youth by caring for her crippled father and managing our affairs." Charles McBride sighed and lightly kissed the back of his daughter's hand as she stood behind his chair with her hands on his shoulders.

"I am sure mother will have much to say about this matter as soon as she arrives," Vern ventured aloud.

"Aunt Rose is coming to Charleston?" Kellie said, surprised.

"We received a letter this morning from her, child. She will be arriving within two weeks. I dare say there will be many changes here when my dear sister comes. She will take over in her usual efficient manner and then perhaps you will have some time for yourself." Charles McBride turned in his chair to look at his daughter.

"You know that I love Moss Rose as well as you, Father. I do not find it tedious to see that everything runs smoothly."

"I do not mean to imply that it is tedious work, child. I only want you to be able to pursue other things. You should be going to parties and picnics with your friends. Why, most girls your age are already married and raising a family."

Kellie had heard all of this before, many times. How she wished her father understood! She *enjoyed* spending her energies attending to Moss Rose, overseeing the repairs on the estate, even spending hours going over the books and receipts. She had wasted too much time in the past in the company of people her own age, and all that it had gained for her was the headache of having to deal with the many young men who had pursued her. She had always found some small disfavor in their suits and now at the age of twenty she had all but given up finding the one who would harmonize with her temperament and heart.

"I would be more than willing to oblige you, Mistress McBride, and serve as your escort to any of these parties or picnics you wish to attend," Blakely Savage offered.

"*What?*" Kellie swung about, incredulity flitting over her features.

"I say, I would be most pleased if you would feel free to call upon me if you are in need of an escort to any of the events your father has mentioned."

Kellie adamantly shook her head. Momentarily flustered, she could barely speak above a whisper. "Thank you for the offer, Lord Savage, but I do not have time for such functions."

"But when mother arrives, you will find yourself with much free time, dear cousin. Do not be so quick to reject such an offer. You know, you are not getting any younger." Vern chuckled, his blue eyes dancing with mirth as he looked from his red-faced cousin to Lord Savage.

Kellie could only stand and gape at her kin, not believing that he would say such a thing in front of company. She felt her face flame with embarrassment. "Perhaps you should heed your own advice, Vern. I do not see you hanging about with a bevy of young women." She straightened, not daring to look back at Lord Savage, for though she found the man distasteful, she knew that he must surely be mortified by her cousin's bad manners.

"Quite true, quite true," Vern said with laughter in his voice. "I shall have to remedy the situation when time permits."

Charles McBride, having at firsthand witnessed the small squabbles between the two cousins, thought to bring about a halt to their conversation before it got out of hand. "Would you care for something to drink, child? I can call Honey and have her bring you something."

"No, thank you, Father. I am going to take a

ride into town and visit Marie. It has been ages since I saw her."

"Is this Marie that you speak of the tavern keeper's daughter?" Blakely Savage questioned.

"Why, yes, Marie Darring is his daughter and also one of my dearest friends," Kellie stated somewhat defensively.

"There was some talk in town this morning about her father." Knowing all eyes were upon him, Lord Savage, with his usual aplomb, made a fuss about straightening out his vest before going on. "As the story goes, it would appear this bandit known as the Falcon intervened once again and saved the day. Of course, the British are not sure where the tavern keeper got the twenty shillings for his license, but last evening one of our fine British officers was robbed as he was delivering the tax money from the harbor to our kindly Elroy Beeking. It would also appear that old Mab Fisher's brood of children have new shoes on their feet this day."

Kellie had heard much talk about the man the entire countryside was calling the Falcon. For the past year it seemed that he had surfaced in Charleston, helping those in need and pitting himself against the British. There was talk that he was a smuggler and hauled fine wines, laces, silks and even cotton and molasses in the hull of his ship without paying the high taxes the English forced upon the colonies. "Do the townspeople think, then, that it was the Falcon who gave Mr. Darring the money for his taxes?" Kellie ventured, and her heart seemed to hammer a bit wildly in her chest with the image in her mind of a dark figure riding over the countryside defending those less fortunate.

"Who is to say truly?" Blakely Savage observed. "Upon my word, these colonies are getting to be not a fit place for a decent man to live; what with all this rabble shouting for equality and outlaws such as this Falcon roaming about under cover of darkness and attacking our good keepers of the law."

"You are quite right, my Lord," Vern said. "What is to become of us all if a few take it upon themselves to try and disrupt our royal Crown's proclamations?"

As Kellie looked at her cousin, he in turn winked at her playfully. She would have liked to question her cousin about what he *truly* thought of the British imposing their will upon the colonists, but thinking better than to do so in front of her father and Lord Savage, she told herself to seek him out at a later time.

Saying her goodbyes to her father and cousin, she turned to Lord Savage. "I thank you again, sir, for your help in getting Vern released from the guardhouse. My family is in your debt, and if there is anything we can do in the future to repay you, please let us know." Kellie turned and started down the steps, but was halted in midstride.

"Why, yes, madam, there is something, now that you mention it, that you can do to repay me," Lord Savage called to her.

With some surprise, Kellie turned back. She had not expected to be taken up on her offer so soon. She in truth had only spoken as a matter of politeness. "What, pray tell, my lord, could you wish of me?" Her emerald gaze lighted on the three men; obviously, her father and cousin were just as surprised as she, and were both looking at Blakely Savage and waiting to hear what he was to say next.

"I have been asked to tea upon the morrow and I would like for you to accompany me. These affairs can bore one to death, I am afraid, but when the banker's wife, Mrs. Dunely, asked me to join her and several of her lady friends, I felt I could not refuse."

Kellie groaned inwardly at his request. She could hardly abide such affairs as afternoon teas, where the ladies of town sat about and gossiped over the latest styles and the unfortunate ones who had not been invited to their small gathering. But as she looked at Lord Savage, she knew that she must accept him. Had she not just offered to repay him for his help? How could she in good grace refuse him such an innocent request? Though she dreaded the thought of spending the afternoon in his company, she slowly nodded her head.

A large grin appeared over Blakely Savage's face.

"I certainly do appreciate your consent, madam. I fear the ladies have some ulterior motive in inviting me. Married women forever have this matchmaking look in their eyes when they observe confirmed bachelors."

Vern roared with laughter at these words, until he was abruptly silenced by a look from his cousin.

"Of course, my lord, I will be pleased to accompany you." Kellie knew the feeling of those that were happily wed desiring to have the rest of the world in a like situation, and as she looked at Blakely Savage, she felt some inner compassion for him. Could he truly help his primping ways? she questioned herself. Perhaps he did overdress, and his powdered wig and face did not help his appearance, but he did not appear to be a harsh man. Perhaps she had misjudged him somewhat, she told herself.

"Then I will bring my carriage about tomorrow at noon," Blakely Savage said as he, too, shot her cousin a silencing look.

"There is truly no need, my lord. I can simply meet you at the Dunely's house." Though Kellie had accepted his invitation, and though she did feel somewhat ashamed of her earlier treatment of him, she did not wish to be seen in his gilded carriage. The less that was said about her and Lord Savage, the better, she thought.

"I will not hear of it, madam," Blakely Savage retorted. "I shall enjoy the ride out here to Moss

Rose. It is not often that I get the chance to get out into the fresh air. I will more than enjoy picking you up."

Again Kellie saw the mirth play over her cousin's features. Thinking that he was laughing at her expense, she straightened her spine. "At noon then, my lord," she stated as she left the veranda and mounted her horse.

For a full moment the gentlemen did not speak. Blakely Savage's gray gaze watched the beauty on horseback and followed her with his eyes down the long drive of Moss Rose.

"What say you, gentlemen, we go into my den and have a goblet of brandy and one of those fine cigars that you brought home for me, Vern?" Charles McBride broke the quiet of the lazy afternoon. As Vern pushed Charles's wheelchair toward the double front portals, Lord Savage stared for a few more seconds in the direction the young woman had taken.

The Spoon and Hound Tavern provided a dim, cool respite from the late afternoon heat. Kellie entered through the front door. There were few patrons, and as she looked about the common room, her eyes rested upon Samuel Darring. She greeted him with a becoming smile.

"Good day to you, Mistress McBride," the tavern keeper called across the tavern as he poured a mug of ale and set it down in front of a traveler. "If ye be looking fur Marie, she be in her room above." He pointed a finger up the stairway. "She took sick a bit ago and her mum sent one of the boys off to fetch the doctor."

Kellie would have liked to talk to Samuel Darring about his imprisonment in the guardhouse and the rumor that the Falcon had helped him gain his release, but upon hearing that Marie was ill, she hurried toward the stairs.

She knocked gently, then eased the door open to Marie's small chamber. The room was in partial darkness, as the drapes were drawn. Seeing the form beneath a mound of covers upon the bed, Kellie called out softly, "Marie, are you awake?"

"Come in, Kellie," came the reply, swiftly followed by a hoarse cough, and a light-brown, sun-streaked head poked up from the covers.

"Your father said you were ill. You sound terrible." Kellie sat down on the small chair at the bedside.

"I've had this cough for a few days now and after serving breakfast this morning I began to feel faint from the heat of the kitchen. Mum said I was to take to my bed. She sent for the doctor. He should be arriving soon." The pixie-faced young woman spoke between bouts of coughing.

"I am so sorry," Kellie stated. Her friend worked from sunup to sundown helping her family at the tavern. Kellie knew that her father's arrest must

49

have come as a hard blow, and now, on top of everything else, Marie had taken ill.

Marie sat up and fluffed her pillows behind her back. A large grin spread over her clear, lightly freckled features. "I will be fine." She reached over and patted her friend's hand. "You are such a dear for being concerned about me. But now, tell me about that good-looking cousin of yours. How is Vern?"

Kellie laughed outright, feeling reassured that Marie was not as ill as she had first feared. "That rascal is well, I assure you. I left him not long ago with Father at Moss Rose." She left out the fact that she had also left Lord Savage. She knew that her friend's sense of humor at times was much like her cousin's. For a certainty, Marie would tease her were she to hear that Kellie was to take tea with Blakely Savage upon the morrow.

"I was so alarmed when I heard that he had been taken prisoner by the redcoats. Is he truly all right? They did not harm him, did they?" Marie's dark brown eyes were laced with concern.

"Why, my dear Marie, one would think if they did not know better, that you were love-smitten by my cousin." Kellie giggled, knowing full well the feelings that her friend had harbored for Vern for the past few years. "No, they did not harm his thick hide. He was released, his ship given back to him, and he is now hale and hearty, which at the moment is more than I can say for you."

50

Marie slumped back against her pillows at the news. "I was so afraid for him, Kellie. I had hoped to come to you at once when I heard of his arrest, but then my own father was dragged away from the tavern by the British soldiers."

Kellie saw her chance to ask the questions that had been in her mind since Lord Savage had spoken about the Falcon. "Marie, how did your father get out of the guardhouse?"

"Why, he simply paid the tax that was owed." Marie brought her hand up to cover her mouth as she coughed once again, and when she glanced back at Kellie a guardedness darkened her features.

"Yes, I thought that. But how did he get the coins for the tax?" Kellie probed. "There is a rumor that the Falcon robbed a British officer last evening and then your father, of a sudden, had the coins for his release from the guardhouse, and also, mysteriously, Mab Fisher's children all have new shoes. Do you know if this is true?" she questioned, sure that their friendship permitted no secrets between them.

"I have heard none of these rumors. I have been ill the day through," Marie stated softly.

"Oh, Marie, is it not the most romantic thing? A dark figure swooping down upon the oppressors and giving his gains to the oppressed?" Kellie exclaimed as her head filled with the dark image of the Falcon as he roamed the countryside through the lonely nights seeking justice.

Marie looked at her friend in surprise. She had never known Kellie McBride to be rash or given to any sudden flights of fancy, but as she looked at her friend, she noticed a softness about her features that spoke of hidden daydreams. "I have never thought of you as one to be interested in the happenings between the British and the colonists. At least we have never talked about such things before."

Kellie was taken aback by her friend's words. There seemed to be criticism in her tone. "I guess that, in truth, I have not thought about the plight of any except those close to me," Kellie confessed. "I have been so busy with the running of Moss Rose, there has not been time for me to take notice of what has been happening about me."

For a moment neither woman spoke. It was as though Kellie had just made a discovery, hit upon a rare truth about herself, and Marie had witnessed the revelation.

It was at this moment that Marie's mother burst into the room, announcing that Doctor Bingham had arrived and was downstairs having a mug of ale, and would be up shortly.

As Maggy Darring left the chamber with much fussing about Marie and her covers, Marie all of a sudden grabbed hold of Kellie's hand. "I need your help, Kellie," she stated abruptly.

Seeing the seriousness of her friend's face, but

thinking it one of her ploys to get a message to Vern, she smiled. "Whatever you need, my sick friend."

Marie sighed out her relief. "I have a message." She dug beneath her pillow and held out a sealed envelope. "No one must see this, Kellie."

"Of course, I shall let no other's eyes except Vern's see its contents." Kellie grinned widely.

"No, Kellie, not even Vern is to see this. You must promise me that you will do exactly as I say."

Seeing the concentration on her friend's features, Kellie felt her stomach turn over as she wondered what she had gotten herself into. For the second time that day, Kellie regretted her hasty compliance. "What is this, Marie?" she at last questioned as she looked at the envelope in her hand.

"You must take this tonight to the Swain's Wing Inn." Her words were spoken low as though she feared that other ears besides her friend's would hear.

"But the inn is over ten miles from town," Kellie exclaimed. "I would not even get there until late in the night. And who, pray tell, am I to give the letter to? Do not tell me you have a new love in your life and have at last given up on my cousin?"

"No, no," Marie was quick to object, her honey-colored curls bouncing upon her shoulders. "There is no other for me except Vern. You have but to go to the inn and sit at the table nearest the stairwell. You will be instructed what to do."

"What is this all about, Marie?" Kellie questioned as her hand gripped the envelope tightly in her fist. Even as she asked, she knew deep down that the delivery had to do with the patriots' cause.

"The less you know, the better off you will be. I would not even ask this of you, but there is none else I can trust. The message must arrive tonight, and I am too sick to take it myself. Please do this one thing for me. I will send one of the boys from the kitchen to tell your father that you will not be returning home until late. I will say that you are sitting with me because I am ill."

Kellie saw no way to refuse as she looked into her friend's dark, pleading eyes. Before she could have uttered a word to further question her, the door was thrown wide and Maggy Darring and the doctor swept into the room.

"Take my cloak next to the door there on the peg, Kellie. The air has a chill and I would not wish you to take sick."

"Your guest shall have to be on her way, miss. You will need all the rest you can get if you are to recover quickly." Dr. Bingham shooed Kellie out of the chamber.

"Come tomorrow for a visit, Kellie. We have much to talk about," Marie called out to the retreating figure of her friend.

Kellie drew Marie's cloak closely about herself.

She was chilled, as much by fear as by the coolness of the night, as she made her way toward the Swain's Wing Inn. Her emerald eyes sought out every shadow along the rutted road.

Never would she have believed that she would find herself in such a foolhardy situation! How had she allowed Marie to talk her into such a dangerous undertaking? She had no idea what the note said and she did not know what kind of people she was going to contact. The only thing she had been sure of by the desperation in her friend's manner and tone was the fact that what she was embarking upon was very dangerous. She was sure that it had something to do with the upheaval in the colonies. And if her assumption was correct and she were caught by the British, her fate would certainly be sealed.

As the moon moved higher in the darkly clouded night, Kellie controlled her nervousness with some inner force and concentrated on each step her stallion took along the way. It was well into the evening when at last she spied the dim lights of the Swain's Wing Inn and with a sigh, she dismounted as she reached the yard and gave her mount over to the care of the stable boy. She placed a small coin in his hand, and thanked her good fortune that she had not gone to town this day completely penniless.

The inn was filled with travelers and local patrons, Kellie noticed, as she cautiously made her way into the lighted interior. Pulling the cloak tighter abut her figure and keeping the hood over her golden curls, she tried to make herself as small and inconspicuous as possible as she looked about the busy room. Remembering with some nervousness all that Marie had told her, she glanced toward the stairwell, but to her surprise she glimpsed a lone gentleman at the small table. He was drinking at his ease from a pewter mug.

What should she do? she wondered. Should she perhaps approach the man? Was *he* the one she was to entrust the envelope to? But before she could put any decision into action, a small, harried, serving girl approached her and with a quick manner asked if she would like to sit at a table. Kellie nodded her head, deciding that the best thing for her to do was to wait awhile and watch the man at the table. If he appeared to be waiting for someone, she would make some kind of approach. "Please bring me a mug of warmed cider," she said, forcing the words from her fear-constricted throat as the serving girl led her to a small table near the hearth. She sat nervously on the edge of the straight-backed wooden chair.

The girl brought her a mug of warm cider and asked if she would like her to take her cloak. From the corner of her eye Kellie noticed the gentleman near the stairwell rise from the table and start toward the front door.

"I would like a different table." She ignored the

girl's question and stood. "That one over there will suit me." She started across the room, leaving the serving girl to follow with the mug of cider.

"But mistress, it is warmer by the hearth. Are you sure?" The girl questioned as she finally caught up with Kellie at the stairwell.

"This table will be fine. I will just leave my cloak on."

The young girl looked strangely at the newcomer, nodded her head, and hurriedly went off to serve another table.

Kellie felt the eyes of several men upon her as she sat alone and sipped from the mug of cider. Not daring to look up for fear of attracting unwanted attention from one of the male patrons, she kept her gaze lowered.

The minutes ticked past slowly without event, until an hour went by and still Kellie sat alone at the table. Silently she began to berate herself for being a terrible fool. Why on earth had she even agreed to Marie's pleadings? She could be home in her warm, safe bed, instead of sitting alone at an inn, waiting for a stranger to approach her, if indeed anyone was going to approach her. Her mind swirled in a riot of confusion.

At that very moment the door of the inn swung wide and the clatter and noise of the common room seemed to cease as three redcoated soldiers entered. Stern and imperious, their eyes scanned the interior of the inn. Instantly Kellie lowered her head back to her mug, her heart beating at a wild pace as fear gripped her insides.

Expecting to be singled out at any moment as a traitor and dragged from the inn, Kellie was relieved when she glanced up and found the soldiers occupied at the table she had earlier been seated at near the hearth. The young serving girl was taking their orders amid loud laughter when one of the soldiers pulled her into his lap. His voice was teasing and loud as he propositioned her services for later that night.

Kellie's first thought was to flee while the soldiers were distracted by the young girl and before they noticed her sitting all to herself near the stairwell. Slowly she set the mug of cider down and, pulling the cloak about herself, she started to rise.

As she was about to step away from the table and make her way as quietly as possible to the front door of the inn, an older, buxom serving girl came to her side. "Mistress, go out the back way. Through the kitchen and out into the yard. Go quickly now and be silent. No one will notice your departure."

Afraid to follow these instructions but even more frightened not to, Kellie, her hands clutching the folds of the cloak, took the few steps near the stairwell that would lead her out into the kitchen.

Great gulps of air were expelled from her lungs as at last she found herself in the large, warm, busy kitchen. For a few seconds she leaned heavily against the door that separated her from the soldiers in the common room. Noticing that the kitchen help had paused in their work and had all turned around to stare at her, she quickly made her way out the swinging back door.

The fresh air hit her full force as she stepped out of the heated kitchen. Looking about the backyard of the inn, her only thought was to find her horse and get herself away as quickly as possible. Glimpsing the stables, she started down the stone steps and across the yard.

As she neared the side of the stables, a dark cloaked figure stepped before her. Fearing the worst, Kellie opened her mouth to scream, all of the night's frightening experiences welling up within her.

With a quick movement, the large figure caught her about the waist as one hand covered her mouth and muffled a scream before it left her lips. "Be quiet!" a deep-timbered voice hissed next to her ear.

Kellie's eyes were twin saucers of fear as she felt her heartbeat slamming against her chest.

Slowly, as though not trusting her, the hand lowered from her face, but still the stranger's arm held her tightly against his broad chest. "Why are you here? Where is Marie?" The dark-clothed and cloaked man questioned in low, deep tones.

"Marie . . . Marie is ill. She could not keep this appointment and asked me to take her place."

Kellie's words rushed out in a strangled gasp.

"You should not have gotten involved in this, Kellie McBride." The man pulled her with ease into a small growth of trees.

Hearing her name, Kellie's curiosity stilled her fear. "You know who I am?" Her sea-green eyes sought out the man's face in the darkness.

A low, husky laugh filled her ears. "I know of you indeed, mistress." The tone now was more of a caress that left gooseflesh rushing over Kellie's arms.

"But who are *you?*" Still she could not make out his identity. "What do you want of me?" Her reason for being at the inn and her earlier terror had completely disappeared at the sound of his voice and with his arms so tightly about her.

"Did Marie not give you something to deliver to me?" he questioned her.

Nodding her head very slowly, it dawned upon Kellie who the man had to be. "You . . . you are the one they call the Falcon!" she exclaimed, her voice rising in dismay and alarm.

"Keep your voice down, mistress," he cautioned, but instead of covering her mouth once again, his finger lightly caressed her lower lip and ran a light path down her delicate jaw line.

"You are the smuggler and highwayman that all of Charleston is talking about!" she whispered, heeding his warning. "Marie did not tell me that it was *you* that I would be meeting!"

"Usually I do not come myself on such business, but this message that you are carrying is of great importance to me and those who wish for their freedom."

"Their freedom?" Kellie asked.

Again the pleasant laughter filled her ears. "My little innocent one. Do you in truth not even know what you have been caught up in?" Still the finger laid against her smooth flesh as he asked this question almost to himself.

Kellie all but melted under his touch and without a will she could but stare up at his shadowy features, her eyes lingering on the night blackness of his hair against his dark collar.

"Marie should not have gotten you involved. This is a dangerous business that we have with the British."

With these words some of her senses returned. "There are British soldiers at the inn." Fear settled about her anew as she thought of what would happen to this man known as the Falcon if he were caught here near the stables, and also what would happen to her if she were caught in the presence of the outlaw.

The Falcon must have sensed her rekindled fear. He quickly tried to reassure her. "I watched the soldiers go into the inn. They will spend some time drinking and wenching. Do not fear while you are with me. I will protect you with my very life if the need arises."

With some strange spell of wonder wrapped about her, Kellie listened to his words of reassurance, and did not fear. She felt safe and somehow protected while standing next to him. But reason told her that as long as they lingered near the stables there was a danger of them being seen. Drawing out the envelope that Marie had given her, she handed it over to the Falcon without saying a word.

For a moment longer he held her about the waist, enjoying the feel of her slim body next to his own. Responding to a stronger force of will, however, he released her. "The hour grows late, and you should be home in your bed. I must see that this message is given into the right hands."

"When will I see you again?" The words slipped from her lips without thought. Kellie wondered at her own boldness.

The green of her eyes were like glittering jewels; their sparkle triumphed over the darkness as the Falcon gazed down into her lovely face. Instead of answering her question, he drew her cloak tighter about her and positioned the hood around her face so that her golden curls were out of sight. "Do not be so foolish again, little one. You are too rare a treasure to risk your life in such a game of chance."

"But what of *you?*" she parried, and after a moment of silence, she ventured, "*Who* are you? What is your name? Do you live in Charleston?"

There were so many questions and she had so little time! For at any moment she knew they would be parting and perhaps she would never see him again.

"My identity must remain my secret for the time being. Our country depends on it." For a moment he raised his hand as though to reach out to her again, but he brought it to a stop in midair. "Do as I say, now. Ride back to Moss Rose and do not be so foolish again. There have already been too many lost to our cause, and you are too precious a gambit to chance."

Never in her life had Kellie felt such an overpowering urge to be held in a man's arms. His voice held her very soul captive, and she experienced an irresistible desire to lose herself forever in the strength of his arms.

"Go now!" The words seemed torn from his throat; his strangled tone convinced Kellie of his own turbulent emotions.

Without a backward glance, Kellie turned and started to the stables. Retrieving her horse as though in a daze, she slowly started down the road that earlier she had traversed from Charleston.

The fear and caution she had felt while en route to the Swain's Wing Inn had vanished. She could still hear the husky seduction of the Falcon's voice, feel the strength of his body and arms encircling her, and see his dark form and the dark hair that brushed over his shoulders. She tried in vain to remember his handsome, chiseled features but the darkness of the night had hidden much that she would have wished to commit to memory. The color of his eyes, the way his lips slanted when he smiled down at her, the contour of his nose, all of these she had to form within her mind, and the picture that resulted she knew was beyond compare.

In the few minutes that she had shared with the Falcon, she had experienced feelings that she never knew existed. There was a strength and authority about him that filled her entire being with heady illusions of what could have occurred between them. If only this man had been one of those who had courted her! If only it had been the stranger called the Falcon who had come to Moss Rose and begged for her hand, instead of the fortune-seeking young men that had plagued her father's doorstep over the past few years!

The stranger called the Falcon . . . be he smuggler, highwayman, or patriot, it mattered little to Kellie at the moment. Somehow the chance meeting had changed her; she knew that she would never be the same again. "The Falcon," she whispered aloud to the night wind, and felt her heart flutter at the mere saying of his name.

Chapter Three

Pulling back the lace draperies, Honey let the bright sunlight flood the bedchamber. "Wake yerself up now, Miss Kellie. Ye done slept most of the morning through and yer papa be chafing for yer presence downstairs."

Sleepily Kellie pulled the soft down and silk coverlet over her head.

"I swear, girl, I don't know what's gotten into ye lately." Honey shook her large cropped head as she went about the room gathering up the clothes that Kellie had discarded the night before. "Why, lately you've been staying abed later and later. And this mess!" she scolded as she held up an armload of lace and silk.

Kellie groaned, knowing that she would find no sleep with this tyrant chiding her. With a yawn, she slowly pulled the coverlet beneath her chin. Looking toward the black housekeeper and the mound of clothing in her arms, she felt somewhat guilty for her behavior. For the last two weeks, several mornings had passed just like this one. Being a night courier had definitely changed her usually orderly lifestyle! By the time she found her way back to Moss Rose and climbed the servant's staircase, it was the early hours of the morning and all she could do was strip herself of her clothing and fall into bed.

"The boys have brought up hot water for your bath; it's waiting for you in the bathing chamber. You had best be quick, for that fancy lord is downstairs with yer cousin. They're all waiting for ye to go with them to town to pick up Miss Rose."

"I completely forgot that Aunt Rose was arriving today!" Kellie exclaimed as she scrambled from beneath the warm confines of the bedclothes.

"I reckon ye *did* forget," Honey chastised, one dark brow raised at her young mistress before she left the chamber.

Kellie pulled off her nightgown and hurried into the adjoining bathing chamber, where she lowered her body into the warm depths of the scented water. With a soft sigh, she shut her eyes as she felt the full satisfaction of the comforts of home.

"Lord," she murmured as she began to lather her legs with the rich rose-scented soap that had been left on the small table near the brass tub. She was so tired! She had gone back several times to the Swain's Wing Inn with messages that Marie had entrusted to her. She had been frightened of these nightly escapades, but each time that Marie had asked for her help, she had been unable to refuse. The uppermost thought in her mind had little to do with the worthy cause the colonists were fighting for—she simply wanted to see the mysterious Falcon one more time.

She assured herself that the inner quaking of her body and the feelings of lightheadedness when she thought of the dashing smuggler were not the reasons for seeking him out, but that she had to get word to him for his own safety.

The afternoon she had agreed to take tea with Blakely Savage, the ladies of the town talked of nothing else but the exploits of the man called the Falcon. There was also gossip about the new governor arriving in Charleston and his sworn oath to capture the Falcon and put an end to smuggling in the Charleston area.

As the ladies had talked, Kellie felt her insides convulse at the thought of the handsome Falcon swinging from an oak limb. She had to warn him, she told herself daily, and the only way that she could get in touch with him was to put herself in league with the patriots who had sworn their allegiance to a cause that was not only dangerous but deadly.

She had not seen the Falcon in all of her subsequent visits to the inn. A different man had met her to take the message, leaving her with only words of assurance that he did indeed know the

Falcon was safe, but he did not know how to get in touch with him.

She was growing frustrated with taking such risks and ending the evening with overwhelming disappointment. The Falcon came and went without anyone knowing his true identity, yet he seemed to know every move the British made.

Rinsing her body of the sweet-smelling soap, Kellie felt almost defeated. The governor was to arrive in Charleston aboard the same ship as her aunt. If the Falcon did not take care, he would be captured and imprisoned or even worse, and she had been unable thus far to get word to him of the governor's plans.

Not wishing to linger any longer in her bath, Kellie dressed, brushing out her waist-length golden curls. She pulled the lengths of the tresses back and secured them with a silk bow. Shortly she left the chamber and approached the small group awaiting her downstairs.

"Why, my dear, you are breathtaking as usual and well worth every minute of the wait." Blakely Savage had been the first to glimpse her coming down the stairs and, leaving the other two men, he held out his arm to her and escorted her to her father and cousin waiting in the foyer.

"And you, Lord Savage, are always the gentleman," Kellie replied, greeting him warmly. She had found his company to be not so unpleasant as she had feared. Over the past weeks, he had become a frequent guest at Moss Rose; she had to admit that his quick wit and refined manners were a welcomed change from the men who usually visited her father's home. Though his wig and his fussing manner still annoyed her, she found that Blakely Savage had somehow grown on her. "You shall be going with us, my lord?" she questioned as they reached her father and cousin.

"Most assuredly. I would not wish to miss out on the opportunity to meet your dear aunt. I have my carriage and thought that perhaps you would join me on the lonely ride to town?"

"Of course, I would be pleased to ride with you, my lord." After placing a kiss upon her father's brow, she allowed Savage to hold her lace shawl for her.

As the small group reached their designated carriages on the cool, balmy fall morning, Blakely Savage, in his usual manner, fussed over his own olive and gold attire and then took some moments settling the warm lap robe securely over Kellie's knees. "I must say, mistress, this shade of blue suits you very well."

Kellie glanced down at the velvet décolleté with its cream-colored lace bodice. "Thank you," she replied, finding his fussing somewhat amusing. "I in turn would like to say how dashing you look this morning." She took in his olive knee-length jacket with its gold braiding and large gold buttons, and matching britches and gold vest.

"Why, thank you, madam. I do take pride in my appearance, as you know. But I wanted to look especially fine for our trip to meet your aunt." There was a trace of laughter in his high-pitched voice.

Kellie grinned widely with thoughts of what Aunt Rose's reactions would be to the alarmingly gaudy figure of Lord Savage.

The ride into Charleston was pleasant as the couple engaged in some light bantering. Lord Savage introduced a more serious tone into their conversation when he began to tell her about the news circulating in Charleston that morning.

"It would appear that late last evening, the Sons of Liberty gathered once again, but this time in front of Elroy Beeking's home. Apparently, they burned an effigy of Beeking right there in his front yard, and called for tar and feathers. The militia had to be called out to quell the rebels, and two of their lot were captured."

"Who were those captured?" Kellie questioned with a hollow feeling in the pit of her stomach.

"Why, I believe their names were Jeffery Stark and Ned Bowlings. But do not worry yourself about them."

"Why on earth would I not worry about them? Why, I have known both young men since we were children. Their mothers must be frantic with worry over them."

"I am sure that those good ladies are well aware that their sons are no longer in the guardhouse."

"Where did the redcoats take them then?" Kellie asked fearfully.

"Oh indeed, they *were* taken to the guardhouse after the soldiers had hurried the rest of the crowd from the streets, but it would apear that once again the outlaw known as the Falcon saved the day."

Before Lord Savage could say any more, Kellie sat up straight against the cushioned seat and with widened eyes, she gasped aloud, "The Falcon?"

"Aye, word has it there was a daring breakout in the early hours of the morning. Reports hold that Fess Turner roused himself from a drunken stupor long enough to glance out his chamber window, to see a large man dressed all in black flying through town on the back of a horse, with two young men following close behind."

"Was anyone hurt?" Kellie questioned as her heart raced wildly in her chest.

"The guard, when discovered, had a large goose egg on the side of his head, but it would appear that no others were the worse for wear."

"Then the Falcon got away?" Her voice held an anxious note that was not lost upon her companion.

"The rascal got clean away as usual," Savage stated in a high tone. "It would seem our new governor will have his hands full with this blackguard."

Kellie swallowed hard and slowly nodded her

head, relieved that once again the Falcon had escaped danger. "What of Ned and Jeffery? Will they not still be in danger? I would expect that the soldiers are out this very moment looking for them. Oh, their poor families if they are found hiding them!"

"I am sure that this Falcon fellow has taken care of his fellow rogues, Kellie. They say he has a very fleet vessel. I am sure that at this very moment those two young men are having a lively time of it with the rest of that band of cutthroats."

Blakely Savage never failed to rouse her ire when he spoke in such a high-handed manner. Did he not realize that companions of the Falcon's were like thousands of others who wished to be free of the choke hold of British tyranny? But she knew Lord Savage would never relent. He was loyal to the Crown, and had no toleration for anyone who was not a dutiful subject, no matter the cost to themselves or their families. Well, at least the Falcon and Ned and Jeffery were safe, she thought, as she relaxed against the seat and spoke no more on the subject.

As Lord Savage's gilded carriage drew close to the Charleston docks, it became apparent to Kellie that many of the townspeople had turned out for the arrival of the new governor. There were also many redcoated British soldiers on the docks; Blakely stated that this was to prevent the Sons of Liberty or other radicals from causing a scene like the one that had taken place the night before.

Despite the presence of the soldiers, gay talk and laughter rose from the quay. Lord Savage and Kellie alighted from the carriage and found themselves close to a group of ladies who were watching the approaching ship with excitement.

"Why, Lord Savage! Did you and Kellie McBride come out to welcome the new governor to our fair town?"

As an elderly lady's gaze took in the pair, Kellie witnessed an expression on the woman's face that bespoke of the gossip that would surely be circulating at this afternoon's tea. Speculation about the relationship between the unlikely pair, Kellie knew, would be on the tips of everyone's tongues.

"No, not exactly. My Aunt Rose is arriving and we have come with my father and cousin to meet her," Kellie said, hoping to dispel any gossip about herself and Lord Savage.

"Come, Kellie. I see that the passengers are starting to disembark," Blakely Savage said, taking her elbow and moving her away from the ladies intently scrutinizing the pair.

Kellie groaned inwardly. He had been in the habit, of late, of calling her by her first name. It had not bothered Kellie, but now she was confident that she would be the topic of the gossipmongers' next meeting. There was little for her to do but hold her head high and follow where Blakely Savage was leading her, through the dense crowd and toward her cousin, who was already standing at the end of the gangplank.

By the time the pair made their way through the crowd to reach Kellie's cousin, Vern was holding a tiny woman tightly in his embrace. "Aunt Rose!" Kellie cried aloud and as the woman turned in her direction, Kellie saw that her aunt had seemingly not aged a bit since the last time she had seen her, years ago.

Rose Fielding moved quickly to embrace her niece. "Why, my dear girl, you have grown into quite a beautiful young woman!" For a moment Rose Fielding held her at arm's length and with a single, precise glance took her in from head to slippers. "Vern has written me of your hard work at Moss Rose and how you have had little time to yourself. That shall be set aright now that I am here. We shall not *abide* any further neglect of your future from this day forth!"

There was little sense in arguing with her aunt, Kellie knew. She would bide her time now and find a more appropriate moment to explain to her that her greatest pleasure was in helping to run her father's home.

"Who is this at your side, my dear?" Rose Fielding questioned in her no-nonsense way, taking in in a glance Lord Savage's long white powdered wig, pale face, and olive and gold dress.

"This, Mother, is Lord Blakely Savage," Vern broke in, making the introduction with a wide grin on his face.

"Savage?" the elder woman pronounced the name, her sharp gaze studying his features as though to seek out his worth beneath the white powder and cheek-rouge.

"At your service, madam," Blakely Savage intoned, making a flourishing bow there on the docks, his high-toned voice rising over the noise of the crowd.

For a moment Rose Fielding seemed taken aback by his manners and tone but quickly regained her composure, trusting that in time she would comprehend his place in the lives of her niece and son.

"Well, let us not stand about any longer here on the docks. This crowd is deafening." Looking toward her son she said, "I trust that Charles is awaiting us in the carriage." She took hold of Vern's arm and started to lead him away from the gangplank. "You will, of course, be coming with us?" she questioned, directing her attention to Lord Savage.

"Of course, madam. I would not miss such an event as your homecoming."

"Good, then. Let us not dally here. There is an awful chill in the air." Rose Fielding was ramrod straight as she started off in the direction of the carriage, her head nodding in greeting as she was recognized by several of the people milling about.

For a moment Kellie watched after the small, correct figure of Rose Fielding, having forgotten what an orderly, determined little woman she was. Life at Moss Rose would certainly be different with her in residence! A sigh escaped her lips when she realized that one of the first things on her aunt's list would be the welfare of her niece. She was pulled from thoughts of her aunt's imminent arrangements when she heard her name spoken at her side.

"I see that you have come to get a first viewing of our new governor," Elroy Beeking declared.

"I am afraid not, Mr. Beeking," Kellie replied, addressing the odious ex-governor. "My aunt has arrived in Charleston today. That is my reason for being here at the docks."

"Well then, I am sure you can spare a few minutes to be at my side to meet Governor Mansfield. I assume that you have given more consideration to the conversation we had in my office that dreadful day that your cousin was detained. As acting governor of this town, it is only fitting that you stand beside me when Governor Mansfield sets foot in Charleston." Beeking's watery eyes lecherously devoured Kellie's figure before settling on the enticing swell of her neckline.

"You received my answer that day, Mr. Beeking. And I am of a like mind today."

"Tsk, tsk. I will give you all the time you need to come to your senses and see the benefits of becoming my wife. After all, a woman of your age and, shall we say, *firm-mindedness,* does not get offers of marriage every day."

Kellie was flabbergasted by the man's incivility. She angrily turned her back to him and started to make her way after her aunt and cousin, but was instantly brought up short by a firm hold upon her arm.

"Do not be foolhardy, madam—"

At the abrupt halting of his speech Kellie found herself free of his grasp and, turning to see what could possibly have caused him to retreat, she saw Elroy Beeking stumbling backward, and heard his scream of outrage as he went flying through the air and landed with a loud splash in the water near the gangplank.

"Oh, do excuse my clumsiness!" Blakely Savage exclaimed as he stepped around the gangplank and peered down at Beeking, whose small periwig was dripping wet and askew upon his nearly bald head and whose boney arms were flaying about wildly in the air. "I did not see you there, my good man. An accident, you know." Turning to Kellie he offered her his arm. "I think, madam, that your family is awaiting us."

Elroy Beeking looked to the man that had been the cause of his mishap in disbelief. "Why, you . . . you . . ." he sputtered, still flaying about in the water. "Get me out of here you gawking good-for-nothings!" he yelled to the soldiers who had hurried to the gangplank to see what the commotion was about.

Kellie found it difficult to keep from laughing.

She had witnessed Blakely Savage's hefty thrust, which had sent Elroy Beeking into the water on his backside. Her emerald eyes sparkled with mirth as the soldiers rushed about to lend assistance to the frantic man. When Lord Savage offered her his arm she took it willingly and gave it a little squeeze of thanks.

"Did you ever doubt, madam, that I would come to your rescue?" Lord Savage said as the pair walked away from the docks. The outraged exclamations of Elroy Beeking filled their ears as the soldiers hauled him out of the water.

Once in Lord Savage's carriage, Kellie gave vent to the glee she had been holding in check. She laughed until she felt the sting of tears upon her cheeks. "Did you see the way he flew backward? Did you see his face? He was so surprised!" she said breathlessly.

Blakely Savage sat back against his cushioned seat with a smile on his lips, delighting in his companion's pleasure. "Oh yes, my dear Kellie, I witnessed it all."

"Of course you did," Kellie murmured. "And I do so appreciate your assistance."

"Anytime, my dear, anytime. While in my company you have nothing to fear. I shall always guard you as the greatest treasure."

Kellie's laughter quieted somewhat as she heard the seriousness of his tone, and for a moment her emerald eyes studied him. But quickly her lips curled up again as Blakely offered, "Why, I feel quite assured that if the opportunity arose and I had to deliver you from this villain known as the Falcon, you could very well depend upon me."

Kellie had to control her mirth as she looked across the space of the interior of the carriage to Blakely Savage and compared him to the man she had met the night at the Swain's Wing Inn. The Falcon was the very epitome of manhood, and Lord Savage did not begin to measure up, in his silks, satins, powder, and wig.

"You would mock me, madam?" Blakely questioned as he glimpsed her obvious amusement.

"Nay, my Lord, I do not mock you. I only pray the opportunity never arises for you to face the Falcon," Kellie answered truthfully, for she knew the Falcon would not be the rival that Elroy Beeking had been.

"A dinner party!" Rose Fielding declared upon her arrival at Moss Rose. "We shall hold a small dinner party so I can get reacquainted with old friends. Perhaps I shall even invite the governor. It never hurts to cultivate the right connections."

And as though her words had created the affair, the evening was upon them, the crystal chandeliers were alight, vast amounts of food had been prepared, and the guests were beginning to arrive.

Taking one last minute to look over her appearance in the mirror, Kellie studied herself critically. Her gleaming blond hair was fashioned atop her head in ringlets, with tiny pearl hairpins holding the coiffure in place. Her rustling gown of pale pink satin belled out in yards and yards of material, fitted tightly about the waist, the bodice boasting rows of tiny seed pearls and plunging low to enhance the deep valley of her swelling breasts. The sleeves were delicately puffed at the shoulders and then tapered tightly from elbow to wrists. Her slippers of matching satin were also trimmed with tiny seed pearls.

Kellie knew that she looked her best. Her cheeks flushed lightly, her petal lips were shaded with a touch of rouge, and her emerald eyes sparkled beneath the thickness of her long lashes.

At first she had been against her aunt's plans for a dinner party, but as the day drew closer and the seamstress finished her gown and the household at Moss Rose grew livelier with preparations for the affair, Kellie could only relent. After all, it had been some time since Moss Rose had held a party of any kind.

Making her way downstairs to the parlor, Kellie was greeted warmly by her cousin, who left the company of the two young women he was talking with to come to her side. "Why, dear cuz, you are absolutely breathtaking this evening." He drew her arm into the crook of his own and pulled her into the parlor.

Several couples and a few young ladies and gentlemen were sitting about the room as Rose Fielding played the gracious hostess. Kellie spoke to each in turn, and glimpsed Blakely Savage in all of his finery in conversation with her father and another gentleman that she had not as yet met but assumed to be Governor Mansfield. Sitting in the chair next to him was Elroy Beeking, and standing in attendance close at hand were two redcoated British officers.

"This is my daughter, Governor," Charles McBride proudly proclaimed as he held his hand out in Kellie's direction after Vern had escorted her about the room. "Kellie, I would have you meet our new governor. Governor Mansfield, this is my daughter, Kellie."

"Ah, yes, I have heard much these past days about you, young lady," the gray-bearded and bewigged gentleman stated. His dark eyes took in the young woman and found her a beauty indeed. It was no wonder Elroy Beeking was so set upon claiming the young woman for his own, he thought, with a calculating stare. Not only did the lady have a fair face and figure, but by the look of her father's home, Beeking had been correct when he claimed that she would be wed with a sizable fortune as her dowry.

Kellie's lips curved into a tight smile at his greeting, and she held herself in reserve. The way his piercing black eyes examined every detail of her

81

body irked her. She glanced at Elroy Beeking, who rose to stand at the governor's side with a smug smirk upon his thin features. She was sure he had been the one who had told the new governor anything that he had heard about her. "It is a pleasure, Governor," she softly demurred, at last.

"The pleasure is all mine, my dear. I can see now why our good Elroy Beeking here is so enamored of you. You know, my dear, he swears that you are the only woman alive for him." The governor smiled as Kellie's cheeks flamed. "I do hope that I will be able to help influence you on his behalf, mistress." With this his dark glance went from the young woman to her sire; he wanted to impress upon Kellie's father that the match would please him well.

Charles McBride was not unaware of his daughter's embarrassment, and noticed that most of his guests were paying close attention to the scene at hand. "My daughter, Governor Mansfield, has always had a mind of her own. I declare it will take a special man to claim my daughter's hand and take her away from Moss Rose." With these words McBride laughed lightly to show the new governor that he meant no offense.

"Then I would think that she would give the most serious consideration to Mr. Beeking here. He would make a most splendid husband. He will go far in the service of the Crown."

Kellie could not believe that any man could be so

bold in polite company. She was amazed at Governor Mansfield's lack of tact. To ward off any further attack, Kellie's sparkling jade eyes moved from the governor to Elroy Beeking; she saw between them a sort of conspiracy that boded ill for her future.

It was Lord Savage who once again saved the moment for Kellie. He got to his feet and, clearing his throat, said in a loud voice that was not lost on the guests, "I have been patiently awaiting your arrival, madam. Have you forgotten so easily your promise of showing me the gardens before dinner?" Fussingly he began to straighten out his plum-shaded jacket and then stepped toward her and offered her his arm, disregarding the dark scowl that instantly came over the governor's features.

Kellie gave Blakely Savage a warm smile. He seemed always at hand when she was in need, she thought, as she laid her fingers against his satin jacket and glimpsed the fury upon Elroy Beeking's face. "If you will excuse us, Father. I did promise." She did not await an answer but turned about as Blakely Savage led her through the French doors leading out of the parlor and into the gardens.

"Thank you so much, Lord Savage," Kellie sighed as the cool night air hit her face and calmed her somewhat. "I am afraid that if I had stayed much longer in the presence of those two men, I would have been forced to give them a display of my Irish temper."

"Why do you not call me Blakely?" Lord Savage questioned as though all that had taken place in the parlor was of little consequence.

Kellie was surprised at his words. "You are a dear friend," she said as she wiped away the moisture on her brow. "You always seem to be at hand when I am in need. Of course I shall call you Blakely. It is a simple enough request."

A large smile settled over Savage's lips as he heard her response and witnessed the winsome smile on her soft lips.

For a moment, in the moonlit gardens, Kellie found herself looking into his features and thinking him almost handsome as he smiled down at her. But quickly the illusion disappeared as he took hold of her arm and said that they had best return to the others or her aunt would be in a state they could be hard pressed to soothe.

"I will be more than willing to play the hero this evening and fend off the governor and Mr. Beeking for you, Kellie," he said as he bowed low.

With Kellie's mood much improved she graciously curtsied. "You are certainly most gallant, sir." And as she straightened she added with a bold wink, "Thank you, Blakely." She then walked before him and returned through the French doors.

For a full moment Blakely Savage was rooted to the spot where he stood. His name from her lips was like a melody. Shaking himself from the stupor her intoxicating presence had induced, he followed her back into the parlor.

Kellie, with Blakely at her side, moved across the room conversing with her guests. When dinner was announced, Elroy Beeking, with a determined step, started from his chair and crossed the room to claim Kellie as his dinner partner, but when he was halfway to her side he stopped short as he watched Blakely Savage hold out his arm toward her, and Kellie, with a radiant smile, placed her hand gently upon the plum satin jacket.

He had had about enough of the fancy lord, Beeking seethed inwardly. First he had interfered and won her cousin's release from the guardhouse, when Fielding's imprisonment could have won him her agreement to wed him, and then at the docks the fop had *accidentally* pushed him into the water and he had been unable to greet the governor. It would seem that the self-centered, self-indulgent Lord was becoming more of a problem than he could have imagined.

"Why, Mr. Beeking, I would be honored to share dinner with you," Carolyn Peal exclaimed as Beeking glared at the couple making their way out of the parlor.

It took a moment for him to realize he was being addressed, so consumed with anger was he, but looking down into the pinched, plain features of the young woman so close at hand, he could but offer his arm and declare through clenched teeth, "Why thank you, Mistress Peal."

Kellie found herself sitting between her cousin and Blakely Savage. Across from her, Governor Mansfield was seated with Carolyn Peal between him and Elroy Beeking. Trying to avoid any eye contact with either man, she paid attention to only those at her side.

"I invited Marie to join us this evening, but she claimed her father could not spare her from the tavern. I fear she thinks she will be out of place here at Moss Rose in the company of our guests."

Vern smiled down upon his cousin, knowing well her friendship with the tavern-keeper's daughter and her intention to play matchmaker. "I also invited Marie, Kellie. I think that after this affair I will make my way to the tavern and have myself a mug of ale, and perhaps have a chance to visit her."

This pleased Kellie very much, for sitting next to her cousin was a very pretty young woman that her aunt had invited with the sole purpose of catching her eligible son's eye. Now she could relax with the assurances that her cousin, too, had not forgotten her dear friend.

All through dinner as course after course of the savory repast was served, Kellie felt the brooding eyes of Elroy Beeking upon her. Forcing herself to pay close attention to her food and to Blakely Savage's company as he plied her with humorous accounts of his home in England and his days at court, she avoided having to return her attention across the table. She was, however, distracted from her dinner partner's story when she heard Arthur Dunsley questioning Governor Mansfield about Jeffery Stark and Ned Bowlings.

"What say you, Governor? Will there be a halt to the goings on of the group calling itself the Sons of Liberty? More and more of our young men are being led astray by this rabble. Why, the Bowlings and Stark boys are both from well-respected families, and there is no telling who else has joined the rebel cause."

Governor Mansfield set his spoon aside as though his appetite had disappeared. "One of my major intents as governor of this colony is to bring about a halt to these radicals calling themselves the Sons of Liberty. If the wealthier, more prominent men of this area, men such as Christopher Gadsden, would cease this madness of enticing the lower class rabble into a frenzy with their speeches of 'liberty' and 'rights,' we would have peace. And the sons of your neighbors would not be in hiding as the Stark and Bowlings boys are now. But whether by force or will alone, it is yet to be seen. I promise you that any who go against the Crown shall be forced to pay."

"Why, Governor, perhaps the Crown shall be forced shortly to take another look at this Stamp Act it has imposed. It is claimed that Greenville has devised a means of gaining more coins for the Crown's coffers behind dear King George's back,"

Gladys Meaking stated softly, and several heads nodded in agreement.

Lawrence Mansfield was a firm believer in all that the Crown stood for and as he listened to the woman's little speech, he frowned, finding her words almost treasonable. "Do not let yourself be led into folly, mistress. King George is well aware of those who are faithful and those who would be traitors to this Crown. Patrick Henry and a number like him who think to complain over the unfairness of the Crown's command shall one day soon be regretting each treasonous word that was spoken before the House of Burgesses in Virginia. You colonists are a *ruled* people, whether you will it or not, and as such you shall abide by the Crown's dictates."

"You are right of course, Governor," Arthur Dunsley said, smiling toward Governor Mansfield, who he felt was of a like mind. He also had a great fear that to go against the Crown would endanger his own finances. He stated, "If more people would look toward men such as Benjamin Franklin and James Otis of Massachusetts, who boldly state that it is our due to pay whatever taxes are imposed upon us as citizens of the Crown, there would be peace. We have all fattened ourselves off this new land. What harm is there in tightening our belts for a short time? This group that is called the Sons of Liberty, and even this smuggler known as the Falcon, are but troublemakers who care not a wit but for their own selves." Arthur Dunsley's face had turned a bright red with this speech, which he attempted to deliver with the utmost conviction.

"Was it not this Falcon who set free the two young men from the guardhouse after they had been caught burning an effigy at your front door?" Blakely Savage intoned as he held the eyes of Elroy Beeking, and watched that man squirm uncomfortably in his seat.

Elroy Beeking curtly nodded his head, disliking the turn the conversation had taken. Indeed, he would not soon forget the effigy that had been hung on his front porch and set aflame. He had been asleep in his bed when he was awakened by the clamor in his front yard. When he looked down from his upstairs window he saw the gathering crowd, heard the shouts, all manner of vile slanders upon him. "Haughty tyrant," "merciless parasite," "first-born son of Hell!" were among the well-versed phrases that had filled his ears. As the crowd's tempers worsened he had heard the threats of tar and feathers. He had stood in his nightshirt and cap with a terrible fear filling his soul. He had sworn that moment that he would book passage back to England on the next available ship if he survived the night. Only when a number of soldiers arrived a few minutes later was he able to let out his breath, and a small portion of his courage returned. From that evening forth there had been guards posted around his home, and only with the governor's assurances that the crowd would not dare to truly set on him, had he postponed his trip to the motherland until that time when he won the hand of Kellie McBride.

Governor Mansfield also looked across the table at the powdered features of Blakely Savage, feeling some irritation as he noticed the painted beauty mark high upon the man's cheek. He had noticed the way the fancy lord had swept Kellie McBride from the parlor when he had tried to convince her to look with some favor upon Elroy Beeking. He had also watched through the evening as the foppish lord played court to the young woman at her father's dinner table. And now he was questioning Beeking about an evening the ex-govenor would obviously much prefer to forget. Swallowing a sip of wine, he took the opportunity to answer Blakely Savage's question. "The Falcon's days are numbered, you can be assured of that, sir, and with his downfall shall come the capture of his band of cutthroats. They shall all swing together, my lord."

"You are so sure, then, that you shall be the one to capture this Falcon and put his days as highwayman and smuggler to rest?"

A large smile, almost a smirk, settled about Governor Mansfield's lips with this question. "Aye, my lord, I am sure that *I* shall be the one to put an end to all of the Falcon's treasonous activities. This very day, we added two additional British naval vessels to our efforts to comb the Charleston coast for the outlaw. Captain Burgess Sutterfield of the *Golden Rover* is in command of our small fleet. He has made a personal vow to deal harshly with the Falcon. He is also carrying aboard his ship the stamps that the Sons of Liberty thought to confiscate from Mr. Beeking's house. Let the rebels try and halt the Crown's interests again, and we will make short work of them."

Kellie clutched her hands tightly within the folds of her gown as she listened to all that was being said. Her features paled with each word the governor uttered. It was with some surprise that she felt Blakely Savage gently squeeze her hand as though offering her some small assurance.

"You sound as though you have everything worked out then, Governor. I drink to your success." Blakely raised his glass as did the others at the table but for Kellie, and they all loudly toasted the governor on his future success in Charleston.

Lowering his glass, Governor Mansfield's dark eyes took in the pale features of Kellie McBride. "Forgive me, Mistress McBride, for such talk at your table. I had only thought to assure you that nothing would be lacking in my duties as your new governor. I was sent here to quell these radicals and I do not take the job lightly."

Kellie's gaze lowered to her clenched hands and as the governor watched her with a suspicious light in his piercing gaze, Rose Fielding spoke up. "I agree, gentlemen. There has been enough talk of duty and causes. Why don't we retire to the parlor and I shall play a tune on the spinet for your entertainment."

Blakely Savage was the first to rise from his seat. "How can one resist such a delightful invitation, Miss Fielding?" he said, and the rest of the group began to vacate the table.

For the rest of the evening Kellie played the gracious hostess beside her aunt, but inside she felt miserable. She was even more anxious to warn the Falcon about Governor Mansfield's plans for his capture. Even at this very moment, she thought, he could be being chased by this Captain Sutterfield, who had taken on the Falcon's capture as a personal quest, or caught in some other trap of Governor Mansfield's making. She had to get word to him of the danger he was in, but she was powerless to devise a plan to see this through.

As Blakely Savage and several other guests left, and Governor Mansfield, Elroy Beeking, and the two soldiers also said their farewells, Kellie at last was free to make her way to her chamber. After kissing her aunt and father good night, she made her way up the stairs.

Once in her bedchamber, Kellie paced about the large room. She went over and over in her mind all that Governor Mansfield had said about the Falcon. Her one meeting with the daring smuggler had changed her world forever. He was always in her thoughts, but this night he seemed bolder and more dashing than ever in her mind. How would she be able to live with herself if he were to be caught and hanged? Was he so terrible? He was fighting for a cause that he believed in strongly — indeed, one that most of the colonists believed in, whether they proclaimed their beliefs aloud or not.

As she changed out of her dress and into her nightgown, she felt the full frustration of her inability to help the Falcon or to change the plight of the colonists. She had done all that she could, she told herself. She had risked her own life time and again to carry messages for the patriots. She had also told Marie and the men at the inn that had received the messages that she wanted to warn the Falcon of the danger he was in. What more could she do?

She tried to take her mind off of these affairs by reading from a book of sonnets that she kept by her bedside, but this did not serve to relieve her of the thoughts plaguing her mind. Had she, in fact, done all that she could? Was there not some way she could get word to the Falcon? *There had to be!* She threw the book aside and again was on her feet and pacing about.

Finding herself before the hearth gazing into the dimming flames of the fire, she brought to mind the image of the Falcon that she secretly secured there. She brought his dark, handsome features into focus in her mind's eye, until he was as close to her as he had been that night, that night, which seemed so long ago.

"Drat!" she scolded herself. What kind of simpleminded twit was she becoming over a man she did not even know? Why should *she* be the one to have such concern for his welfare?

With that thought she wrapped her robe around herself and left her chamber. Perhaps some fresh air would relieve her of these images of the Falcon. She shivered slightly as she remembered the feel of his hands about her body as the silk robe grazed her flesh, and with such thoughts she hurried down the stairs.

The downstairs portion of the house was dark and quiet. Her aunt and father had retired and Vern had gone to town, as promised, to visit Marie. Traversing the parlor, she easily slipped out into the gardens.

For a few minutes she walked about the tiled patio on bare feet, then started across the trimmed lawns. Beneath a large oak there was a stone bench that on occasion Kellie had visited when she wished to be alone to gaze on the bountiful beauty of the gardens.

The gardens at Moss Rose had been her mother's pride. Though Elizabeth McBride had been taken from this life when Kellie had been young, she could remember fleeting images of her golden-haired mother. Again she felt the loss of her mother deeply. How she needed a woman to confide in! A woman who would listen to her problems and would understand her inner self, without scorning her or rebuking her for the feelings that were running rampant through her soul. Oh, she could easily enough talk to her Aunt Rose, but her aunt was so straightlaced, Kellie was sure she would be shocked to hear of her meeting with the Falcon and even more horrified to know that her niece was a courier for the patriots. More than likely Aunt Rose would quickly beseech her father to make arrangements to marry her off; and with her luck, the happy bridegroom would be Elroy Beeking or another man of his ilk!

Suddenly, from out of the shadows of the oak tree a figure loomed before her and, fearful, Kellie gasped, her body tensing as she readied to run from the intruder.

"Do not be afraid, Kellie."

The husky voice filled her ears and sent ripples of gooseflesh along her arms. Without being able to make out his face, Kellie knew who her nighttime visitor was. "You!" she gasped. "What are you doing here?" Her eyes quickly surveyed the gardens to see if there were anyone about.

"No one knows I am here. The house is dark and the servants abed." His deep voice caressed her as he drew closer to the bench.

For a time Kellie could not speak. She was mesmerized by his presence and his lulling voice.

"I was drawn to your gardens this night, as I

have been other nights, in the hopes of seeing you again."

"You have come here other nights?" Kellie whispered.

"Aye, Kellie. Other nights I have been led here, but this night my desire to catch a glimpse of you was even stronger. I have brought you a gift, but I fear that it is little compared with your own rare beauty." He held out a lone, red rose, the thorns having been removed from the long stem.

"It is beautiful," Kellie whispered as she held the flower almost lovingly in her hand and her eyes sought out his face. "I have gone back to the Swain's Wing Inn with hopes that I, also, would see you once again," she confessed.

"I know this well. I was told of your every visit. But I want to warn you once again to have a care for your safety."

"But I would help in some way! It is as though I have just awakened to the plight of the colonists. Can I now sit back and act as though all the Crown inflicts upon us is of no consequence?"

"There are other ways to help besides risking yourself." The Falcon sat down upon the bench beside her. His dark cloak concealed his figure, his midnight hair glistened beneath the moonlight that filtered through the treetops. As Kellie looked trustingly into the handsome outline of his face, he reached out and drew her body tightly against his own. "What good to triumph over tyranny if *you* are lost in the battle?" he said, and before either knew what was happening, his lips descended, and tenderly closed over her own. As Kellie moved closer into his embrace, the kiss heightened, their lips relentless, as if seeking out some knowledge that was hidden even from them.

With the first stirrings of love awakening within her breast, Kellie clung to the dark, mysterious stranger. She lost all reason and thought in his arms. Never had she been kissed this way, never had she been held so tenderly in a man's arms, never had she surrendered so completely. As his tongue began to probe her mouth gently, she felt her very limbs melting, intoxicated with desire. In that moment she knew that she would do anything to stay forever in his arms. He had but to lead and she would willingly follow him . . . anywhere that he desired.

With an inward sigh of regret, the Falcon put Kellie at arm's length. "I am afraid that we must part once again, my heart." His husky whisper tingled along her spine and drove her mindless to anything except the kiss they had shared, his arms about her, and his softly husky voice filling her ears.

"When will I see you again?" she asked.

"I will come to you." With his words, the Falcon placed a tender kiss upon her soft petal lips as he regretfully rose to his feet.

As though his leaving sparked her to her senses,

Kellie also rose, her hand clutching his dark cloak as she beseeched him to have a care for himself. "Governor Mansfield claims that he will capture you! He has added two more naval vessels to patrol the coast for your ship."

"Do not fear for me, my heart. I will have a care." With these words he held her tightly against his chest, his hand tenderly caressing the warm flesh of her delicate cheek. "You should go now, before someone discovers that you are not abed."

Kellie suddenly felt the full impact of his leave-taking. "Why does it have to be this way? Why can you not tell me who you are?" she implored as she felt tears welling up in her eyes.

"The time is not yet right, my heart. Be patient, we shall not be apart forever." With this he was gone, his figure disappearing through the shadows of the gardens.

Kellie felt a warm ache in the pit of her being as her eyes searched the gardens for the dark figure. Her hand lightly touched her lips where she could still taste the fiery kiss they had exchanged. He had called her his heart. This man that had mysteriously come into her life as a stranger had sworn with his parting words that they would not forever be apart.

As she made her way back to the house, she glanced down and glimpsed the perfect red rose clutched in her hand. Slowly a languid smile settled about her lips. Though turmoil and danger seemed to set upon them from every direction, she no longer felt the fear that had earlier filled her soul. The Falcon had, she knew, claimed her for his very own.

Chapter Four

"Halt, in the name of the Crown! Stand where you are!" The shout reverberated through the once-dark, quiet courtyard of the Swain's Wing Inn. The yell was followed by a stampede of British soldiers, their bayoneted muskets glittering in the torchlight.

"Run mistress!" the man standing next to Kellie hissed, scanning the ranks of the advancing ambush of redcoats with some disbelief as he pushed her in the direction of the stables. Without waiting for her to obey, he turned away, seemingly disappearing into the dark shadows of the night.

Fear the likes of which she had never known took hold of Kellie's very soul as she abruptly came to her senses and, swinging about, made a dash for her horse. They had been caught in a trap! *A trap!* her mind kept repeating over and over as she heard the shouts of the soldiers; with every rattle of their steel sabers, terror raced through her body.

"Catch that one, the other went this way!" the young lieutenant in charge shouted as he sent a group of at least a dozen soldiers off in the direction of the man who had fled through the trees. The rest of the soldiers followed him as he ran toward the stables.

Kellie could feel the wild frenzy of her heartbeat as the blood pumped fiercely in her chest. Reaching her horse, she knew that she had only seconds before the soldiers would set upon her. She frantically untied the reins from the wood railing, and was pulling herself up into the saddle when she suddenly felt a viselike grip encircle her upper arm. Without a moment's hesitation, her only thought being to escape, she pulled the small pistol from the pocket of her cloak and, clasping her eyes tightly shut, pulled the trigger. Instantly her arm was released.

As she swung up into the saddle and kicked at the sides of her mount, she glimpsed the fallen British soldier. She felt the cowl of her dark cloak slip from her head as her mount took flight beneath her.

"Give chase! Get after the traitorous bitch! Do not let her get away!" the lieutenant shouted to his men. He had been first to reach the wounded soldier's side and had seen the wealth of golden curls spill from the black cloak of the fleeing rider.

Never before had Kellie felt the terror that was now coursing through her veins. She knew that it would be only a matter of seconds before the soldiers were mounted and giving chase. With frantic cries of encouragement to her horse, she pushed her mount faster and faster. In a headlong flight, she raced across the pasture at the back of the inn, her instincts telling her to stay away from the roads, where the British soldiers would surely be searching. They would be looking for the man with the packet. Not daring to breathe, Kellie pushed her horse onward through the darkness of the night.

Within moments, she heard the thunder of hoofbeats behind her and the shouts of the soldiers as they caught sight of her cloaked figure. Desperation clutched at her heart as she put the pasture behind her, cleared a small ditch, and started through a field toward the woods.

Quite suddenly, a lone, dark figure on horseback appeared out of the trees directly in Kellie's path. She felt a scream well up in her throat as she realized her capture was imminent. She tried to maneuver her horse to the right and away from him, but as the horseman pulled abreast of her, she heard him shout to her to ride for the coastline. Turning her horse immediately to carry out the man's instruction, it dawned on Kellie with a surge of hope that the intruder was an *ally*. Joyfully, she understood that he had appeared out of nowhere to somehow help her in her deadly flight—he was a patriot!

Riding as fast as her horse could carry her, she did not dare look back to see what had become of the helpful stranger. She had to get away! She could not be caught by the British and charged with treason!

Mile after mile of pasture and field passed beneath her; until gradually she became aware that she no longer heard the heavy sound of hoofbeats behind her.

The coastline was only a short distance ahead, and at last Kellie allowed her pent-up breath to escape. Hearing the labored breathing of her stallion, she slowed his pace, her ears listening intently for any sound of pursuit.

Reaching a stretch of the coastline which she knew well, she dismounted, feeling a deep trembling in every limb of her body. For a time, she wrapped her arms around her horse's neck, as much for support as to show the large beast how grateful she was for the part he had played in her daring escape.

A long, shuddering sob escaped her throat as Kellie at last allowed herself to recall all that had taken place at the inn. Only seconds before hearing the British officer shouting for them to halt, she had handed the man she had met behind the inn the packet with which she had been entrusted. Everything after that seemed to have happened so quickly, she could scarcely believe her part in it had taken place. Again she remembered the sheer terror that had filled her when the soldier had taken hold of her arm, and her own instinctual response to reach for the small gun she had thought to carry.

"I killed him!" Her voice came out in a strangled whisper as the realization of her actions settled over her, and Kellie sobbed, burying her face in the lathered neck of her horse.

Suddenly she felt a firm grip on her shoulders, and Kellie jumped back, her tear-stained eyes wide with terror as she tried to pull away. Her first thoughts were that the British had found her.

The hands held her tightly as a soothing voice touched her ears. "You are safe now. I led them on a merry chase through the forest and then doubled back to find you."

A sigh of relief escaped her as Kellie realized that it was not a British soldier that had found her, but the Falcon. "It was *you?* You were the one who helped me flee the British?" Kellie gasped between stifled sobs.

A deep chuckle left the Falcon's throat. "Aye, my heart. It was I." He tried to keep his tone light, for he could easily feel the trembling of her body and could well understand her fear. In his mind he relived the moment when he had sat in the shelter of the trees behind the inn and watched as the courageous woman had evaded the British troop. He thanked God that he had been the one who had gone to retrieve the packet from the patriot courier. Though the man had fled with the packet, the Falcon was confident that he, too, had evaded capture. The patriot was a smart man, and had been in like situations in the past.

"I shot one of the soldiers!" Her words brought him out of his reverie. "I killed a man back at the inn!" Her voice quieted to a whimper as her tears flowed and she allowed him to hold her tightly against his chest.

"No wonder they were so determined to capture you." The Falcon let out his breath against her soft curls. He reviewed the full scope of the night's dealings and thought about how very different the outcome might have been if he had not been in the area. He was silent as he gently stroked her slim back.

Between her soft sobs, Kellie tried to explain what had taken place at the inn. "It was a trap. I had just handed over the packet to the man I was to meet when the soldiers came out of nowhere and surrounded us. There was so little time, and I was so afraid."

"The man you gave the packet to was not captured by the British?"

"I . . . I do not think so. Oh, I am not sure! It was so dark and after he warned me to run to my horse, he disappeared so quickly. All I could think to do was get away."

The Falcon nodded his head. If the courier had time to warn Kellie to make her way to her horse, more than likely he had had the time to save himself. He was a good man, quick and smart. The Falcon felt confident that the packet would reach the right hands.

"It was so terrible!" Kellie cried, clutching fiercely at his dark cloak. "I thought that I would get away from them, but when I reached my horse, one of the soldiers grabbed hold of my arm! I never thought to hurt anyone! I just wanted to get away!"

Feeling her tremble violently in his arms, the Falcon cradled her against his chest. Scooping her gently up into his embrace, he carried her to a small copse along the beach. Spreading his cloak with one arm, he lowered her tenderly upon it. He went to the horses and led them to a group of trees, securing their reins.

"There was little else you could do, Kellie." He knelt down and in soft tones reassured her, his large hand lightly caressing her cheek, and feeling there the wetness of her tears. "If you had not defended yourself, you would have been captured by the soldiers."

"I was so afraid." Her green eyes displayed her turmoil as she looked into his eyes. "I should have listened to you and given up this game of courier, but Marie could not get away from her father's tavern and the packet had to be delivered."

The Falcon sat down next to her on the cloak and pulled her into his arms, feeling the trembling of her body and the frightened pounding of her heart. He spoke in soothing tones. "My sweet heartling, you are safe now. Try to put this night from your mind. There was no other choice but to save yourself." When he thought of what could have happened to her if she had not shot the soldier! Holding her tightly, he offered her the only comfort he could, as his hands tenderly caressed her golden curls, and his lips lightly pressed warm kisses against her smooth brow.

He spoke softly into her delicately scented curls. He talked of things he hoped would distract her from the happenings of the ill-favored night. His thoughts went to the sea, as they so often did when he needed a respite from troubling thoughts. He spoke to her of the beauty he had seen upon the deck of his ship late at night as he stood beneath a starlit sky; of the shimmer of the moonlit waves as his vessel glided elegantly over the dark, warm depths of the ocean; of the acuteness of one's senses as the spray of the sea, its salty tang, mixed with a tropical breeze, and one gazed out over the expanse, the sparkling blue-green expanse, with awe.

Kellie allowed herself to be embraced by the wonderousness of his words. The night's horror seemed to be of another time and place. All that mattered was the world of his making, the world that he was bringing to her. His hands caressed her upper arms and the smoothness of her neck as his soft words held her enthralled. She felt herself coming alive under his ministrations. The trembling of her body was no longer caused by fear, but by a full awareness of his presence. This man whom so many in Charleston called a smuggler and a highwayman had, from their first meeting, shown her only the most tender care. His strong body molded closely to her own as his tender voice filled her ears. With little thought to her actions, she turned in his arms, her face now level with his. She reached out and lightly, almost tentatively, stroked his strong chin.

Looking into her deep, sparkling green eyes, the Falcon knew he was lost. Her beauty left him breathless. The radiance of her pale curls glistening in the moonlight, the rose-petal shape of her full lips . . . Oh, those lips, those sweet, tempting lips!

The kiss they shared was to both a soothing balm.

"Your lips taste of the sweetest nectar," the Falcon breathed against the side of her mouth, as he pulled her tighter into his embrace. "I have not been able to banish from my thoughts their taste and the feel of you in my arms."

Kellie's head reeled, her hands clutching tightly to the dark silk fabric of his shirt as she gazed back into the swirling blue depths of his eyes.

Slowly his thumb touched her mouth, making a light path down her chin to the creamy smoothness of her throat. With a husky groan, he drew her tightly to him, his mouth capturing her lips in a scorching kiss that left them both gasping. His lips seemed to devour hers. His tongue slipped in between her teeth, rhythmically plying her soft mouth, then plunged deeply, and a swirling heady euphoria ignited from the very depths of their souls.

Kellie felt her body melting from within, hot, fiery molten liquid stealing over her. She was no longer sitting in his embrace, but stretched out upon his cloak with his large form molding tightly against her. Her arms encircled his neck as though holding fast to a safe harbor. All thoughts of the past night flew from her mind. This man who had risked much to save her, his strong arms holding her, and his lips endlessly tormenting her, were all that mattered.

The Falcon's lips traversed a path along the side of her mouth, along her jawline, and down her neck to the gap of her silk blouse. The fullness of her straining breasts tempted him as he felt the pounding of her heart. With ease the tiny pearl buttons parted and the open bodice slipped away beneath his hand, leaving the rose-tipped crests of her breasts swelling under the touch of his fingers as his hot kisses rained down upon her.

"You are exquisite," he breathed against her flesh, the hot touch of his breath electrifying her entire body. Ever so tenderly his warm tongue made tiny circles around the rosebud of one breast as his ears filled with the sound of Kellie's small gasps. His mouth took in the fullness of the delicate mound, sucking lovingly and with skill as his other hand lavished attention on the other rose-peaked nub.

In the distant recesses of Kellie's mind, a small voice of warning cautioned her that she was letting this man go too far. His hands, the feel of his lips, made her body respond in an unfamiliar, uncontrollable way, a way that Honey had warned must be explored only by a husband and wife in the privacy of their bedchamber. But she was powerless to heed any warning now. Her body strained toward the Falcon as her breasts swelled under his caresses and a burning heat began to grow in the depths of her body.

Perhaps it was the fact that her life had been in such peril only a short time ago, or perhaps it was the comfort of the cool, soft sand, the velvet-shrouded, star-brilliant night and the salt air of the ocean's breeze that stoked her senses to a point of no return; she was not sure. She only knew that at this moment, in this space of time, all that mattered was the Falcon. Only the thrilling touch of his mouth and hands as they roamed at will over her body was real. She was beyond the point of turning back. Should she even try to quench the searing flames of desire that throbbed wantonly from the core of her being?

As she lay naked against the darkness of the cloak, the Falcon's shimmering silver gaze roamed freely over the beauty before him. He stood and shed his own clothing, his gaze taking in the golden length of curls that fanned out over the cloak and twined about her lovely shoulders. Her passion-filled emerald eyes sparkled. Her young, lush body generously displayed before him caused his own body to throb with a maelstrom of unquenchable passion. "From the first moment I looked upon you, my heart, I have thought of little besides this moment. Your beauty is incomparable. You are all that any man could desire, all that I will ever want." With this his lips captured her own; he was seized with an urgency only the taste of her could quell.

Kellie moaned softly, his tender words touched her heart; she welcomed his loving assault. Wrapping her slim arms about his neck, she pulled his naked body to her, wanting to be overcome, to be possessed by the Falcon.

His mouth and hands seemed to be all over her body at once. The trail of his mouth parted her lips, then sensuously drifted across her cheek, lightly kissing the creamy texture of her skin as his lips roamed from cheek to ear, and then back along her jawline and down the slim column of her throat. Tasting of her flesh as though she were made of the sweetest ambrosia, he lingered at her breasts, tempting their hard tips with deft flicks of

111

his roaming tongue. Slowly his mouth lowered, traveling over the smooth flesh of her ribs, over the milky-white valley of her abdomen, over the curve of her hips, down a long, shapely leg and back up the other. The heated flame of his kisses lovingly settled within the soft triangle of her being.

Kellie's breath caught sharply in her throat, and for a moment she reached down and captured the dark length of his hair in her fingers to try to pull him back to her, but her fingers slackened without a will as he ignored her protests, his tongue probing the sweetness of her body. Soon his ears were filled with her soft moans as she was lost in a tumult of sensual delights. Losing all reason, Kellie felt within her a throbbing, volcanic storm; she ached for more, rising up to contain peaks of rapture she could never have imagined.

Rising up over her, his manhood throbbing with desire, the Falcon gazed into her passion-filled features, his silver eyes locking with the jade jewels below him. In that instant, there was a promise of tomorrow, for this life and all eternity. Gently he eased her legs apart as his mouth lowered. For a moment his lips played over her own, then locked hers in a kiss that joined them completely and swept away all restraint. The Falcon's manhood gently probed between the junction of Kellie's legs as he whispered her name. "You have touched my heart where no other has dared," he said. "You are mine for now and forever." With one deft stroke, he pushed into her tight warm depths.

With his entrance, Kellie felt her body tense. The pain of his intrusion startled her. Everything up until that moment had been so beautiful. How could such pain exist where once there had been only exquisite pleasure?

Seeing the pain transform her beautiful features, the Falcon held himself back, checking his own desire. "Easy, sweet, the pain will soon vanish. The first time is always thus." His lips tenderly kissed her mouth and then gently kissed her eyelids, her soft cheeks, only to return to her mouth.

Kellie forgot her pain as once again the fires of passion began to ignite. Her body, not able to lie still under his ministrations, cautiously began to stir.

It was only a short time before Kellie was swept up into a brilliant realm of passion. Tentatively her hips moved against his own. She discovered for herself the sweet fire of his manhood as he filled her entire being.

The Falcon held back, not wishing to cause her any undue pain, thus giving her a time to adjust to his manhood within her. He wanted the first time to be beautiful for her; he wanted to give her all the time she needed. His lips worshiped her face as he began to feel her stir beneath him. Her hands wrapped about his back and her nails anchored themselves gently in his skin. His body

113

slowly began to move in rhythm with hers.

Looking deeply into her jade eyes and seeing there only passion, none of the earlier pain, he began to move with an increasing boldness of strokes. Gathering the fullness of her buttocks in his hands, the Falcon pulled her fully against him, allowing more of his love tool to enter her warm depths. With the throbbing life of him completely filling her, Kellie cried aloud to the dark night, her satin legs wrapping about his hips, helping him to gain the full bounty of her love. Her body trembled with the sheer ecstasy that consumed her. She met the Falcon's every thrust, until the very center of her being seemed to shatter into a thousand spiraling brilliants. She gasped at the completeness of the release, clinging to the Falcon, his name escaping her lips.

The Falcon savored the knowledge that she had fully shared the joy that his body could bring to hers. He looked down into her face, glimpsing there her wondrous beauty and dazzled eyes; he marveled at how completely he, too, had experienced passion's rapturous heights.

Clasping her tightly in his embrace, the Falcon could only dare to believe the experience they had shared. There had been many women in his past, that fact he could not deny, but never had he known such complete fulfillment in any other's arms. "Oh, Kellie McBride. My heart, my love. You are incredible, the most wonderful, beautiful woman I have ever known." He sank to the petal-soft lips beneath his own, as though wishing to drown forever in their sweetness.

Kellie lay upon the dark cloak as though stunned. She was sure that nothing could compare with what she had just experienced. She was lost to bliss as she accepted his kiss, her ears filing with his gentle words.

They lay upon the Falcon's cloak, their limbs entwined. For some time, Kellie's arms held him against her. But these moments ushered back her reason, memories, conscience. The voice in the back of her mind dimly questioned once again. What had she done? How is it that she could enjoy such an act with a man she knew nothing about—nothing but that he was wanted by the Crown for treason!? Had she no shame for her actions? She did not even know the Falcon's true name!

But Kellie McBride was a woman who was used to taking responsibility for her actions. She would not cry now that she had been set upon, or deny the fact that she had not only enjoyed what had happened but that she had been a willing participant. She pushed the voice from her mind. As the warmth of his body enclosed her, she knew that everything would turn out as it should. After all, had he not called her his love, his heart? Surely he would tell her everything now, and they would be able to declare their love to all.

Kellie was just beginning to feel lulled by these thoughts when the Falcon pulled himself away from her, leaving her chilled by the ocean breeze.

"You had best dress now, my sweet," he said. "You should return to Moss Rose before someone discovers you gone."

"But I thought we would go to Moss Rose together. We could talk to my father," she said, leaning upon her elbows and looking up at the Falcon as he pulled on his tight-fitting black breeches.

Looking down at her with silver-blue fathomless eyes, the Falcon smiled thoughtfully for a moment before bending down and lightly caressing her cheek. "What we shared I will carry in my memory always. But you must understand, it is impossible for me to claim you at this time," he said softly.

"But . . . I thought that after . . ." Her wide eyes carried the meaning of her unfinished sentence.

"What we have shared this night will be between us a seal of love. The day will come soon when we will be able to acknowledge to everyone that we are each other's."

"Can you not even tell me who you are?" Kellie questioned him as she began to pull on her blouse. If he believed that he could not publicly come forth and claim her now, at least after what they had shared he could confide some of his secrets in her.

"It is still best for a time that you do not know. There is too much at stake, and I would not have you forced to admit to the British that you have any knowledge of me. It is not only you that I think of, but your family." As he glimpsed the glimmer of tears forming in her emerald eyes he moved toward her. "I trust you with my heart, my sweet. But I can risk you no further."

Slowly Kellie nodded her head, understanding his reasoning but not wishing to accept it. Was she only to have the memory of these few minutes shared upon his cloak to hold in her heart? She would have no name to put to the handsome features, no knowledge of his life when he was away from her. And then of a sudden the thought struck: What if he were already married? Perhaps after this interlude with her under the stars, he would return to a warm home and a lovely wife! And children! she thought with horror. As far as she knew, he could have a brood of children that pulled at his legs before he left on his nightly raids! What had she done? How could she have surrendered to the passions of her body that *his* body had evoked? She had given herself to a man she knew nothing, absolutely nothing about!

Her distress must have been written upon her features, for leaning over, the Falcon tenderly took her lips. "You are the beating of my heart. There shall never be another for me now that I have tasted of your love."

117

Kellie stared into the silver eyes before her trying to determine for herself the truth of his words. Her fears seemed to melt away as easily as a first winter's snow as she beheld the warmth and tenderness of his gaze. Her lips rose to meet his, drinking in the assurance she needed.

The Falcon rode with Kellie to the long lane of Moss Rose. Before they parted they again shared a kiss they both knew might have to last them for some time.

"Do not carry any more messages for our cause, my love. There are others who are called to do such dangerous work. I want you to stay home where you are safe until the troubles of this night have abated."

Kellie remembered with a start what had happened at the Swain's Wing Inn. "The soldier! Do you think that I truly killed him?" she said.

"Nay, my sweet. But that is all the more reason for you to keep yourself out of trouble's way. The British will be searching for the courier who shot their man, and also for the man you gave the packet to." He could not be sure, of course, that she had not killed the soldier, but she had shown him the small gun that her cousin had given her for her eighteenth birthday, and he doubted that it could have done much damage. But he intended on making sure she steered clear of harm.

"But what if somehow they find out that it was me at the Swain's Wing Inn tonight?" Kellie said desperately. She pictured a troop of British soldiers riding out to Moss Rose with orders for her arrest.

The Falcon was quick to reassure her. "No one could have recognized you, Kellie. Rest easy on that count. They only saw a woman with golden hair. They could not have known it was you."

Reason seemed to return to her with his words. Slowly she nodded her head, wishing that she never had to part with him. He seemed to offer her so much strength and reassurance. When she was in his presence, nothing seemed to frighten her for long.

"If there is need for you to get in touch with me, send word through your friend Blakely Savage. He will be able to send me your message."

"Blakely Savage?" Kellie gasped, not believing her ears. "Why on earth would such a man as Lord Savage be able to get word to you?"

"I have known Blakely for years now," the Falcon said, smiling widely. "You could say that we are very close, though he spouts out loudly enough his fond arguments for British tyranny; our political beliefs are different, but in truth we are well known to each other."

"I can not believe this! Lord Savage has never mentioned that he knows you!" Kellie remembered all of the conversations they had shared, and how Blakely Savage had talked of the Falcon only as a dastardly traitor.

"I am afraid he considers me a bad apple, but

119

he cannot deny our past relationship." The Falcon kissed her quickly one last time. "Do not forget my words. No more acting as courier, and if you need me, let Savage know."

Kellie hastily agreed as she watched him disappear into the darkness of the night.

Riding slowly up the lane to the large house, Kellie's thoughts were in a whirl as she tried to sort them out. So much had happened in the short span of just one night! She was no longer the person she had been this morning, but had been changed into a woman at the Falcon's hands. She vividly recalled each touch, each whisper they had shared upon the beach. Never had she known such wondrous feelings; not for a second would she deny a moment of what she had shared with the Falcon. He had shown her such delight, such rapture, and though she had little previous knowledge of such things, she knew that no other man could have been so gentle and yet so masterful at the same time.

She pushed from her mind all thoughts of the happenings at the Swain's Wing Inn. The Falcon was right. There was no way they could identify her as being the courier who had shot the soldier." She would hold her own guilt for having committed such an act and pray that the man would live.

She would keep only thoughts of the Falcon in her mind, thoughts of the time when he would no longer have to live a secret life of highwayman and smuggler. She left her horse in the stables and made her way to her bedchamber. That night her dreams were of a dark figure with silver eyes who reached for her over the endless expanse of the sea.

Stretching languidly upon her soft down mattress, Kellie awoke contentedly. She had dreamed of the Falcon the night through. The morning sunlight filtered through her chamber windows. If only she could lie abed the entire day with thoughts of him!

Kellie yawned, knowing that this was not to be. Already she had overslept, and there was much for her to do. The accounting books for Moss Rose had been lying on her father's desk for some time, and she had promised herself that she would go over them this morning and complete the time-consuming work. Aunt Rose had asked her to accompany her into town today, but she had declined, saying that the books had to be put in order.

Pulling herself from the satin covers, Kellie knew that if she did not work on the books, her aunt would be upset and think ill of her. She would more than likely declare to her father that Kellie had used the excuse of working on the books to avoid going with her and visiting some of her friends.

"Drat!" she declared softly as she began to dress in a wine-and-cream-colored velvet dress. Life seemed to be becoming more difficult with each passing day.

From the moment she left her bed, thoughts of the soldier she had shot had assailed her mind. Though she tried to force such thoughts away with images of the Falcon, the fear of not knowing if the soldier had died from the wound she had inflicted would not disappear.

After a decent time of sitting behind her father's large oak desk in the downstairs study, Kellie set the ledgers aside and decided to go into town on her own and seek out Marie. Perhaps her friend would have some information about the soldier she had shot, and she could put her mind to rest.

The Spoon and Hound Tavern was unusually busy when Kellie entered through the double front doors. There was a tension in the air that seemed to settle about her. Seeking out Marie, she paid little attention to the hustle and bustle around her.

"I tell ye, it were the Falcon himself I saw standing as bold as ye please on the top mast of the Crown's vessel, the *Silver Star*. Lonny here was at me side and watching, too, and I be swearing, now, that I sees the flash of a gold chest beneath his arm as he swung from a rope to the docks." A large, burly man sat with a small group at a table across the common room and boasted aloud as he gulped down the warm ale in his mug.

"Can ye be believing it? There be talk that he got clean away with the past six month's taxes," another man declared with some awe. "The *Silver Star* was to be leaving Charleston at noon this very day for London."

"Aye, we can all be believing it. He be a daring rogue, that one. But damn me if I, for one, don't be applauding his actions." The man called Lonny spoke in lower tones, as though not wanting his words to go any farther than their table. "Why should our coins be going to England when we could be using them right here in Charleston? The Falcon be the man who will see that our gold gets to those in our own parts, who are much more in need of it than old George sitting high and fancy upon his throne."

Talk of the Falcon's daring exploits seemed to be on the tips of everyone's tongues. As a meeting place of sorts, the tavern was the perfect spot for the men of town to lift a mug and gossip over the day's events.

Marie, like the other serving girls at the Spoon and Hound, was busy rushing about to make sure that mugs were filled with ale and orders taken for those that were hungry. Glimpsing Kellie as she stepped through the front portal, she hurriedly made her way to her side. "Did you hear the news?" she questioned in an excited tone.

So consumed with thoughts of what had taken place the previous night at the Swain's Wing Inn,

Kellie immediately assumed that Marie was talking about the British soldier who had been shot. Word must have spread quickly, she thought, as she slowly nodded her head. "I need to talk with you a moment."

"There is little time now. As you can see, the place is jumping, what with everyone talking about the Falcon."

"The Falcon?" Kellie asked stupidly. She had expected that Marie would question her about what had taken place at the Swain's Wing Inn. Being so distracted with her own problems, she had paid little attention to the people around her, but with Marie's words she saw the men gossiping at the tables and heard the name of the Falcon in most of their conversations. How had anyone found out that it had been the Falcon who had helped her flee from the inn last evening? she wondered as her gaze once again settled upon her friend. "How could they have found out that it was the Falcon?" she breathed at last, her fear growing by the moment. If they knew that the Falcon had played a part in her escape, did they also know that *she* had been the woman acting as courier?

"Why, half the town saw him riding away from the docks this morning on that big black horse of his," Marie said, looking at Kellie strangely as she noticed her pale features.

"Riding away from the docks?" Kellie asked.

"You have not heard, then?" Marie questioned,

wondering for an instant what Kellie had thought she was talking about. Kellie shook her head, and Marie began to explain. "The tax money collected throughout Charleston for the past six months was to leave for England today upon the *Silver Star.* The Falcon and several of his men went aboard ship early this morning and, overpowering the few guards, they stole the Crown's chest of gold!"

"Did he get away?" Kellie's heart hammered wildly in her chest as she envisioned the danger the Falcon had been in and, holding her breath, she awaited Marie's answer.

Her friend smiled broadly. "As ever, the Falcon staged a daring escape for all to witness. Those about the docks say they saw him swinging from the top mast of the *Silver Star* to the dock below, where his horse was waiting. His men disappeared into the crowds."

"Thank God they escaped safely," Kellie said breathlessly.

"I am afraid the British are not of a like mind. They have been searching houses along the streets this morning for any of the men who took part in the robbery. They say Governor Mansfield is fit to be tied, and swearing that someone will pay for this treason." Marie laughed as though the whole affair were a jolly good joke. "The governor has not been here a fortnight and already he has lost the tax money that was to go to England!"

Kellie could well imagine the state that Governor

Mansfield was in. The man did not appear to be one who would take kindly to being duped.

"If it was not about the Falcon and the theft of the tax money that you wished to talk to me about, what was it?" Marie questioned. She watched as another group of men entered the tavern and knew that she had precious few minutes to spare before her father would be casting stern glances in her direction.

"Have you heard anything about what took place last evening at the Swain's Wing Inn?" Kellie's emerald eyes watched her friend's face intently, daring to hope that news about the shooting had not been circulated. If the British had kept the incident secret, perhaps it meant that the soldier had not been seriously injured.

"A few soldiers were in the tavern earlier and I did overhear one of them saying that a soldier had been shot, but with all of the excitement over the Falcon"—she paused and then her eyes widened—"Oh my God, Kellie, was he shot at the Swain's Wing Inn? But you delivered the packet last night! You were there! Did the man you delivered the packet to get away? I am sure he had no other alternative but to shoot the soldier! At least you were not harmed!"

"The courier was not the one who shot the soldier," Kellie whispered softly. "He was the first to see that the soldiers had set a trap. He got away after warning me."

Gazing intently into Kellie's face, the full import of her friend's words settled slowly over her. Marie pulled Kellie toward the kitchen urgently. "It was *you? You* shot the soldier? she questioned in disbelief.

"I did not know what else to do! We were ambushed—suddenly the soldiers were all around us. I ran to my horse and almost got away, but I was apprehended. I do not even know how I was able to do it, but suddenly my gun was in my hand and I fired at the man who was holding me."

Marie set the serving pitcher on a small wood table in the kitchen and patted Kellie's shoulder. "You were very brave then. As you said, you had no other choice. If you had been caught, I do not need to tell you that not only would your family have suffered, but the entire cause would have been threatened. The packet that you carried held valuable information. You did the right thing; had I been in your place, I hope I would have done no less."

"Perhaps the British will be so busy with the Falcon's activities, they will think little of the happenings of last night," Kellie said.

"The soldier was only wounded and will live; I heard an officer say so. Try to forget about it all. You should not carry any more messages for a time. I am sure now that the packet contained information about the tax money aboard the *Silver Star*. The British will be more determined than ever to have someone's head over this whole affair and will be watching the Swain's Wing Inn day and night. There shall have to be a new meeting place arranged. For a while you had best stay a distance from any kind of work for the cause." Marie worried that the wounded soldier would be able to identify Kellie as his assailant if he were to see her again.

"The Falcon was of a like mind. He told me not to act as courier again."

"The Falcon knows what happened?" Marie looked at her friend intently.

"He came to my rescue at the inn. If not for him, the British would have caught me. He led them away and then doubled back and made sure I got safely home."

Marie only nodded her head, cursing the fact that she had so little time to talk to her friend. She wanted to question her further about the Falcon. There was something about her friend's manner that led her to believe she was not disclosing all. "The Falcon is a very smart man," she said. "You should heed his advice well. He knows the state of the colonies and has eluded capture by the British because he knows when to strike and when to retreat." Though Kellie had become valuable to the patriots' cause, Marie knew that nothing was worth the chance of her being caught and imprisoned. "I must be getting back to the common room now," she said, "before my father seeks me out. I will try to steal away to visit you soon." Marie embraced her friend, hoping that Kellie would heed her words of caution and stay at home for a time. There was always the chance that when the soldier recovered, he would recognize her in town and name her a traitor.

Saying goodbye to her friend, Kellie made her way through the front doors of the tavern, all but running into Elroy Beeking and Governor Mansfield on her way out. The men had a group of British officers following closely upon their heels.

Governor Mansfield took Kellie's elbow in an attempt to steady her footing on the sidewalk. "Why, Mistress McBride, what a pleasure to see you again," he said. His piercing, dark eyes ran the length of her figure. "I had plans to call upon you this afternoon at your father's house."

Kellie tried to regain her composure. Of all the people in Charleston she could have run into! she thought. "Governor, Mr. Beeking," she stammered, acknowledging the men. "I was just on my way to my carriage."

"I am sure you can spare us a moment or two," Governor Mansfield stated matter-of-factly.

"What is it that you wish to speak with me about?" she asked. The thought crossed her mind that her fears had not proved to be phantoms. Were not the governor and Elroy Beeking coming to arrest her? Had the governor not said that he was going to go to her father's house? Was this moment not presaging the time of her imprisonment?

Governor Mansfield directed the soldiers behind him to go about their business. "Do not forget, I want Tom Peterson questioned and brought to me at once. He might have had something to do with the robbery this morning, since his boat was confiscated last month. Bring the rest of his family, too. Perhaps one of the women will tell us something if Peterson does not."

Kellie swallowed nervously. All the horrors of the night before flashed through her mind.

"I am sure you heard about the tax money stolen from the *Silver Star?*" Mansfield stated abruptly.

Kellie nodded her head. "I . . . I was just visiting my friend Marie Danning and did hear mention of it at the tavern," she confessed.

"Oh, yes, Marie Danning. A lovely little thing. Charleston is a town with many beauties, but all must be measured against you, mistress."

Elroy Beeking's eyes traveled lasciviously over Kellie's figure.

"As I was saying," the governor continued, "the tax money was stolen, and I have it on good authority that a message was delivered to the traitors last evening, a message that informed the patriots that the tax money was aboard the *Silver Star.* There is no other way the Falcon could have known about the chest of gold, for only a very few of the most trusted men knew of its where-abouts."

Kellie's heart and mind were racing. Why was the governor telling her all of this? Did he suspect her involvement in the patriots' cause?

"Last night a British soldier was shot as he attempted to detain a traitor to the Crown," the governor stated.

He wants to frighten me, Kellie thought. *He thinks I know something and he's trying to make me confess.* Kellie took a deep breath. She'd be damned if she let him win that easily. "What on earth does all of this have to do with me, Governor? Are there no more families like the Peterson's that you can question?" she asked.

"I am getting there, mistress." His tone was hard and his dark eyes studied her intently. "You see, I know who it was that shot the soldier."

Feeling her face drain of all color, Kellie nervously questioned, "You know who it was?"

"The courier was a woman, and we think the Falcon helped her in her escape."

Kellie gave an inward sigh of relief. *He does not know who it is,* she told herself. *He knows only that it is a woman.* "Then why do you not arrest this woman?" she asked coolly.

"I was given the information that the woman was about your size." His jet-black eyes once again traversed the length of her figure. "She also betrayed a wealth of golden hair when her cloak fell away."

He knows! she thought. He knew it was her! He was only playing with her for a time as a cat would play with a poor defenseless mouse. "There are many women in Charleston with blond hair, Governor," she said, forcing herself to look him straight in the eye.

"Perhaps not as many as one would think, mistress. There is also the fact that the wounded soldier caught a glimpse of the woman's face."

No! Kellie thought. *This could not be true.* She was sure she had turned away when her cloak had fallen back. All the soldier could have seen was her hair. "What are you implying, Governor?" she said somewhat angrily.

"Well, we do have a small problem, my dear. As you know, an accusation is all that is needed for an arrest. The description the soldier has given of the woman courier fits you, Mistress McBride, uncomfortably well."

"I assure you, Governor, I was at home all last night."

"Perhaps, my dear, perhaps. But unfortunately the soldier's testimony has put you in a rather unlucky position. I'm afraid I must be *assured* of your loyalty. As I see it, there would be little to gain for any of us if you were to be arrested and sent to Halifax to stand trial for treason."

Kellie gasped aloud, her emerald eyes going from the governor to Elroy Beeking. "You would

132

not dare arrest me!" she exclaimed. "No one would believe you!"

"It matters little whether anyone believes me or not, mistress. If you are arrested for treason and stand trial, your family's properties, slaves, and monies will be forfeited to the Crown."

"You cannot do this terrible thing!" Kellie said desperately, looking from Governor Mansfield to the loathing, unsympathetic expression of Elroy Beeking.

"Perhaps there is a suitable alternative," Governor Mansfield stated as though upon a moment's reflection. He glanced toward Elroy Beeking with a slight smile playing over his features. "My duty as governor in this colony is to assure that the Crown's interests are served. With this thought in mind, I shall set this proposition before you. You, mistress, will have your own choice in the matter."

Kellie's fear was mounting with each word he spoke. The full horror of her situation unfolded before her. Whatever his proposition, somehow she knew that any alternative to imprisonment, granted by Governor Mansfield, would leave her unconditionally compromised.

"As I said, the choice shall be entirely your own. Either I shall declare you a traitor to the Crown, or you shall of your own free will marry within the month!"

Kellie gasped in disbelief. "*What* did you say? Did I hear you right? I must marry within the month?"

"Not one day over the last of the month, I say. I wish to be assured of your loyalty. Suspicion has been raised that you were the woman at the Swain's Wing Inn last night. I am willing to be sympathetic, under the circumstances. After all, idleness can be dangerous. I am convinced that a husband would keep you busy with his needs and the needs of a home. There would be no time for *causes*."

With wide eyes Kellie stared at the governor. This was her choice. She either would be arrested as a traitor or she would have to marry. "You cannot force such a thing upon me, Governor!" she cried. "How on earth could I find the man that I would wed in so little time?" Both situations were insane! How could she make such a choice between the two? She could not allow herself to be arrested. Not only was her own life at stake but her family's as well. But on the other hand, a speedy marriage was impossible. The Falcon was the only man she could share vows with. He was the one of her heart; after what they had shared, she could take no other as her husband. And he had declared that the time was not yet right for him to come forth and claim her.

The grin the governor bestowed upon Kellie proclaimed that advantage he held over her. In gloating tones, he thrust the barb deeper. "You have not far to look for a suitable mate, Mistress. Elroy

Beeking, our good ex-governor, is more than willing to see to it that you and your family are not compromised by any suspicions that may be cast upon you. You have but to agree to become his wife, and your future and that of your family will be secured." Governor Mansfield smiled. Whether she was the woman who had been at the Swain's Wing Inn or not, he would have his way, along with the portion of her dowry that would come to him for arranging a match between Kellie McBride and Elroy Beeking.

Kellie gazed in horror at the governor and then upon the odious features of Elroy Beeking. The whole affair was but a ploy of the governor's and Beeking's to force her into marriage with the loathsome man. Governor Mansfield had no idea who had shot the soldier. He saw the incident only as a means to threaten her into agreeing to wed Elroy Beeking. Her anger flared. "No!" she declared heatedly. "I have already refused Mr. Beeking, and even under such a threat as imprisonment, I shall not agree to such a union." She glared her distaste at Elroy Beeking, causing his face to flame as his thin hands fluttered about the lace collar at his throat. "Arrest me if you will, but I will never marry this . . . this . . ." *scheming bootlicker,* she finished silently, turning on her heel and hurrying to her waiting carriage.

"By the end of the month, mistress!" Governor Mansfield shouted into the carriage window as the

135

vehicle started to pull away. "If you have not wed, then you shall pay the price. Again I say, the end of the month!" As her carriage continued down the dirt street, Governor Mansfield turned back to his companion. "I would put a quick halt to that temper of hers, were I you, Elroy, as soon as the vows are spoken," he said.

How dare the man threaten her in such a manner? Kellie fumed as she clutched her hands tightly in the folds of her gown. If he had thought to get away with such a scheme, he would soon find that he was sadly mistaken. She would go to prison, she would wear rags and beg on street corners, she would . . . she would . . . Her thoughts roiled in a feverish rage as she imagined all that she would do before she would agree to marry Elroy Beeking. Not even if he were the last man on earth . . .

She began to regain her composure as she left town and the carriage started toward Moss Rose. Her reason began to return. Of course she could not be charged with treason and arrested. It was out of the question. She would have to come up with a plan, for she knew without a second thought that Governor Mansfield was not a man to go back on his word. If she did not do something to save herself, he would without doubt follow through with his threats.

The Falcon! He would see her out of this situation. He would come forth as soon as he heard of her dire circumstances and declare his love for her. They would wed before the end of the month and her family would be saved.

Of course he had said that the time was not right last night, but everything was different now. Wasn't it?

She tried to calm herself and plan the moves she would make. She knew she could not go to her father with the governor's demands. He would surely be furious and demand that she be charged and given the chance to defend herself. But remembering the governor's words, she knew that her family would lose everything during the time she would be in Halifax to stand trial. And her father would never agree to the governor's bribery scheme. The only person she could seek council from was Lord Blakely Savage.

She would seek out Lord Savage and have him get word to the Falcon. Though she hated the idea of telling Lord Savage about the ordeal she was in, she saw no way out. He was her only means of getting word to the Falcon.

She sat back with a sigh against the comfortable seat of the carriage. Yes, the Falcon would surely save her from the likes of Governor Mansfield and Elroy Beeking. They would wed, and soon. Everything would turn out for the best. A small smile played about her lips as she again remembered the previous night. Perhaps the governor was unknowingly doing both her and the Falcon a favor by issuing his demands. A warm flush heated her body as she envisioned the Falcon's strong masculine body. Though she knew little of the man, she did know that for all her life there would never be another for her.

Chapter Five

The morning sun had not broken through its shroud of gray clouds. Feeling a chill settle over her due to the early winter weather, Kellie stepped closer to the warm hearth.

"Why would anyone claim that this blackguard and I know each other?" There was a touch of outrage in his voice as Blakely Savage rested comfortably against the wing-backed chair. "And you say that you have an important message for him, and that I should be the one to get it to him?" His bewigged head shook back and forth as his gray eyes studied her agitated movements.

"I was not told directly that you and the Falcon were friends. I was told only that you knew each other and that I could get a message to him through you." Kellie did not want to tell Savage that it was the Falcon himself who had given her this information.

"I have already told you, Kellie, that you would do well to avoid such men as this Falcon. Perhaps I can better help you. Why not tell me the problem and allow me to decide?"

Kellie had known before she came to Savage Hall that it would be no easy task to persuade Blakely Savage to get word to the Falcon for her, but she had not counted on his being this stubborn. "It is a personal matter, Lord Savage. I would not have come to you with such a request if there was any other way."

"Blakely, please. You promised to call me Blakely."

Kellie relented with a sigh as she took small steps around the parlor. Her whole life seemed to be hanging by a thread and he was concerned over forms of address! "Of course, Blakely. Will you help me?" Her jade eyes beseeched him.

"I am afraid that it is not as easy as you seem to think. Can you not tell me something about what you need to relay to this scoundrel?"

Kellie clasped her hands together nervously. She had hoped to avoid answering any direct questions about her need to speak with the Falcon. The fewer who knew of the situation the governor had placed her in, the less chance, she had reasoned to herself, of her family finding out. Seeing that she was getting nowhere with Lord Savage by being evasive, she decided that she would have to take him somewhat into her confidence. "I am not sure where I should begin." She sighed and sat down on the edge of the settee.

His gray-blue eyes held her, not giving her much comfort as she tried to form the words that would soften what she would reveal to a man who did not hide the fact that his allegiance was to the Crown.

"Why do you not start at the beginning?" Blakely Savage offered. "As a friend, you will find me most loyal. I would never betray anything told to me in confidence."

"Thank you, Blakely. I only hope that after I tell you my problem, you will not wish to withdraw your offer of friendship."

"Never!" Savage stated boldly as a small smile flitted about his lips.

"In truth, I do not know how all of this came about." She glanced down at her clasped hands, finding the lie bitter upon her tongue. There was little help for it though, she told herself. She had to get a message to the Falcon, but she could not tell this man the circumstances that had brought her to such a sorry plight. He would never understand her nefarious deeds. He would condemn her as surely as he did the Falcon, if he knew of the help she had given the patriots' cause.

Lord Savage did not speak, but patiently waited for her to continue.

"Yesterday I went to town to visit my friend Marie Darring. At the tavern I learned that two nights ago at the Swain's Wing Inn a British soldier was shot as he attempted to stop a courier who was passing a message to one of the patriots." She swallowed nervously and took a deep breath.

"I heard of the dreadful affair," Savage offered as his gray eyes searched her features. "Rumor has it the Falcon had a hand in the ordeal. I hope that your wish of getting a message to him is not with the intention of providing more gossip for the wagging tongues of Charleston."

"Of course not," Kellie replied. He certainly was not making this easy! "I must speak with the Falcon because Governor Mansfield and Elroy Beeking are using the incident at the Swain's Wing Inn to blackmail me!" There, she had gotten a portion of the truth of her situation out, now she could only pray that Lord Savage would indeed keep what she was telling him to himself.

"Blackmail? How so?" Savage sat up straighter in his chair as at last he appeared to give her his full attention.

"The courier who shot the soldier was a woman, and according to Governor Mansfield was of my size and likeness."

"What has all of this to do with you? You spoke of blackmail?"

Kellie took another deep breath as though to fortify herself. "The Governor and Elroy Beeking approached me when I was in town yesterday, and declared that either I wed by the end of the month or they shall have me arrested for treason. They shall accuse me of being the woman at the Swain's Wing Inn."

"This is outrageous!" Lord Savage jumped to his feet and glared down at her. "How dare he make such demands? Does he have any proof that you were the courier?"

"There is no proof, only suspicions. If I do not comply, I am sure the governor will carry out his threats. If I am arrested, my family will lose all that they own." Kellie's voice cracked as a tear slid down her cheek.

"Perhaps I can talk to the governor," Savage claimed. "What is the advantage in forcing you to wed? And if he has no proof to offer, he can charge you with no crime."

Kellie shook her golden head back and forth. "He thinks that by giving me so little time, I will be forced to marry Elroy Beeking. The two of them have come up with this scheme against me."

Savage sat back down in his chair as though his breath had been knocked out of him. "You are sure this is his reason?" he questioned, though he knew she was not mistaken in her claim. The governor and Beeking had made it obvious already what their intentions were toward Kellie McBride. Looking at the distressed features of the young woman across from him, he softly questioned, "What part does the Falcon play in all of this?"

Kellie did not know how to answer him; she blushed scarlet as the gray-blue eyes watched her intently. She could not possibly tell Lord Savage what had taken place between her and the Falcon. "I . . . I thought perhaps he could help me," she stammered.

"In what manner, madam?" A dark brow arched above one gray eye. "If your hopes are that he will sway the governor, you are mistaken. The governor would never listen to an appeal from a criminal."

Slowly Kellie shook her head, feeling the heat of her flushed features spreading over her entire body.

"If this is not your intent, I have cause to wonder if you hold thoughts that this villain will rescue you by some other means before the month is out?"

Not able to respond, Kellie could but look down at her lap.

"How far has this relationship gone between you and the Falcon?" He easily glimpsed her answer in the emerald eyes that rose up to meet his. "I see then," Blakely stated uncomfortably.

"He is not as you think," she said. "He is good and kind and fights for a cause he strongly believes in."

"I must warn you, Kellie, I see little good coming from your going to the Falcon with this. From what I know of him, he is not the kind who comes forth to assist a lady in her time of need."

"I have no other choice," Kellie uttered almost

144

inaudibly.

"Surely there are other men in Charleston who would be more than willing to claim you as their bride," Blakely offered.

"It . . . it is too late for me to go to another." Let him think what he would, she told herself. She had no other choice but to get word to the Falcon, and this man was the only means she knew of to gain her desire.

Seeing her agitation and distress, Lord Savage sought only to comfort her. "Then there is no choice but to get word to the scoundrel."

Kellie brushed away the tear on her cheek and managed a smile. "Thank you, Blakely."

Blakely Savage nodded his bewigged head. "Again I warn you, madam, do not place all of your hopes on this rogue. You would do better with the time left you by looking to some other gentleman to share your future with."

Kellie did not answer. He had agreed to get word to the Falcon, and that was what she had come to Savage Hall for. Lord Savage may not think the Falcon a man of honor with gentlemanly intentions, but *she* had seen a side of the smuggler that no other had. He had declared that she was his heart and that they would be together one day. Surely his declarations had meant something to him as they had to her, and he would not see her wed to another.

The days passed swiftly as Kellie anxiously awaited word from the Falcon. Each night in her dreams the Falcon came to her and offered his love and protection, but with the morning light, she faced the reality of another day's passing and the time drawing near when she would be forced to account for her deeds.

Two weeks flew by. Kellie tried to lose herself and her thoughts in the work that needed her attention at her father's estate. She became nervous and edgy as each hour passed. She expected the Falcon to boldly step before her and make his declarations known to her and her family. Blakely Savage had sent word to her a few days after she had been to Savage Hall; her message had been delivered to the Falcon. Now all she could do was wait.

There was but one week left to the end of the month. Not able to abide the isolation at Moss Rose a day longer, Kellie had the stable boy saddle her horse. She had decided to venture into town. She had not heard from Marie and thought perhaps her friend would have some news of the Falcon. Thoughts of him being ill or wounded hounded her. Mayhap Marie would be able to give her some hope, some small bit of reassurance . . .

Entering the town square, Kellie noticed a small group of townspeople standing about. As she drew closer, she saw a woman imprisoned in the wooden stocks that had been little used over the years.

"Molly Fisher!" She gasped as she hurriedly dismounted and ran to the woman's bent form. "Why on earth have you been put into the stocks?" Kellie questioned as she leaned down to address the elder woman. Her emerald eyes sparkled with ire as she looked around at the men and women standing off to the side and watching the scene from a distance. None dared to get too close to the imprisoned woman, with thoughts that her ill fortune may in fact be passed on to them.

Glimpsing several of Molly's children standing back with woeful expressions on their faces, her fury increased. What on earth could this kindhearted woman have done to deserve such cruel treatment? "Let me get you some water." Kellie hurriedly crossed to the mercantile store and took a dipper of water from the outside water bucket.

Brushing back the gray strands of hair from the woman's face, she held the dipper of water to her lips as Molly thirstily drank the cool liquid.

"Thank you, Kellie, but you had best go on about your business now. The governor has declared that I must stay in the stocks for the length of the day and I would not wish for you or any other to be treated as harshly if caught speaking with me."

"But why are you in the stocks? What did you do to be punished in such a manner?" Kellie questioned heatedly as she felt her hatred of the governor and the Royal office he stood for increase in measure.

Molly only shook her head, not wishing for Kellie to linger in her presence. It was one of her older sons who stepped forward and, taking Kellie's arm led her to the sidewalk and away from his mother.

"What happened, Bobby?" Kellie asked the young boy who stood taller than she.

"It was my little brother Harry that brought the governor's wrath upon us, Mistress Kellie," Bobby began to explain. Kellie had to search her brain to remember which one of Molly and Mab Fisher's children was named Harry.

"Harry and some of the younger children were playing to themselves as me Mum and I and a couple of the older boys were gathering clams, when the governor and two of his officers came down to the wharf. Well, little Harry, he always has had an eye for something shiny, and when he saw the governor's scarlet jacket and all those gleaming buttons, he went right up to him and reached out to touch one of the buttons."

A small smile flitted about Kellie's lips as she envisioned the tiny, dirty hands reaching out to the governor.

"You guessed right, mistress. Little Harry was covered with mud, as he and my brothers and sisters were making little mud cakes. But me Mum saw no reason for Governor Mansfield to slap him so hard on the hand."

"He hit little Harry?" Kellie could not believe her ears—how could anyone dare to slap such a sweet little boy as Harry Fisher? Now that his image came to mind she was reminded of the towheaded boy's winning smile for everyone he met.

"Of course when me Mum and brothers heard little Harry crying out we hurried over to see what was the matter, and when me Mum took in the scene, she rushed right up to the governor and told him just what she thought of such a large brute striking such a small child."

"And he put Molly in the stocks because of what she said?" Kellie could well believe Governor Mansfield's scorn when confronted by a vengeful mother trying to defend her child, but such punishment was unreasonable!

"The two soldiers grabbed hold of her and Governor Mansfield ordered that she be put in the stocks until sundown," Bobby dejectedly stated, his bright blue eyes returning to his mother's crumpled form.

"Is there anything I can do?" Kellie felt her spirits sink even lower, as she fully realized the extent of Governor Mansfield's power in Charleston.

"Nay, mistress. It would only make things worse for me Mum. I be looking after the younger children till she is freed."

"Please tell your mother that I will be out to see her soon," she instructed, and with another glance of sympathy cast in Molly's direction, she pushed her way through the crowd on the sidewalk and slowly made her way to the tavern.

Marie had little encouragement to offer Kellie. She had heard little of the Falcon in the past few weeks, and could only assure her friend that there had been no word of his being wounded or ill. It would appear since the British had set up the trap at the Swain's Wing Inn that there had been little activity of any kind on the part of the patriots. Even the Sons of Liberty had remained quietly in the background over the past weeks. "I did hear that a load of smuggled goods was brought into Charleston and distributed, and that Governor Mansfield has increased the British patrols on all of the Charleston roads."

"Then the Falcon must still be in the area," Kellie reflected aloud, which gave her friend a moment's pause.

"Well of course he is still in Charleston! He would never leave the cause of the patriots. There is still much work that needs to be done. The British seem to grow in numbers every day."

"Governor Mansfield seems to have a tight hand over all of Charleston," Kellie added solemnly. "Right this moment Molly Fisher is in the stocks."

"I heard about Molly's troubles, but at least she will be freed this evening. That is more than can be said for the young men that will be forced to serve two year's service in the Crown's navy."

"What?" Kellie had not heard of this latest outrage.

"You have been keeping yourself at Moss Rose of late, so of course you have not heard the news. The governor has sent out a proclamation that at least a dozen of Charleston's young men will be pressed into service in the Crown's naval force. Their names have not been circulated as yet and there are rumors that some of those who think they are on the governor's list have already left Charleston.

"How can he do this?" Kellie questioned in outrage, but she already knew that the governor could do what he wanted, there being no higher authority in Charleston. After all, looking at her own circumstances, she knew that no offense was beyond him.

A group of men entered the tavern and Marie knew there was little time left to visit. "He will do as he desires until he is stopped. If we sit back and allow England to rule us, then we will have to live with such tyranny. But if we stand up and fight for what we believe in, perhaps one day we will be able to live in peace and not have to fear what tomorrow will bring." Marie embraced her friend and returned to her duties.

Kellie had much to think about on her ride back to Moss Rose. The Falcon was still in Charleston and he had received the message that she needed to speak with him. She could not understand why he had not yet come to seek her out. She could only hope that he would come soon. There was still a week left until the end of the month. Perhaps he was so busy he had not had the time, she reasoned. After all, Marie had said that smuggled goods had been brought into Charleston. That would mean that the Falcon had been gone, for days perhaps, on his ship, and on his return he had heard of all the other atrocities that Governor Mansfield was inflicting on the populace, and of course he was busy making plans to help in some way. He would come to her as soon as he was able, she told herself once again. She only hoped that he would come in time. Perhaps she should send him another message, she thought, as she gave her horse over to the stable boy and started into the house.

As Kellie entered the front door, her aunt Rose met her in the foyer. "That fancy-dressed Lord Savage has been waiting for you in the sitting room." Rose Fielding made a sour face, informing Kellie in no uncertain terms of her distaste for Blakely Savage.

Feeling her heart skip a beat with thoughts that perhaps Lord Savage had brought her word from the Falcon, Kellie rushed past her aunt, not wishing to linger a moment longer than necessary.

"You look well refreshed after your ride," Blakely Savage said, greeting her warmly as Kellie entered the sitting room.

Kellie smiled in return and asked without preamble, "Have you brought me some word from the Falcon?"

Seeing no way to avoid dampening the excitement he had glimpsed on her features, Blakely shook his head as he took her hand and pulled her toward the settee. "I am afraid I have not received any word from that wiley outlaw."

"Then why are you here now?" Kellie blurted out, as all her hopes for rescue seemed to shatter with his words.

"You have but a week left until the end of the month. I thought that perhaps you had made a decision." Lord Savage seemed not to take offense at her outburst.

"How can I make a decision when I have not heard from the Falcon?" Kellie wanted to shout at him, but controlled herself, feeling repentant for her earlier rudeness. It was surely not his fault that she had not heard from the Falcon. Lord Savage had done all that he could to help her.

"I told you not to count on a man who plies his trade under cover of night. You cannot trust a man of his nature."

"Could you not send another message to him? Perhaps he did not receive the first; perhaps something has happened to him!" Kellie said, for admitting to herself that the Falcon did not care about her plight after all they had shared was too horrible to bear.

Lord Savage hated to see such distress upon her beautiful features, but there was little he could do. "You must listen to reason now, Kellie. The message has been delivered to the Falcon and he has not responded. You must now think of yourself. You have only a few more days until the decision is taken out of your hands. Governor Mansfield will then be the one to decide your future. Of course you must not allow yourself to be arrested. Your only other alternative is to wed."

"What would you have me do?" Kellie cried aloud. "Only the Falcon can help me!"

"You can look to another," Blakely stated boldly. "The Falcon and Elroy Beeking are not the only men in Charleston."

"I have already told you that that is impossible!" How could she take another as her husband when she had already given the Falcon the prize that should only be given to a husband on his wedding night? she questioned herself.

Blakely waved her words away with a brush of his hand. "There are plenty of men who would overlook this one slight, er, iniquity. We have but to determine an agreeable mate for you."

"You are not serious!" Kellie exclaimed aloud.

"Aye, serious indeed, madam. You have no choice. I have given this a great deal of thought in the past two weeks. Perhaps Jonathan Bitner would be the right man. He owns a fine bakery shop. Or Andrew Bosworth. He is a tad older

154

than you, but he could provide well for all your needs."

"Jonathan Bitner? Andrew Bosworth?" Kellie could not believe her ears. Both men were well over sixty years old! Was she to be a wife or a nursemaid?

"We must remember your situation." Blakely's high tone filled her ears. "You are not in a position to be choosy. But if you think Bitner and Bosworth too old, perhaps John Carpenter would fit the bill. I hear he is looking for a wife to care for his six children. It may be a bit difficult at first, but I am sure you would adjust."

Kellie could do nothing but sit with her mouth wide open as she looked at Lord Savage. "You must be jesting," she at last returned.

"Do not be testy, Kellie. I am trying to help you."

"I can well do without your help, if these men are your solution," Kellie declared with some agitation.

"There is one more choice." Lord Savage's gray-blue eyes narrowed.

"And, pray tell, who is this unlikely candidate?" Kellie questioned, wondering who next he would consider as a possible spouse for her.

"Why, myself, of course." He continued before she could respond. "You must admit, I am not as old as Bitner and Bosworth, nor do I have a house full of children who need mothering. And I do have the added advantage of wealth to see that you are comfortable."

"You are not serious!" Kellie stared at the satin-and-lace-bedecked man across from her and for a moment held back the strong desire to laugh outright at his proposal.

"You must admit that this solution would benefit us both. You would have a husband and I would have a beautiful wife who would stand at my side at parties and other functions. This would certainly put a halt to the matchmaking matrons I am the unfortunate prey of."

"I . . . I could not possibly allow you to make such a sacrifice."

"Then you will agree to wed Elroy Beeking?" Lord Savage intoned, and when she did not answer, he added, "We would be a suitable match. We get along well together."

"But what of the Falcon? What about what we have already shared?" Kellie could barely think faced with the overwhelming prospect of marrying Lord Savage.

"We will forget the Falcon, of course," was his reply.

How could she forget the Falcon? she silently asked herself. Could she forget his kisses? His touch and the husky murmur of his voice next to her ear? No! She would never be able to forget him! "I could never be the type of wife that you deserve, Blakely," she softly offered. Her heart belonged to another whose memory was impossible to escape.

"And what sort of wife do you suppose I am in need of, my dear?" Blakely leaned closer to her on the small couch. "My needs are few. My manservant sees to most of them. I ask only for a small amount of your company upon occasion, and that you do no injury to my name."

"But what about . . . what about?" Kellie could not get the words out, but the heated flush of her face told him all.

His pale eyes sparkled. "As I have told you, my needs are few," he said.

His meaning was clear. Kellie pondered this. Perhaps an illness at a young age had rendered him incapable of performing in the marriage bed, or perhaps an accident . . . and then a horrible thought struck her: What if he had no desire for a woman because his attractions did not incline toward her sex? "Would you like to talk about it?" she at last got out, thinking that after all she had shared with him, he might be in need of a willing friend to listen to his own hardships.

"I would rather speak no more on the subject. Suffice it to say that another woman's virtue is quite safe in my company."

"Oh!" was all that Kellie could say.

"You see now that the most practical solution for both of us is for you to agree to marry me."

"But this is insane!" Kellie argued. "I cannot

possibly agree to wed you or any other besides the Falcon."

"Not so insane, madam as I am sure you will soon realize. Your choices are few; I believe that your agreeing to become my wife would be the lesser of two evils put before you." Blakely rose to his feet and started to the door of the sitting room. "You still have a few days to think over my proposal. I shall be awaiting your answer." With this he exited the room, leaving Kellie alone with her thoughts.

Kellie awoke to a light rain tapping against the leaded panes of her chamber windows and, snuggling deeper into the warmth of her covers, for a few minutes she indulged in the comfort of a secure world. She had been lost within her dreams of the Falcon. They had been running hand-in-hand through a vast meadow of sweetly scented flowers. She had felt the sheer happiness of being in love and at peace. But with the morning came reality and with it, the knowledge of what would never be.

She had but one day left to make a decision. Tomorrow Governor Mansfield and Elroy Beeking would be at her father's door to demand either her arrest or her consent to wed the ex-governor.

She had lain awake late into the night and had at last forced herself to face the truth. The Falcon was not going to rescue her from the fate that tomorrow would bring. It was up to her to see that her family was protected.

Pulling herself from the warmth of the covers, she hurried to the hearth and stoked the flames within the fireplace. For a moment she stood before the fire and shivered; she felt the chill of the room, but there was a cold in her very soul that she would be hard-pressed to dispel.

Stepping to her wardrobe, she pulled forth a dark brown woolen gown that was as somber as her mood. Once dressed and fully set on her course of action, Kellie left her bedchamber. She was relieved to find the downstairs portion of the house empty.

Sending word to the stables for Jerome to bring the carriage around, she waited on the front veranda as she secured her cloak tightly about her.

Her wait was a short one and soon she was settled comfortably against the cushioned seat of the vehicle. Kellie felt as numb inside as out as Jerome started the carriage down the long lane of Moss Rose. As the conveyance halted before Savage Hall, Kellie swallowed nervously as she gazed up at the towering stone building. The gray, rainy weather seemed to magnify its forbidding aspect. She slowly made her way from the carriage to the front double doors.

It was Blakely Savage himself, resplendent in blue twilled silk, who opened the large double doors after her hesitant knock. With apparent surprise on his features, he beckoned her inside the front foyer.

Taking her damp cloak from about her shoulders, Savage smiled as he took in her sedate beauty. "You are out and about early this morning, Kellie," he greeted and with a wave of his hand, he directed her toward the long hallway that led to the parlor. "Come and get yourself warmed." He motioned for her to walk before him, admiring the graceful swaying of her skirts as he followed her.

"This is certainly a pleasure that will serve to brighten this miserable day." His gray-blue eyes fixed upon Kellie as she settled herself on the settee.

"I hope I am not arriving at a bad time." Kellie took in his elaborate outfit of blue silk and gold braid and, remembering his hasty answer to her knock, she thought that perhaps he had been on his way out.

"No, I am completely at your disposal," he hurriedly reassured.

Kellie was unsure how to approach the subject that was uppermost in her mind. "As you know, Blakely, it is now almost the end of the month."

"And you have as yet to hear anything from your friend the Falcon?" Lord Savage inquired as he rested back against his chair.

Feeling her face flame and knowing he would

not make her admission any easier, she slowly nodded her head, trying to keep a firm grip on her temper. After all, she told herself, Lord Savage had been correct in stating that he was the lesser of two evils in the matter of her future. "I have not given up any hope that the Falcon will come forth to save me, my lord."

"Quite sensible on your part, madam. Now, I can only assume that at this late minute, you have considered my proposal and reasoned out the wisdom of it?"

Kellie nodded her golden head.

"I take this not altogether convincing movement of your head to mean that you shall become my wife?" Blakely rose to his full height and before Kellie knew what he was doing, pulled her to her feet. "Time is short, then, my dear. I have already spoken to Father Dunley with the hopes that your good sense would reconcile you to the matter. He is awaiting our arrival at his parish to perform the ceremony."

Kellie was completely taken aback. She had not planned on everything happening so quickly, nor had she anticipated his having made arrangements with the priest. His ability to take over so quickly astounded her. "But there is still a day left!" she gasped.

Lord Savage frowned down at her. "One day left for you to dream of the Falcon coming and claiming you?" His manner seemed to instantly harden toward her.

"I was not thinking of the Falcon, but of my family, my lord," Kellie defended herself. "My father would never forgive me if I married without his knowledge, let alone his blessing."

Lord Savage relaxed somewhat. "Of course, I was not thinking. Charles must be witness to his only daughter's nuptials. The weather is foul; we cannot expect to bring your family into town. I am sure Father Dunley will not mind coming out to Moss Rose."

Perhaps deep inside Kellie had desired one last day to give the Falcon the opportunity to come forth and proclaim his love for her, but pulling herself together, she realized that by coming to Savage Hall she had already made her decision and could not back out. "I will be expecting you this afternoon," she said softly.

Kellie was in a daze as Blakely Savage led her back into the foyer, bundled her into her cloak, and helped her into the McBride carriage.

The ride back to Moss Rose seemed to pass all too quickly for her. She clutched her hands together in her lap. How was she going to explain her hasty plans to wed to her father? She could well imagine her family's reaction when Blakely Savage and a priest suddenly appeared on their doorstep! Her father would more than likely have a seizure, her aunt would swoon, and her cousin would think she had taken leave of her senses! It would be best, perhaps, if she said nothing of the affair until Lord Savage and the priest appeared. She entered the house and silently made her way back to the security of her chambers.

For the rest of the morning and into the early afternoon Kellie sat before the hearth in the comfortable needlepoint chair that was positioned before the small fireplace. She felt numb as she reflected on her hasty decision to wed Blakely Savage. Though she had had little choice, she now felt as though her fate had been taken out of her hands, and her destiny was being swept all too quickly in a direction that was little to her liking.

If only she had never become involved in the patriots' cause and she had never gone to the Swain's Wing Inn that fateful night when the soldier had gotten shot! If only she had never met and fallen in love with the Falcon! "If only . . ." she breathed aloud to the empty chamber.

She could still be living in her comfortable, secure world at Moss Rose, she reflected inwardly. She would never have discovered the plight of her fellow man or the full scope of the British tyranny that was forced upon those who could well rule themselves. She would never have known that the touch of a man could make her heart beat wildly in her chest. She would never have known the joy of becoming a complete woman at the hands of the one and only man she could ever love.

She had played the game to the fullest and now

she had lost all, she scolded herself. There was little sense in bemoaning her fate. She had set the course and would do well to make the best of whatever life had left to offer her.

As Blakely Savage's bride there would be little of the love and passionate joy that she would have shared with the Falcon. Savage had told her outright that he would not desire her as a wife in the sense that most men would a loving spouse. She would have his friendship and his company; she could expect little else besides his protection.

She was being selfish, she knew, as she sat and thought of the wretchedness of her future. Blakely Savage was willing to give her his name, knowing full well that she was not the chaste bride that most men expect to wed. He knew that she loved another man, but still he offered her all that he had in order to see her remain out of prison or the wife of Elroy Beeking.

Pulling herself out of her lethargy and swearing to herself that she would make Blakely Savage the best wife she could, she began to pull the woolen dress from her body. She heard the delicate gilt clock upon the mantel chime the hour of three. She would put the Falcon from her mind, she promised herself. She would devote her life to seeing Lord Savage comfortable and not allow him to ever regret that he married her. She thought of his powdered wig and pale features, and of his silks and satins, and imagined herself enabling him to attain a more masculine image. A small smile came to her lips with this thought. Perhaps her life would not be so miserable. She would live in a fine house; her every whim would be granted. What more could any woman desire? She forced from her mind the unbidden thoughts of a star-brilliant night in the Falcon's arms with the soft sand as her bed.

Dressing in a creamy beige satin gown, Kellie fashioned her hair in delicate ringlets atop her head. If within she felt a dark foreboding, without she would be a beautiful bride that any man would be willing to claim. She would not dishonour Lord Savage by portraying herself as anything other than a most willing accomplice to the ordeal ahead.

The family was gathered in the small parlor and as Kellie entered the room, Rose Fielding took in her niece's attire and was quick to speak up. "I do hope you have no intentions of going out in this dreadful weather."

"No, Aunt Rose, I thought to join you all here in the parlor."

"Then you do us a great honor, my dear," Charles McBride said as a large smile came over his features. "You do indeed brighten up this gray afternoon. Come and sit near me, my dear."

Kellie obediently sat in the chair next to her father's wheelchair, opposite her cousin, who sat and watched her in silence.

"We were talking about John Vern's trip to London at the end of the year. If there is aught that you wish for him to bring back for you, my dear, you had best make a list. I for one want designs on the latest fashions and more bolts of that brocade material, but of course in different shades than what you brought back on your last voyage." Rose Fielding went on and on about the fashions in Charleston and how little they compared with those of England today.

Kellie relaxed, knowing that she would not have to add to the conversation. Rose was in her element when talking about the fashions of the day.

Presently a knock sounded upon the front portal and Kellie stiffened as she heard Honey's heavy footsteps making her way to the front of the house.

"I wonder who would be foolhardy enough to venture out in this foul weather?" Charles questioned as the small group expectantly awaited for Honey to announce the caller.

Lord Savage and Father Dunley followed the housekeeper into the parlor. "Good afternoon, Charles, John, ladies," Blakely greeted as he entered.

Kellie kept her gaze lowered to her hands clutched tightly in her lap. However would she explain all of this to her family?

"Would you gentlemen care for a cup of something warm to take the chill off?" Charles offered graciously as he looked from one man to the other and wondered what this unlikely pair were doing coming out to Moss Rose in such ill weather.

"No, thank you, Charles, I am afraid that Father Dunley can only spare us a short time," Lord Savage replied.

"I take it then that you have not come for tea?" Charles questioned.

Slowly Kellie's emerald eyes rose to Lord Savage.

In the few seconds that they looked into one another's eyes, Savage glimpsed her turmoil. A smile slowly flitted about his lips as he made his way around the couch and stood directly behind Kellie's chair. Placing both gloved hands upon her shoulders, he squeezed gently in an attempt to impart to her some of his strength. "I see that Kellie has been shy about making the announcements." He paused as he held the attention of everyone in the room.

"Announcement, Lord Savage?" Rose queried, her sparkling blue eyes pointedly glaring at his hands on her niece.

"I am sure that this will come to you all as a surprise. Kellie has graciously agreed to become my wife, and Father Dunley is here to perform the service."

"*What?*" Charles McBride would have jumped out of his wheelchair had he been able, but all he could do was look from the powdered face of Lord Savage to his daughter, who slowly nodded her head. "You have agreed to this? To become the man's wife?" he questioned incredulously.

Rose Fielding looked at the couple with disbelief; John Vern sat on the settee with a wide grin on his handsome features. "Could it be that at last my little cousin has found true love?" he quipped, earning a heated glare from his mother.

"Let it be enough to say that Kellie and I have come to an agreement. I am in need of a wife and she has given her most generous consent."

"Kellie, you have truly agreed to this marriage?" Charles McBride could not believe that his beautiful daughter, who had shunned any number of handsome young men, had agreed to wed an overdressed fop.

Kellie thought again of the governor's propositon—that she be married or face imprisonment. "Yes, Father, Blakely is the man that I wish to marry," she stated.

A loud moan escaped Rose Fielding's lips. Charles lightly tapped his fingers against the arms of his wheelchair as he peered at his daughter and tried to read more into her words than she had disclosed. "When did you decide this? I had thought that when you married, daughter, it would be in the church, with your friends and family in attendance."

Kellie could easily see the hurt and surprise on her father's face, but there was no help for it. She could not tell him of her need for a husband's protection before the end of the month. "Blakely and I have decided that we need only have a small ceremony. All that I desire is you, Father, Aunt Rose, and Vern to be witness."

"Once I won her agreement, Charles, I am afraid that we decided not to wait any undue length of time. Father Dunley has brought all the necessary papers. We but need to speak the vows between us." Blakely eased Kellie from her seat with a slight pressure on her shoulders.

Kellie silently thanked Lord Savage for his taking control. If left to her, she was unsure how she would have handled her family. But Lord Savage had been firm, and his manner was one that would not be put off.

"Well," Charles sighed aloud. "I guess you two know what you're getting into."

Rose started to protest; she had envisioned her niece wedding a young man of good standing, but never would she have dreamed that Kellie would have chosen such a one as Lord Savage.

Charles cut her off before she could give vent to her thoughts. "Kellie knows her own mind. She has been given leave to make her own choice of a husband, my dear Rose. And if Lord Savage is that choice, we shall not hinder her."

"But . . . but perhaps she needs more time to think this out clearly." Rose wanted to demand that her brother at least force the couple to wait the proper period of betrothal, but the forceful stare that Charles directed at her quickly silenced her on the matter.

Lord Savage took Kellie's arm and pulled her before the warm hearth and Father Dunley stepped before them. Within minutes the small wedding party was formed and the vows quietly spoken.

After the signing of the nuptial papers and the leave-taking of Father Dunley, Charles raised his glass to toast the newly wedded couple. John Vern shouted his hearty congratulations, and Rose sat silently on the settee as though stunned throughout the whole affair.

Honey had stood silently by the parlor doorway for the duration and, wiping her tear-stained eyes, made her way to Kellie's side.

"Child, child, I'm just not truly believing that you done and got yerself married." Honey wept, and blew her nose loudly on the large, cotton handkerchief that she had been dabbing at her eyes with.

Kellie felt the sting of her own tears as she was enfolded in the large, comfortable embrace. Overcome with emotion, she could not speak. The dear woman had been much like a mother to her, and now this portion of her life was at a close.

It was Blakely Savage who appeared at her side and softly spoke. "You are welcomed at Savage Hall anytime, Honey. Your mistress will miss you, though I am sure she shall return to Moss Rose often enough."

Kellie smiled her appreciation at his kindness toward Honey. And Honey, brushing a tear from her cheek, also smiled, though weakly. "Ye be a good man, Master Blakely. Ye best be good to my little girl here."

"That is a promise, Honey," Blakely stated warmly, not at all offended by Honey's familiar tone.

"I be getting a few of Miss Kellie's things together now. She can't be leaving without some of her own things, and ye best send someone over tomorrow for the rest. I be having everything packed and ready."

"I always thought when I married that everything would be perfect." Kellie's voice sounded almost childlike as Honey rushed off to tend to her mistress's belongings.

Blakely Savage felt her pain and taking her elbow he gently led her back to her father's side. "We had best leave soon. I would like to get back to Savage Hall before dark."

Rose Fielding made her way to her niece and drew her aside as Savage was handed one last goblet of brandy by John Vern. "Dear, I only wish I could have known about your plans; I would have had the time for the mother-daughter talk most young girls receive upon the occasion of their wedding vows." Rose felt it her duty to attempt to answer any questions Kellie might have about the wedding chamber.

Kellie saw the distress on her aunt's face and, placing a kiss upon her cheek, she thanked her for caring. "I am in truth not that young, Aunt Rose, and besides, Honey has over the years told me all that I should need to know." She felt a small pang of guilt for her deceit, for she had already learned well the pleasures of a young bride. Honey had left out much about the experience that she had learned from the Falcon's touch, but Kellie could not tell her aunt of her knowledge, nor could she explain that there would be no joining between her and Blakely Savage in the marriage bed. She would forever have but that one night with the Falcon to hold in her memory, and no other but the Falcon and now her husband would ever know her secret. *The Falcon,* the name twisted in her chest like a sharp knife. He had betrayed her! He had left her at the mercy of a cruel fate, and she could never forgive him. She hoped never to see his handsome face again, his masculine body, and midnight hair.

"Are you ready, Kellie?" Lord Savage came to her side and pulled her from her thoughts. As Kellie looked at her aunt, she glimpsed a curious look on her features, as though she had seen something in her niece's face that had piqued her suspicions. Flushing lightly, she nodded her head to her husband, quickly kissed her aunt, and then said her goodbyes to her father and cousin.

As careful of his wife's attire as he was of his

own, Blakely helped Kellie to don her cloak and pulled the hood up securely over her head before ushering her out of the front door and into his carriage. "Are you comfortable?" he questioned as he tucked the warm lap-robe over her skirts.

"Yes," Kellie replied in a weak voice. Now that the marriage ceremony was over and she was truly wed, she felt an exhausted lethargy envelope her entire body. It had all been too much for her. First the governor's threats, her days and sleepless nights of awaiting word from the Falcon, and now the reality of her marriage to Blakely Savage.

Lord Savage must have understood her exhaustion, for as they approached Savage Hall he explained that her chamber had been prepared and she would have time to change and relax before dinner.

Kellie smiled her gratitude at the kind man who appeared to always have her needs in the forefront of his mind.

As he helped her from the carriage and she began the walk up the stone steps to Savage Hall, she fully realized that her life had forever changed. She was no longer the carefree and independent young woman she had been. She was now a married woman, forced by the fates into a loveless union. With a will stronger than she imagined herself capable of, she straightened and started into the house. She at least was sure of her husband's friendship, she told herself. Blakely Savage, though different from most, had offered her security. His protection and friendship would see her through the years ahead, and she would do her part to be a good wife to him.

Chapter Six

The parlor was illuminated by candlelight flickering from silver sconces lining the walls. The warm glowing coals from the fire in the stone fireplace greeted Kellie as she entered the room. Her attention was drawn to a small table set with crystal and china, and with a warm smile directed at Blakely Savage, she said, "This is a beautiful setting for our marriage supper."

Savage was pulled from his thoughts as his eyes took in the delicate beauty of the woman he now called his wife. "I thought we would be more comfortable in here. There is much we must learn of one another, Kellie, and I thought that this eve should be the beginning," he said in a serious tone.

Having changed her clothes and spent some time alone putting her thoughts in order, Kellie felt relaxed and ready to begin this new chapter of her life. "There will be plenty of time to get to know each other. After all, we are now husband and wife." She advanced farther into the room, noticing that her husband had also changed his attire. His jacket and pants were more subdued than anything he had worn in the past, and she had to admit that she found the dark, neutral colors of his present ensemble much more to her liking.

"Would you care for a glass of wine?" Savage went to the table and filled two glasses with a dark amber liquid.

Kellie wondered at his grave expression. "I take it that you have already found some cause for regret in our arrangement, my lord?" she questioned as she tasted the wine.

"Nay, Kellie, never regrets. I hope that you will be of the same mind when you get to know me."

"But I do know you, Blakely." He looked rather startled, she thought, at this statement. "You are a most dear and generous man," she explained.

"Come, let us sit down. Thomas will bring in our dinner shortly." Savage pulled out her chair and waited for her to sit, and for a moment he lingered behind her as he looked down at the soft curls atop her head.

By the time Savage's manservant brought in the covered trays containing their meal, Kellie had started on her second glass of wine.

Silence descended over them as Thomas left them with their dinner. Kellie found she was famished, for she had partaken of no food all day. She ate ravenously while Savage, in a brooding mood, studied her across the table.

With a soft sigh on finishing, Kellie sat back against her chair. Looking toward her husband, she noticed that he had barely touched his plate. "Are you not hungry, Blakely? The meal is delicious," she said.

"There are some things we must discuss, Kellie," Lord Savage announced abruptly.

Holding up her glass for him to fill it once again, Kellie grinned. "If you are worried that I will somehow involve you in my dubious affairs, I can promise you that I will never bring disgrace to your name. I plan to use great care from this day forth in my dealings with the patriots."

Savage's eyes narrowed as he filled her glass. "I have expected that your days as a rebel would now be over, madam."

Kellie wondered at the change of his voice. He had never taken such a tone with her before. "I hardly consider myself a rebel. I was thinking that perhaps I could do some work for the patriots without being a courier. There must be something else that I can do."

"I will not allow you to further involve yourself," he replied. "It is too dangerous. Have you not already seen what it could cost you? Prison is not a very glamorous place for a woman to spend her days." Blakely's tone was unyielding as he all but glared across the table at his wife.

"Oh, pooh," Kellie said, feeling lightheaded from the wine. "You sound almost like the Falcon." She instantly regretted she had made the statement as memories of the smuggler flooded her mind.

"He was right," Blakely stated softly.

Kellie felt her anger surface as she recalled the unfaithfulness of her lover. "He was never right! He thinks only of himself. *You* were right when you called him a blackguard!" She drained the last drops of her wine and again lifted her glass, but Savage shook his head.

"I think, madam, you have had enough. And I also think it is high time I informed you of who the Falcon truly is."

Kellie's hand stilled upon the thin, crystal stem of her glass as she stared at her husband. She felt strangely disoriented. "You know who the Falcon is?" she whispered.

Savage slowly nodded his bewigged head.

"Why didn't you tell me before?" she demanded.

"You must understand that things could have been done no differently. The Falcon's identity must have remained a secret until after we were wed. I had thoughts of not revealing all to you yet, but it would be impossible to live under the same roof with you and not have everything out in the open."

"You do not have to apologize, Blakely. I can well imagine your fear of the man, and what you risk by revealing his name." Kellie imagined how the Falcon must have threatened her husband into keeping his secrets.

Blakely sighed deeply. "You do not understand. I hold no fear of this man called the Falcon, for he and I are one and the same." There, he had said it, he thought, reaching for his wine glass.

It was several moments before the full import of his words settled over Kellie. She looked fully at the man she now called husband, taking in his large wig and powdered face. Suddenly she burst into laughter, tears running down her cheeks at the ludicrousness of his confession.

Savage shifted in his seat, rather uncomfortable with her outburst. "Kellie, you must listen to me and let me explain," he started.

Kellie lifted a hand to stop him, her jade eyes glittering with amusement. "My lord, you have no reason to feel threatened by the Falcon! The moment I spoke my vows, I swore to be faithful to you and you alone. Though our marriage shall be one in name alone, I would never give you reason to fear that I would in any way tarnish your name or your trust. I will never see the Falcon again, I promise you."

"But I *am* the Falcon," Savage insisted, startled by her reaction. He had expected surprise, perhaps even anger, but never this shaming amusement!

Kellie rose slowly to her feet, keeping her hands on the table to steady herself. She would retire to her room and forget that Lord Savage had made such a wild confession. She was sure that tomorrow he would appreciate the fact that she had given him time to gather his thoughts. And perhaps on the morrow she would talk to him about a change. Mayhap a smaller wig to cover his head. For a second she wondered if perhaps he was bald. Whatever; with less powder on his face and in somber dress, perhaps he would be able to recover some sense of masculine prowess. "If you will excuse me, my lord, I think I will retire to my chamber. I fear the wine has gone to my head."

"But we must finish this discussion! You must see the truth of my words!" Savage implored.

"Not this evening, Blakely. I am truly tired." Kellie turned to the door. If she did not exit soon, she feared that she would say something to hurt him, which she did not wish to do. He had been so kind to her! She could only blame herself for his desiring to prove himself something other than what he truly was.

Savage watched her leave the parlor. He poured himself another glass of wine. He had tried to tell her, he told himself. Now all he could do was *show* her!

Kellie could barely contain her amusement as she made her way up the spiraling stairway to her chamber. Closing the door, she leaned heavily

180

against it, and her laughter filled the room. What a strange day it had been, she reflected. Suddenly sobering, she realized that she knew very little of her husband. He had been a welcomed companion in the past, and had always shown her every kindness; even the appointments of her bedchamber reflected his thoughts to her comfort. But now she wondered at the evening's happenings. Was Lord Savage's insecurity so great that he had to plague her with such wild imaginings? To think he thought she would believe him to be the Falcon! She envisioned Blakely Savage within the comfort of his well-appointed carriage; and the Falcon on his large black stallion riding across the countryside with his pistol brandished.

"Oh, indeed, Blakely is the Falcon!" she giggled as she began to pull her gown from her body. She felt light-headed. Her eyes wandered to the large canopy bed in the center of the chamber, and she longed to lay her body down and sleep. It had been a long day; much had happened and tomorrow would likely see her just as weary. She was not one to sit back and let life go by. She was now a wife, and in her mind there were many duties it was now her responsibility to see to, to ensure that her husband's home run smoothly. The strange little manservant, Thomas, she was certain, did not give the attention to the household that she would.

As her thoughts went to all that she would do upon the morrow, she pulled the gown and underclothing from her body. Suddenly the connecting door of her chamber flew open. Earlier when Savage had shown her the room he had made mention of the door that adjoined his own chambers, but at the time she had felt assured that the door would be little used.

Kellie stared in disbelief as Blakely Savage strode boldly into her chamber. She clutched the gown to her bosom, her underclothing and petticoats in a pool about her ankles. "What do you want?" she gasped.

"Is it so strange that a husband would come to his bride on their wedding night?"

"But . . . but you said—" Kellie stammered as he drew closer to her.

"Have you truly listened to all that I have said?" His steel gaze held hers.

"You claimed that there were few needs you would look to a wife to meet," Kellie said fearfully.

"And indeed my needs are few, Kellie."

She marveled at his voice, which was no longer high-pitched but husky and deep, sending a quiver of gooseflesh down her arms and back.

"It would seem that you have not given your full attention to all that I have told you. I fear that this has been my own fault, for I could not risk losing you."

Kellie was riveted; she gave not a thought to the way her body trembled.

"Did you think that I would ever let you go to another? Allow any other man to touch your skin or kiss your lips?" His gaze lingered over her naked shoulders. "Nay, Kellie, you have always been mine." With these words Savage pulled the wig from his head, freeing strands of jet-black hair, which fell to his shoulders.

Kellie stood spellbound, mesmerized by his words and entranced by his actions. As a cloth materialized in his hand and he began to wipe away the powder on his face, she murmured, "It is truly you!" She clutched at her gown in agitation.

"Yes, I am the Falcon!" he exclaimed.

His words pulled her from her stupor, and instantly she was filled with rage. "You dared to play this great hoax on me?" she said. "You allowed me to trust you? To confide in you? Not you but Blakely Savage? You betrayed me! I waited for you these past weeks to come to me!"

"I was always near," Savage said softly. "You must understand, I could not disclose my identity. There was too much at stake, danger to you and your family."

"So you allowed me to marry a man I did not love? A man I believed offered only friendship and the protection of his name?"

"Blakely Savage and the Falcon are the same! I could not allow you to go to another and I could not reveal my identity before we were wed," Savage said. "Is it not enough that I love you? As Blakely Savage or the Falcon, I desired only you."

His words seemed to come to her from a distance. Her pride had been wounded, her trust shattered. Her mind whirled, both from the wine she had taken and from the shock and deception she was feeling. How could he have done this to her? She had to get away from him, as far away from this nightmare as possible! Reaching out, she grasped hold of the robe she had earlier draped over the chair before the hearth.

Savage drew closer, his hand taking hold of her naked arm before she could clothe herself. "We must work this out. You are my wife!"

"Your wife?" Kellie glared at him, her sparkling jade eyes searing him with the disloyalty she accused him of. "You duped me!" she shouted and pulled her arm free. "I would rather work things out with the devil himself than with you! Marriage to Elroy Beeking or imprisonment would be preferable!" She started to pull her robe over her shoulders and in the process let fall her gown.

Savage's gaze took in her bountiful form and his breath caught in his chest. "Your beauty astounds me," he whispered.

"No!" Kellie gasped as she secured the robe and

started for the door; her only thought was of getting away from him. She had to find a place where she could think. She had to sort out the revelation that her husband was not the man she had thought him to be.

Kellie reached out for the doorknob but before she could make her escape, she felt her waist encircled and she was suddenly lifted from her feet. "Put me down! You lied to me!" she screamed.

"And where do you think you are going?" The deep, husky voice she knew as the Falcon's questioned next to her ear, his large frame pulling her tightly to him.

"Anywhere away from this house, away from you!" she shouted as she wriggled and kicked to win her release.

"Nay, my fiery-tempered little bride, you shall not run away from me or Savage Hall. We are going to stay in this chamber until we straighten out this whole affair." Savage was just as determined as she; he had not won her consent to marry him as Blakely Savage, just to have her flee him upon their wedding night. In his mind she was his, as their vows had proclaimed. She had always been his. He only needed time to convince her of this fact.

Kellie seethed openly. How dare he force her to stay in his company? In her mind, he was the reason for all of her problems. If she had not met him at the Swain's Wing Inn perhaps she would not have become so involved with the patriots. And if she had not come to Savage Hall with her problems and the governor's demands, she would never have married Blakely Savage. Oh, this was all so confusing! Her mind swirled at the thought of his proximity. Blakely Savage, the Falcon—she had thought them so different! How could she have been foolish enough to trust either one of them? "You tricked me into marrying you," she declared as she tried to pull away from his arms.

"Do you forget so easily that it was you who came to Savage Hall in search of the Falcon? It was you who waited until the last moment, in the hopes that I would come to you and make you my bride? *Both of us desired this union.*"

As the truth of his words hit her, Kellie's anger slackened as did her body in his embrace. "I thought it was Blakely Savage that I was confiding in. I believed it him that I wed."

"And you did, my heart." Savage put her down and turned her about to face him. "It was Blakely Savage who held you upon that strand of beach. It was Blakely Savage who you sought out with your problems, and it was he who was always near to see that no harm befell you. I am Blakely Savage, Kellie. I am the one who held you against my heart, who kissed your lips, and who was your friend in your time of need."

"But how could I have not known the truth?" The emerald-green eyes that roamed over his face were glazed with wonder and disbelief.

Gathering her again into his arms, Savage made his way to the chair before the hearth and sat down. He held her on his lap, for he feared that at any moment her wrath would return and she would try to flee him. "I have had over two years to perfect my dual identities, Kellie. Blakely Savage and the Falcon are so different, no one can tell they are the same person without my revealing it. Very few know of my two lives, but I could not keep this secret from you any longer." His silver eyes watched her features to read her reaction to his words. "I desired you as my wife and wished us to share all the joys and pleasures such unions bring. Perhaps I would have desired more time to fulfill my oath to fight the British, but the choice was taken out of my hands. I could *never* have allowed you to belong to another. Governor Mansfield's demands that you be wed only brought us together sooner."

The soft, husky tremor of his voice seemed to touch her heart as Kellie was enfolded in his presence. Her head swam as she looked into the warmth of his gaze. "It is still hard to believe." She shook her head as though to try and clear her mind.

Savage placed both hands against her face. His

187

head descended slowly as his eyes locked with hers. "It is enough that we both want this," he breathed against the side of her mouth before his lips covered her own.

Their lips were undenying; the kiss they shared consumed them. Savage's tongue eased between her teeth; he drank deeper of the heady nectar of her wine-sweetened taste.

Kellie drowned in his attentions. "This is the Falcon," she told herself. "The Falcon is Blakely." And slowly her arms entwined about his shoulders, her breasts pressed against his chest. This was the man she had kissed in the gardens at Moss Rose, the man who had taught her the meaning of fulfillment, the same man with whom she had spoken the marriage vows. Blakely Savage and the Falcon, they *are* the same man. Her heart sang with a joy she thought she had left behind her.

Savage welcomed her response, placing fevered kisses along the sides of her mouth and her delicate chin. He declared his feelings aloud. "Kellie, I have dreamed of this moment. I have lain awake nights here in this cold house, and in my lonely bed have thought of nothing but holding you, of having you here to share my heart."

Kellie could not answer him, she was lost to the sensations of his lips upon her, his hands soothingly caressing her throat and his fingers running over the edge of her robe.

"You are the only woman I have ever wanted as my own. You fill me with such a fierce desire to hold you, to share all of my days and nights with you." Again his lips took hers, but this time Kellie's own tongue sought his, circling and caressing, to plunge deeply within the chasm of his soft mouth.

With a slight movement of his hand, Blakely untied the sash of her robe. Her tender flesh was revealed to his gaze; a creamy pale splendor framed by folds of royal-blue satin. As softly as the touch of a firefly, his hand lowered to the tip of her breast; he felt the peak harden at his touch.

Kellie gasped as waves of heat washed over her body. She could not think, she could barely breathe. She leaned fully against him, her breast filling the cup of his hand as his thumb lightly rubbed back and forth against the erect nipple. As she drew back slightly to catch her breath, Savage's lips plied her throat, lowering across her collarbone to the tops of her breasts, making a path from one taut peak to the other. Taking one tip within his mouth, he suckled gently and ran his teeth lightly over the erect nipple.

Kellie moaned, throwing her head back as wild sensations raged through her body; her breasts strained, her hands entwined within the midnight strands of his hair.

His own body throbbed with the need to lose itself within her sweet folds. Savage stood with Kellie still in his embrace, letting the blue satin robe fall to the floor. He carried her to the canopy bed, and with the tenderest of care he laid his wife down upon the pale satin coverlet. His hands smoothed back the mass of wild golden curls as his gaze traveled the length of her exquisite body. "You shall never regret that you are my wife, Kellie. I will spend the rest of my life making you happy," he breathed as he began to shed his clothing.

Kellie seemed caught up in a whirlwind. The sensual feel of the satin coverlet beneath her naked body, the alluring, husky tremor of Savage's voice filling her ears, and the spellbinding hold of his passion-filled eyes made her tremble with anticipation.

In what seemed only seconds he was lying naked beside her. "From that first afternoon when you came to Savage Hall on behalf of your cousin, I was enchanted by you. Your beauty, your spirit, everything about you made me oblivious to anything but making you my own. That night upon the beach only confirmed my desire to make you mine." Savage held both hands to the sides of her face and looked deeply into her eyes.

Kellie pulled his head down toward her; their lips met and held. In his embrace, all thoughts fled her mind. His lips began a slow path of seduction over her body; she could but close her eyes, captive to his fervent desires.

Blakely left not an inch of her body unattended. He seemed to be everywhere at once. He branded her his own, laying claim to her lips, throat, breasts, abdomen, and slim, shapely legs, lingering at the junction of her legs until Kellie cried out in feverous desire.

Rising above her, Blakely captured her lips as his throbbing manhood pushed into her warm, velvet sheath, bringing a cry of rapture to her lips, and causing her body to shudder as she felt the fullness of him within her.

Her hands roamed over his muscle-rippled back. Enveloped by his powerful strength, Kellie rose up to meet each sensual thrust. Every inch of her being was attuned to his masterful skill.

Savage glimpsed the passion on her features as he looked down into her beautiful face, and a surge of love and adoration filled his body. He had risked much to claim this moment, but for Kellie McBride he would risk his very soul, he knew. With this thought, his mind took flight. His body was consumed by the feel of her beneath him; her fingers stroked his back and set his body aflame as her soft moans of passion filled his ears and speeded him toward the brink of total fulfillment.

The incredible beauty of the moment brought tears to Kellie's eyes as she was overwhelmed by the most delicious feelings of rapture. From the very depths of her body, soul-shattering brilliants of luminous color erupted, sending what seemed like sparks of firey diamonds coursing through her limbs, causing her body to quake and tremble uncontrollably, as she moved upwards on the wings of passion's bliss.

As Savage felt the contractions of Kellie's body, a deep rumbling began to grow in the depths of his chest and from his lips burst her name, *Kellie,* as he was hurled over the thin precipice of reality and achieved an incomparable release within her.

For a time neither could speak. They clung together, their sweat-sheened bodies joined as the pounding of their hearts mingled. They tried to conquer their own breathlessness.

It was Savage who recovered first, brushing his lips lightly against Kellie's. "You are even more incredible than I remembered," he whispered.

Kellie's only response was the shuddering of her body as his kiss rekindled the ambers of passion in the center of her being.

Savage chuckled lightly against the nape of her neck. He had feared that when she regained her senses she would again bombard him with anger. She took him by surprise with her willingness not to put some distance between them. Pushing some of the golden curls away from her cheeks, Savage gazed tenderly into her emerald eyes. "You amaze me, my sweet. Never have I know another like you."

"My lord?" Kellie questioned.

A dark brow quirked over a silver orb before Savage kissed once again the kiss-swollen lips below him. "Do you not mean Blakely?"

"Blakely, the Falcon, my lord. Are not all the same man?" Kellie replied.

"And husband?" Savage queried.

A small sigh escaped Kellie's lips and brushed against Blakely's cheek as he looked down upon her. The dim lighting from the fireplace illuminated the chamber and cast golden shadows across the large oak bed. "That too," Kellie said softly. "Would I now shun my own desires and spite myself in the process? You were right. It was the Falcon I sought to be my husband. It was Blakely Savage whom I trusted as a friend and who stepped forward to see me out of my dire circumstances, and it is you, my lord," her fingertips gently caressed the outline of his strong chin, "you who are both my friend and my lover, my husband."

Overwhelmed by an inner surging of joy, Savage laughed aloud as he held Kellie in his grip and rolled about the bed. "I have gained a marvelous wife. A woman who knows well the benefit of setting her anger aside." Savage could have shouted aloud with his happiness. The relief that filled his heart was beyond words. He had been unsure what he would have done if she had regained her anger and demanded that he allow her to leave Savage Hall. All he knew for sure was that he could never have let her leave him.

"Oh, but Blakely, I have not totally set my anger aside. You will indeed pay a price for all you have put me through." Kellie smiled sweetly as her fingers tugged at the dark hair upon his chest.

"I will pay any price willingly, my heart. I will swim the widest ocean. I will walk barefoot across firey stones. I will—"

Kellie did not allow him to finish. "I am afraid, my lord, that it will not be that easy," she coyly stated, as she pushed him over on his back and leaned her elbows on his chest. "You will find that I am not that easy to live with. In fact, I fear my father and cousin quite despaired at times. I do not take easily to orders. I have a rather unfortunate temper, I . . ."

Blakely silenced her as he wrapped his arms around her slim, smooth back and pulled her forward. "I will suffer all of these things without complaint, my sweet. For I have already partaken of the generous compensation that having you as my wife will provide."

"You have been given fair warning then, my

lord." Kellie bent her head toward him, her mouth nibbling lightly at his chin, her body flushing from the raw heat of lying upon the full length of his naked, powerful form. "You know that the governor and Elroy Beeking will be furious when they learn of our marriage," Kellie said, as much to distract herself from thoughts of her husband's body as to hear Savage's opinion on the subject.

"You shall see their reactions for yourself soon enough," Savage stated and had to hold tightly to Kellie as she drew back from him.

"What are you talking about?" she demanded.

"I sent our good governor and Elroy Beeking an invitation to tea tomorrow at noon. I thought you would enjoy sharing the good news of our marriage at my side."

For a moment Kellie did not respond but only stared down at her husband. Slowly his words took effect, and a small smile settled over her lips. "I would not wish to miss the event," she said slyly. She savored the image of the governor and Elroy Beeking standing in shocked outrage when greeted with the news that she had fouled their horrible schemes.

"I had hoped you would look upon this as an opportunity for a little revenge," Savage said.

"Perhaps you know me better than I thought," Kellie admitted. "But do you think it wise to flaunt our outwitting of them to their faces? It

195

could be dangerous for you. The governor has sworn to capture the Falcon. He might see our marriage as a personal affront. He could wait for you to make a wrong move." A touch of fear crept into her voice as she thought of this threat to her husband's safety.

"No fear there, my love. Governor Mansfield will get his feathers ruffled somewhat at being outsmarted, but have no fear that he will discover my identity as the Falcon. I have had years to develop Blakely Savage into the epitome of a lazy fop. It would never cross anyone's mind that I am anything other than what I appear." Savage settled Kellie against his side, his arm beneath her shoulders as he held her tightly.

"I still know so very little about you," Kellie said quietly. She, herself, had not been able to tell that Blakely Savage was the Falcon. And as close as they had been, she still knew very little about him.

"And what is it that you would like to know?" Savage's hand gently caressed her cheek, roaming over the soft texture of her delicate features.

"I would like to know why an English lord such as yourself would go to such elaborate lengths to terrorize the British." Kellie's sea-green eyes looked deeply into the face that so lovingly gazed upon her.

For a moment quiet claimed the chamber. Only

the tightening of Blakely's arm about her and the slight pressure of his hand against her throat indicated that he had understood her question.

At last his words came so softly that Kellie had to strain to hear them.

"My father is the Earl of Gillingham and I am his eldest son. My younger brother, Emory, knew that he would not inherit my father's holdings, and one summer morning he announced that he was setting forth to make his mark in the world.

"I was loath to have him leave England, for we had always been close. My father, though, knew of Emory's unrest and gave him his blessing.

"Emory took with him a modest inheritance that our grandmother had left him upon her death. He came here, to Charleston. He purchased Savage Hall with a portion of his wealth and with the rest he lived simply, devoting his time to what he loved best—his painting."

Kellie did not interrupt. She felt the wild beating of her husband's heart, and knew that the story was not an easy one for him to tell.

"For the first two years, Emory wrote home often about his life here in Charleston, but then the correspondence stopped. It was almost a year later that we were sent word that Emory had died aboard a British naval vessel."

Taking a deep breath, Savage continued. "My father was devastated, my mother heartbroken, but I was confused as to why my brother had been aboard a British ship. I sought passage to the colonies to find out for myself the reason for my brother's death. What I found out changed my confusion to anger. I learned that my brother had gone into town one day to post a letter, when he was somehow caught up in a demonstration along the docks. Apparently, a group of young men had been protesting against the British for pressing unwilling men into service in the Crown's navy. Emory was among a number of protesters who were gathered up and forcibly taken aboard a British ship."

"Oh, no!" Kellie gasped.

Savage continued, his voice laced with anguish. It still hurt him deeply to tell the wretched tale. "Emory died two months out to sea. I spoke with one of the other young men who had been pressed into service that fateful day, and he told me of the harsh conditions aboard the ship. Dysentery was rampant; only three of the men who left Charleston that fall morning returned after their time of service. The rest, as Emory, died, far from their homes and families."

For a few minutes Savage remained quiet as he relived the first few months after he had arrived in Charleston. He had witnessed firsthand all the outrages that the British Crown inflicted upon the colonists.

"So, the Falcon," Kellie ventured after a time of silence.

"I swore to avenge my brother, and make the Crown pay for all the injustices it feels it is its right to inflict upon the colonies."

"Thank you for telling me about Emory," Kellie whispered sadly.

"My brother would have loved you, sweet. He would have demanded that you allow him to paint your portrait if he had set eyes upon you. He would have captured the wild spirit that is inside of you." Savage turned back to her and, holding her tightly, covered her mouth with his lips, devouring the sweet taste of her, losing all thoughts of brother and duty in the miraculous folds of her flesh.

Long into the night as the flames within the hearth burnt down to embers, the couple indulged their passions, whispering soft words of love, and rejoicing in the fact that they were man and wife.

Kellie felt a velvet-soft caress against her cheek. Slowly she forced herself to open her eyes. Instantly a smile came to her lips as her husband appeared beside her, a bloodred rose in his hand.

"Good morning, love," he murmured as he bent toward her, taking her lips in a gentle morning greeting. "I thought you could use some sustenance, and went downstairs for a tray. Thomas will be up shortly with a bath."

Kellie smiled dreamily as she snuggled beneath the warm coverlet, her gaze taking in the handsome man who set the rose against her pillow and settled a tray upon the bed. He was dressed in a pair of dove-gray trousers and a loose fitting white cambric shirt. His hair hung loose about his shoulders, framing his tanned, sculpted face.

As his silver-blue gaze once again settled upon her, Kellie felt herself flush as his glance took in her disheveled hair and drowsy features.

"You are even more beautiful in the morning, my love." He reached out a hand and brushed some of the soft tendrils back from her face. "I must confess, you make a very tempting picture, and I would enjoy nothing more than to spend the day here in bed with you, but alas, the morning grows late and we must not forget that our guests will be arriving for tea."

His words brought Kellie out of the dreamlike lassitude that had settled over her. "I forgot that the governor and Elroy Beeking were coming." She pulled herself into a sitting position and gathered the coverlet over her breasts.

"I would have allowed you a little longer time to rest, but it takes me such a damnably long time to attire myself to Lord Blakely Savage's satisfaction." Savage buttered a piece of warm bread and handed it to her.

A large smile brightened Kellie's face at the prospect of watching her husband transform himself into the preposterously overdressed Lord Savage.

Savage took a bite of the savory ham and smiled at her. "You look very pleased with something."

"Will I be allowed to help you dress, Blakely?" she asked.

Savage gave her a wicked grin that brought a blush to her cheeks. "I can not think of any greater pleasure than your assistance in such a matter."

"I . . . I *meant* can I help you with your wig and powder?" Kellie stammered.

Leaning over, he kissed her cheek. "Any help you can give will be greatly appreciated. Unfortunately, Thomas's talents do not extend to powder and rouge."

Kellie could well imagine the difficulty the small, dark-clothed manservant had experienced in helping his master with such things. Before she could voice her thoughts, a knock sounded upon the door, and Kellie retreated deep into the covers of the bed. Savage called permission to enter.

Thomas stepped into the room dragging a large brass tub, which he placed before the hearth. Closely behind were two young houseboys with buckets of steaming water.

Kellie peeked over the coverlet to watch Blakely's odd servant as he directed the boys in their work and then in a fussing manner laid out large fleecy towels and an assortment of bath oils and soaps.

Before leaving the chamber, the small man's dark gaze returned to his master.

"That will be all for now, Thomas," Savage stated. Thomas gave a slight nod and he and the two boys left the chamber.

"He does not say much, does he?" Kellie ventured as she again set up against the pillows.

Savage chuckled amusedly. "Nay, sweet, but you will find Thomas a most valuable servant. He came with me from England and has always been loyal to my family."

"I am sure you are right," Kellie stated, but in truth the small man made her feel most uncomfortable.

"Come, love, before the water grows cold; Thomas would be loath to carry up more buckets to heat it." Savage pulled her naked form from beneath the covers.

Feeling somewhat embarrassed standing naked before her husband in the light of day, Kellie hurried toward the tub with the desire to sink her body in the shelter of the warm water. As she stepped over the tub's edge, Savage caught up the length of her golden hair and pinned it atop her head.

Kellie lowered her form until the water covered the tops of her breasts and with a sigh she allowed the warmth to encase her.

Savage stepped around the tub to inspect the vials of bath oils Thomas had set out. He finally poured a small amount of rose-scented oil in the water and then handed Kellie a bar of soap of the same fragrance.

Having assumed that he had already bathed before waking her, Kellie was surprised when her husband began unbuttoning his shirt and loosening his trousers. "What are you doing?" she exclaimed as he stepped naked toward the tub, and she took in in broad daylight the towering, masculine length of him.

"Why, I thought to share your bath with you," he stated as he stepped over the rim.

Kellie jumped up, her eyes wide. "You can't! We can't! I mean, the tub is much too small!"

Blakely's laughter filled the chamber as his arms circled about her waist. "I assure you, we will both fit." He pulled her down with him, the rose-scented water spilling over the rim and dampening the carpet.

Indeed, it was a tight fit. Kellie blushed furiously as she felt Blakely's manhood harden against her thigh. As his mouth sought hers and his hands swept lightly over her body, she quaked with heady, anticipatory delight of what was to come.

Their lovemaking was a wild, frolicsome joining of their passions. Blakely ravished her body, storming the floodgates of their desires. They were caught up in a world where only she and he existed, where only they belonged.

With her body shuddering in its climax, Savage lifted her in his arms and carried her to the bed, their bodies glistening with droplets of water. There they concluded their passionate play.

With his breathing coming out in ragged gasps, Savage rolled over next to Kellie and pulled her body tightly against his own. "Perhaps I was a bit hasty in inviting the governor and Beeking to tea. I would much rather spend the day here in your arms," he said breathlessly.

Kellie pushed against his chest. "Oh, no, Blakely, you promised! I would not miss their reaction to the news of our marriage for anything." Though she had to admit that the thought of spending a full day locked in a room with Blakely Savage more than thrilled her senses, she had anticipated the meeting with the governor and Elroy Beeking and was eager to see their reactions when they realized the trap they had devised had only compromised themselves.

"You are a vixen at heart, my sweet. The day should prove interesting." Savage leaned back against the pillows and watched Kellie as she slipped off the bed and went about the chamber, gathering her clothes for the day ahead.

She gazed out of the multicolored paned glass windows to the sea below, which crashed wildly against the jagged cliffs, and a small smile flitted over her lips. It had been only yesterday that her world had appeared somber and gray, much like the weather today. But overnight all her fears of a loveless future had changed into fulfillment of her dreams.

Her gaze swept over the great room. Indeed, Savage Hall was magnificent. The marble floors were covered with plush Persian carpets, large pieces of mahogany and oak furniture were placed before the huge fireplace, and tapestries and paintings of priceless value hung over the stone walls.

Standing before the hearth, Kellie admired the painting hanging over the marble mantel. The scene captured on canvas was similar to the one she had witnessed as she stood at the windows and looked down to the sea.

"This was my brother's last painting." Savage silently approached his wife and stood behind her, his hands lightly lowering to her shoulders.

"It is beautiful." Kellie remembered the tragic ending to the young man who had been so talented and sensitive that he had the ability to capture the beauty of the sea and the cliffs on canvas.

Blakely tightened his grip upon her shoulders and pulled her closer to his chest. Placing a light kiss upon her soft curls, he drew her out of her reverie. "It is almost time for our guests to arrive. Thomas is arranging the tea tray in the front parlor.

Kellie turned around with a grin of anticipation, her eyes taking in her husband with a mixture of disbelief and surprise that the man before her was the same handsome, virile lover of the night before. Earlier she had helped him to don his wig, and apply the rouge and powder, and as he stood before her now, bedecked in lime-green and royal blue, there was no trace of the Falcon in his appearance. "This is going to be such fun!" she voiced with delight. Now that she knew of her husband's twin identities, she could not wait to participate in the charade that scorned the British.

"I would not in any fashion wish to spoil your enjoyment, my love. I would only give a word of warning that you have a care. For now, not only do you hold my heart in your keeping, but my neck also."

"Have no fear, my lord. I will not give the game away," she said.

"I do not fear." He bent his head and drew her lips to his own in a tender caress. Taking out his lace handkerchief from his jacket pocket, he wiped lightly at the lip rouge that had stained her mouth.

Entering the great room, Thomas took in the intimate scene between his master and new bride and softly cleared his throat. "A carriage has pulled up the drive, sir."

"Thank you, Thomas. We shall await Governor Mansfield and Mr. Beeking in the parlor. Please show them in."

With a nod of his head, Thomas left the great room and made his way to the front foyer to await the visitors.

Savage led Kellie into the parlor and with a slight squeeze of her arm and a wink of his eye, he helped her to settle herself in a chair facing the settee. He himself sat in a chair only a few feet from his wife's, and his silver gaze traveled expectantly to the parlor door.

As Thomas showed Governor Mansfield and Elroy Beeking into the parlor, Blakely rose to his feet. "Why, gentlemen, it is so good of you to accept my invitation to tea." Savage's voice seemed to rise easily to the high pitch that the two men recognized as natural to Lord Savage. Kellie thought his ease in the transformation was remarkable.

"It is our pleasure, Lord Savage," Governor Mansfield responded. "We were in the area this afternoon anyway." He grew silent as Savage stepped around the side of the settee and the Governor's dark eyes settled upon Kellie McBride sitting quietly in a chair.

Elroy Beeking also saw Kellie and hurriedly made his way to stand before her. Pulling her hand from her lap, he kissed the back of it. "Why, Mistress McBride, I had no idea that you also had been invited to tea. The governor and I were going to pay a call at Moss Rose later today."

Kellie's only response was to pull her hand from his grip. She could well imagine what their visit to Moss Rose would have been about!

"Do take a seat, gentlemen." Blakely fussed at his clothing as he himself sat and crossed one leg over the other. "I am sure Kellie will be good enough to pour the tea for us."

"It will be a pleasure, my lord," Kellie stated sweetly and smiled enchantingly at Savage.

"Look here, Lord Savage, when your man delivered your invitation to tea, he led me to believe that you had some matters of business to discuss. I'm afraid my time is far too valuable to make small talk over tea. Since we were on our way to Moss Rose, I insist that Mistress McBride allow us to see her home. Perhaps another day there will be time for a pleasurable visit." He was not about to give Lord Savage the upper hand. He had already witnessed in the past Blakely Savage's interference where it involved Kellie McBride, and he was determined that before the day was over, Kellie McBride would agree to become Elroy Beeking's bride.

"My apologies, Governor. I would not think of wasting your time. If you will make yourselves comfortable upon the settee, we shall indeed discuss some matters of great importance. As for Kellie, she was brought to Savage Hall in my carriage, and as a gentleman, I would not dare to allow her to leave by any other means."

Governor Mansfield glanced from Blakely Savage to Kellie McBride, who gazed back at him with a curious glimmer in her eyes. If her thoughts were that Blakely Savage could plead her case before him, and that he would relent in his decree that she wed or go to prison, she would shortly find that she had severely misjudged him. He would not be swayed in the matter. The wealth that the young woman would bring to a marriage was great, and his portion was too substantial to set aside because of a woman's tears or an overdressed lord's interference. He pushed Elroy Beeking toward the settee. "We shall hear you out, Lord Savage," he stated and placed his large bulk on the small couch.

"Fine, fine, gentlemen. If you will pour the tea, my dear," Blakely said, and smiled at the two men who suddenly appeared very uncomfortable.

After the cups were filled and passed out, Kellie sat back in her chair and quietly observed her husband, who was obviously taking great enjoyment in the proceedings.

"It would appear, gentlemen, that Kellie has confided some very distressing information to me, and as gentlemen, I thought that we could discuss the matter in a rational manner."

Governor Mansfield had heard that Kellie McBride had persuaded Lord Savage to intercede on her cousin's behalf when he had been arrested for smuggling. He should have expected no less of her in this situation, he now told himself. But little good it would do her this time, he thought smugly. He was not like Beeking and could not be so easily intimidated. "Proceed, Lord Savage. I am interested in hearing what you have to say." His glance went to Kellie and a smile of pure malice lit up his features.

Savage witnessed the look the governor directed toward his bride and the anger that he held for the two men intensified by degrees. With a will to control his emotions, he coughed lightly into his lace handkerchief and then came right to the point. "At first I thought that Kellie's assessment of her circumstances was a bit overblown, and that is the reason for this afternoon's meeting. I was hoping you gentlemen could reassure both of us that your intention is not to place any unreasona-

210

ble demands on Kellie."

"Unreasonable demands?" the governor sputtered as he set his cup of tea upon the table. "As governor of this town, it is by my authority that the Crown's rights are upheld, and law and order is enforced."

"And does this authority permit you in good conscience to demand that a defenseless woman wed or be imprisoned?" Savage's voice grew shrill in his agitation. Rising to his feet, he began to pace back and forth in front of the settee.

The colors of lime and blue seemed to swirl together in a blur before the governor's eyes. "Any declaration that I make in order to assure that the colonies remain law-abiding and peaceable I make in good conscience, sir." Elroy Beeking nodded his head in agreement.

For a moment Savage stilled his steps behind Kellie's chair. "I see," he at last murmured.

"Then you agree that, with the month at an end, Mistress McBride has little choice but to comply." Governor Mansfield relaxed as Lord Savage appeared conciliatory.

"Kellie and I both came to that conclusion, yes. Of course, she cannot be imprisoned. Besides the fact that the charges against her are ridiculous, she is far too innocent and genteel to withstand the hardships to herself and her family if she were to be arrested. The only choice left to her is the alternative."

Elroy Beeking grinned widely with Lord Savage's words. "You need not worry yourself over the matter, my lord. It is easy to see that you have some sense of loyalty to Mistress McBride and her family, but from here on out, you need not be concerned. I have already declared my intentions, and this very day I am more than willing to grace her with my name and my protection." Beeking's thin chest puffed out triumphantly.

"I am afraid, sir, that that will not be possible." Blakely Savage's tone seemed to fill the small parlor as his gaze held firmly upon Beeking.

"Now see here, Lord Savage," Governor Mansfield interrupted. "You, sir, stated yourself that Mistress McBride would not fare well in prison. The only possible recourse is that the arrangements for a wedding between Mr. Beeking here and Mistress McBride will be made posthaste."

"Indeed, sir, Kellie will not suffer imprisonment."

"Then I would advise you to counsel her on the merits of looking upon Beeking as her husband. For I assure you, I shall see the end to this affair this very day."

"Then, gentlemen, you will both be able to breathe easier, for your duty is now done." As Savage stood behind Kellie's chair, he placed his gloved hands upon her shoulders. The pair upon the couch were witness to the small smile upon Kellie's face and the hard glint in the eyes of Blakely Savage. "Kellie is now my wife, and the lady of Savage Hall, and I will demand all the respect the title affords her!"

Kellie felt like shouting aloud with glee as she watched Beeking's features turn as deathly pale as Blakely's powdered face. For once she saw the overbearing governor staring speechless at her and her husband.

It was Beeking who, in the space of a few minutes, after seeing all of his dreams shattered, jumped to his feet, his face a bright scarlet with his mounting fury. "You lie, sir!" he shouted.

The smile disappeared instantly from Kellie's lips. She had expected his anger, had even looked forward to it, but she had not believed that the spineless lackey of the Crown would dare to insult her husband!

"I do not believe that Mistress McBride would willingly wed a man . . . a man such as . . ." He dared not finish even in the heat of his towering rage.

"*Willingly* wed? Did I hear you correctly, sir?" A dark brow rose archingly over a gray-blue eye as Savage's hands upon Kellie's shoulders tightened somewhat. She was not unaware of the anger that was coursing through him. "It was you and the governor who took any choice in the matter away

213

from my wife. When informed of her plight, I stepped forward to offer my services and my protection. You demanded that she find herself a husband and she has done so. If you do not believe the deed done, feel free to go to the parish and question Father Dunley."

"But *why?*" Beeking looked to Kellie as though still not believing what he had been told. He refused to believe she could have wed the powder-faced fop.

"I would never have agreed to marry *you!*" She spat out venomously. Her green eyes sparkled with the anger that had been building up over the past weeks. "Any man would have been preferable to you! Even one who wears silk, satins, powder, and perfume. Even a man who wishes a marriage in name only is more to my liking than spending the rest of my life with the likes of you!"

Beeking took a step toward her, his hands balled into tight fists. Savage with a single movement was standing before his wife protectively.

Governor Mansfield stepped forward and brought the confrontation between the two men to an abrupt halt. "It would appear, Elroy, that the lady has made her *choice* in the matter. There is little that we can do here." Taking hold of Beeking's forearm, he pulled the man away from the pair and toward the parlor door. He had always been the type who knew the wisdom of standing aside. He had stretched his power in the colonies to its limits with the demands he had made on Kellie McBride. Earlier he would have stood firm upon those threats, but with the revelation that Lord Savage was now the young woman's husband, he realized that a cooler head had to prevail. Blakely Savage was a lord in his own right, and would one day inherit an earldom. He had reached his position as governor by being careful in his dealings with the upper crust. And this moment, he knew, the wisest course of action was for him and Beeking to beat a hasty retreat from Savage Hall. Kellie McBride and Lord Savage had proven the winners in the scheme he had devised. They had won a major battle, but Governor Mansfield was still governor.

Elroy Beeking was not so easily pacified. As the governor pulled him from the parlor, he looked back with a hate-filled glare to the pair across the room. "You will pay one day for this, Kellie McBride!"

Kellie's laughter followed him through the hallway and out into the front foyer, burning Beeking's ears and making him swear allegiance to the revenge he would take.

For a moment Savage's gaze held upon the doorway. "I hope this encounter satisfied you," he said, smiling at Kellie as she rose from her chair and faced him.

"Indeed it did." Kellie smiled back. "I would hope that the pair of them would think twice about their schemes after this affair."

Savage kept his thoughts about Elroy Beeking to himself. He knew that the ex-governor would bear watching for a time. He would allow no harm or insult to come to his wife. "And what was the meaning of your statements about my clothes, and this being a marriage in name only?" He pulled her into his embrace, delighting in her amusement.

"I desired Mr. Beeking to know the full extent of my distaste for him," Kellie admitted. "Besides, Blakely, if you remember well, the agreement we made before our marriage was thus."

"Thank God I made those statements under pretense." Blakely kissed her deeply. "There is no way on earth I could have kept such a promise with you under my roof."

Kellie also thanked God that all had turned out as it had. She dreaded to think of what would have been her fate if Savage had not come to her rescue.

"I think it time that we retire to our chamber, my heart. The Falcon has had enough of the day's charade." Savage swooped Kellie up into his arms and, amid her squeals and laughter, carried her up the winding stairs to their bedchamber.

Chapter Seven

"I forbid it!" Savage shouted across the room at his bride. "I will hear no more on the subject. You will remain at Savage Hall where you are safe!"

"But, Blakely, I promise I will stay out of harm's way. I can help you! I can watch your back!" Kellie implored.

"And for the last time, I am telling you, no!" *Watch my back indeed,* Savage murmured to himself as he pulled his black breeches from the wardrobe. The two had been arguing for the past hour. Ever since the messenger for the patriots had left Savage Hall and Savage had made the mistake of telling his wife he would be going out for a short time after dark. At first he had not realized her intent when she questioned him, and he had without thinking told her some of the information that the messenger had delivered. After all, she was his wife and knew of his identity as the Falcon. But when her jade eyes began to sparkle with excitement and she declared that she was going with him, he had instantly realized his mistake.

"Please, Blakely, I want to help the cause, too. It will be exciting, and I know I can be of assistance to you. After all, I was a courier. It is not as though I do not know what to expect." Her imagination had been running wild ever since the messenger had left and her husband had confided in her the nature of his mission. Her mind was filled with images of the two of them sharing every part of their lives. She had been awaiting just such an opportunity as this. She could envision the two of them riding across the countryside under cover of night, attacking the British, and offering protection to those colonists who were being persecuted by the Crown.

Her hopes were quickly dashed, as Savage swung around to face her, his features dark. "It is out of the question, Kellie. I will be gone only a short time. If our information is correct, the carriage will be on the road leading into Charleston, so everything should be carried out quickly. When I return, we will discuss the matter at length, but for now there is little time, and I refuse to relent on this one subject. You are too valuable to me to risk you to any kind of danger." Over the past few weeks Savage had learned that his young bride was a woman of remarkable conviction and determination. She had quickly set about taking over the running of Savage Hall, much to Thomas's surprise, and he had even found her one afternoon in his study, sitting behind his desk and going over the books and ledgers, studying his holdings in the colonies and in England. He had allowed her to have her way in these matters, admitting to himself the pride he felt in her abilities and sharp mind. But the line was to be drawn when it came to her safety!

Kellie fumed with his declaration. Did he think her a weak-spined female who would be content to sit at home while he was out roaming the countryside and risking his life? Did he truly believe that she would stay at Savage Hall and not worry that the British had caught him or that he had been wounded and lay bleeding along the side of some deserted roadway? If these were his thoughts, he certainly did not know the kind of woman he had married. She stopped pacing about the bedchamber and hastily formed a plan in her mind. She sat down on the small chair facing the dressing table mirror and watched him as he pulled off his satin breeches and changed into the black pair.

"That is better," Blakely said under his breath as he watched Kellie from the corner of his eye. Though he could see that she was still upset, at least she was beginning to show signs of reason. He buttoned his black silk shirt and pulled his ebony hair back and secured it into a queue. Bending down on one knee in front of Kellie, he placed his hands over hers, which were clutched tightly in her lap. "I am sorry that I must refuse you in this matter. But you must realize that you are far too precious to me to risk. Have you forgotten so quickly the night at the Swain's Wing Inn? You could have been killed. I will simply not place you in such jeopardy again. Tonight, there could very well be British soldiers guarding the carriage."

"And what of you? Who will be there to aid you if the need should arise?" Her voice was calmer now that she had made up her mind as to what she would do. Her sea-green eyes locked with her husband's silver ones and for a moment Savage found himself lost under her captivating spell.

Shaking himself to regain his composure, Savage pulled back before he was lost forever to her beauty. He felt at times that he was incapable of refusing her anything. "I will take no foolish risks," he at last responded. "I will be back at Savage Hall before you have had time to miss me."

Kellie knew that it was useless to argue with him. He would not relent. She watched as he walked away from her with the supple grace of a panther. He was every bit the Falcon. Lithe and powerful of form, he had an air of determination that intrigued Kellie; she devoured every portion of him with her gaze.

"I will tell Thomas to bring up a light tray for your supper and when I return I will have the same." As he turned back and gave her one last look, the sheer heat of her emerald eyes seemed to caress him and with a tender smile he was gone, closing the door behind him.

"The hell I will sit up here in this chamber and be pampered and indulged!" Kellie jumped to her feet the minute Savage shut the door. Rushing to her bureau, she opened the bottom drawer. Without hesitation, she pulled out the black shirt and breeches she had fashioned for herself. In the past few weeks, every spare moment she had to herself she had worked on them. She had planned to show them to her husband but the right moment had never arrived—not, that is, until this evening.

Quickly she disrobed, dressing in the black clothes and stepping into a pair of black boots. Lastly, she pinned her golden curls atop her head and secured a black hat with a wide brim over the mass. Looking in the dressing table mirror, she nodded her head and grinned. No one would ever guess her true identity, she was sure.

As she hurriedly started out of the chamber and down the hallway, she ran into Thomas, on his way to her chamber with a tray in hand.

"What on earth?" Thomas exclaimed as he tightened his grip on the tray. For a moment he thought that his master had returned, but on closer inspection, he gave pause. "Madam, is that you?" Before Kellie could answer, he questioned her further. "Whatever are you about wearing those clothes?" His eyes took in the masculine pants and shirt.

"And your *hair?*"

"I do not have time now to answer your questions, Thomas. Put the tray in my chamber. I will be back soon."

"But, madam—" Thomas protested as he realized her intent. He imagined the master's anger when he found that his young bride had left Savage Hall in the dark of night to pursue him.

But he was too late. As Thomas pondered what best course of action to take, Kellie was down the staircase and in Savage's study. She pulled down one of the dueling pistols hanging over the mantel. She took only a moment to check that it was primed and loaded.

The dark night revealed little along the roadside as one cloud after another obscured the moon. Kellie felt little fear, though; in fact, she felt exhilaration sitting high on the back of her stallion and heading in the direction she was certain her husband had taken. She was sure that she was nearing the place the carriage would be approaching. This would be the designated area set for the ambush.

As she neared the outer roads that forked off into Charleston, she pulled her mount to the side of the rutted road. She would stay in the shadows. Her only desire was to make sure that her husband was not harmed. After the carriage pulled away, her plan was to reveal herself and prove to Savage that she was worthy to ride at his side.

Kellie had been in wait only a short time when she saw the glimmer of a carriage lantern in the distance. Slowly she approached, under cover of the trees along the side of the road. She stopped within a few yards of the halted carriage, taking in a small group standing beside it, and looming above them, a rider on horseback.

As Kellie sat and listened and adjusted her eyes to the dim light, she made out her husband on his mount, his pistol pointed at four men beside the carriage, at least two of which she recognized as British officers.

"Now, gentlemen, your jewelry and your wallets if you please." The deep, husky voice of the Falcon filled the air. "There are widows and orphans aplenty, thanks to King George, who will benefit from your generosity."

Loud murmurings of outrage rose to Kellie's ears, but as she watched, all in the group complied with the Falcon's latest request. They pulled their rings and broaches from their fingers and shirt-fronts; their wallets came next, pulled from jacket pockets. All was placed within the small dark bag the Falcon had thrown at their feet.

"We have just one more business matter to attend to, and then you overfed jackals can be on your way."

"We will have no more *business* with the likes of you! You have detained us and robbed us of our belongings. Now, be on your way before the troop of soldiers following our carriage catches up with us and sends you to the fires of hell where you belong!"

That voice! Kellie knew it well. It was Governor Mansfield, and his words struck terror into her heart. A troop of soldiers would be arriving any moment, but still her husband sat relaxed on his horse taking all the time in the world! She started to kick at her mount's sides, believing she should make her presence known to her husband in order to hurry him along in this night's work.

His deep chuckle stopped her in her tracks. "As soon as your driver throws down the leather bags from behind his seat, we shall call our business finished."

Gasps of disbelief filled Kellie's ears as Governor Mansfield and the men with him started to protest. "There are no bags behind the driver's seat!" one claimed.

"You are mistaken, sir," another man declared.

"Do not make me prove my point, gentlemen," the Falcon said as he waved his pistol about in the air menacingly. "Throw down those bags," he yelled to the driver.

"You will pay for this, Falcon!" the governor snarled.

"Any time, I am at your service, Governor."

Kellie heard her husband's reply and saw that his attention was held upon the men before him. Her eyes, however, were fixed fully upon the driver. He seemed to be taking a great deal of time getting the bags from behind the driver's seat, she thought. And then she saw the reason; the soldier was slowly pulling a musket from behind the seat. The barrel lay slanted across his lap. Without another thought, she rode out of the shadows and aimed her weapon at the driver. "Throw down the musket, my good man, or call a forfeit to your life!" She forced her voice to sound as deep as any man's.

The soldier instantly did as he was ordered. The musket dropped to the ground at the side of the carriage. Without another warning, the man fumbled for the leather bags that the Falcon had earlier demanded.

All eyes seemed for a time to hold upon the newcomer. As Kellie glanced at her husband, she saw the surprise on his face rapidly turn to fury.

As Savage retrieved the bags, he held his gaze and his pistol full upon his victims. "Thank you, gentlemen," he snarled. "The patriot's cause this night is strengthened with your help. It will not be forgotten." With that he kicked his stallion and, with a stiff nod to his accomplice, took a hurried pace down the road.

For some time Savage did not acknowledge that Kellie was behind him as he guided them through a field and stayed clear of the road in case Governor Mansfield had not been making idle threats about the British soldiers in pursuit. It would be only minutes before any soldiers in the area would be sent after them.

As they neared Savage Hall, Blakely Savage felt he was enough in control of his anger to be able to confront his wife. He halted his horse abruptly in a copse of trees and, grabbing hold of Kellie's reins, he hauled her to the ground. "What the hell did you think you were doing? You could have been shot! The governor may not have been bluffing — a troop of soldiers could have come upon us and we could have been captured — or worse!" Savage shouted at her, his hands gripping her forearms tightly and digging into her tender flesh. All of his fears for her safety when she had come from out of the shadows with a pistol in her hand flashed before him. "Why, that soldier driving the carriage could have killed you!" he added, his own words driving real fear like a stake through his heart.

"If I had not come forward when I had, *you* would have been the one killed by the driver!" Kellie shouted back, not for a moment about to back down. She knew she had been right in coming forth and aiding her husband. He was only angry at the moment because of his pride, and the fact that she had been right in stating earlier that he may need her help.

"I knew what the driver was about! I expected him to react with a weapon of some sort. I was only allowing him a second more before calling out a warning," Savage heatedly lashed out at her.

Kellie shivered, held by her husband's chilling gaze. "But I thought . . . I thought he was going to shoot you," she mumbled as she realized she may have acted on a dangerous impulse.

As Savage stared down into her beautiful face, he could only heave a great sigh of relief that she had not come to harm. "I suppose you cut all of your hair off too, to complete your disguise?" He pulled the large-brimmed hat from her head, his hands seeking some assurance that his words were unfounded.

"Of course not!" Kellie balked and would have pulled away, but was held still by the strength of his hands in her hair and his body so near.

Discovering the hairpins, Blakely pulled them free and allowed them to drop to the ground. Then he ran his hands through the lovely strands. *She is safe,* he let himself believe. The terror that had been flooding his heart slowly ebbed away. "I should throttle you right here on the spot," he said as his hands caressed her and he inhaled deeply of the rose scent of her tresses. "When I realized that it was you dressed in the dark clothing so like my own, I thought for a second that my heart would halt its beating," he whispered huskily as he pulled her against his chest. He knew that his hands were heavy against her, that his touch was rough and unyielding. His anger and fear were slowly turning to passion. A passion for life, for survival, and for the excitement of living on the edge. A passion for *her* rushed fiercely through his veins.

"You cannot expect me to sit at home while you face untold dangers from the British!" Kellie said breathlessly. *This is insane,* she told herself as Savage began to undo the buttons at the front of her shirt. They had to settle this between them! He had to be made to understand that she was as capable as he or any other man of fighting against the injustice of the Crown. "What is in the leather bags you stole?" she gasped as she felt his hands upon her naked flesh. She was determined not to allow his actions to distract her.

"Later," Savage breathed softly against the side of her mouth.

Later, Kellie thought. Then with a sigh, she surrendered to her own desires. The man had such an incredible power over her! With his touch, she forgot everything.

As they stood beneath the shelter of the canopy of trees, Blakely disrobed them both. His body throbbed with desire as he stood, holding his bride on the leaf-strewn ground, raising her up to meet his need.

Kellie gasped at his swift entry, her legs of their own volition wrapping about his torso, her arms wrapping around his neck as her breasts pressed against the dark hairs on his chest. *Let this be insanity,* she thought. *For it could well be madness!* Their physical joining reclaimed them emotionally as one. A volcanic torrent stormed her heart; broke through to the very core of her womanhood, sending a shower of embers coursing over her body in a kaleidoscope of color.

Holding her tightly against his body, Savage broke the bonds of earth and scaled the starlit heights of heaven. His body shuddered, till one final convulsion emptied him of everything but her name. Clutching his wife tightly, he murmured it over and over; it was branded in his heart.

A small laugh, almost of disbelief, escaped Kellie as Savage gently untangled her legs and set her down. "Can you deny, my lord, that this is a much more enjoyable outcome to your nightly raids?"

Sighing, Blakely retrieved their clothes and helped Kellie to dress before covering himself. "I do not dispute the truth of your words, Kellie, but this night cannot be repeated." His level tone bore none of his previous anger.

After all they had been through this night, she thought, she would keep her thoughts to herself. Let him make all the demands that he wished. He would witness once again, if he left her at Savage Hall, that she would not willingly comply with his wishes for her to stay behind where she was safe and out of harm's way.

As though reading her thoughts, Savage spoke up as he buttoned his shirt. "If forced, I will lock you in our chamber." His silver eyes held hers of green, and through the moonlight filtering through the treetops, she glimpsed the set features on his face.

"You would not dare!" she exclaimed.

"Do not tempt me to it, Kellie. I promise you that I will do everything in my power to make sure that you are safe."

"But did this night not prove anything to you? I was safe! Who would dare question the pistols we brandished?" Her tone softened. Reason warned her that her husband would be better persuaded if she controlled her temper.

"This night did indeed prove something to me," Savage softly replied.

Kellie stared at him, her heart beginning to beat rapidly with anticipation as she waited for him to state the words she so wished to hear.

"I realized, in the moment when I thought you in danger, the full depth of my love for you. You are the very beating of my heart, the breath of my own breath, and I will not, nay, cannot, risk that you be taken from me."

What could Kellie say when faced with such a heartfelt declaration of love? She was still just as determined to have her way in the matter, but she would have to further her cause another time, she cautioned herself. "My own feelings are the same, Blakely," she told him. "I do not think I could endure life without you." Tears suddenly stung her eyes.

"And you shall not be put to such a test, madam. For I intend to be with you when we are both old and gray and bouncing our grandchildren upon our knees." His voice was tinged with laughter. "Come now, love, it is frightfully cold out here. Our warm hearth at Savage Hall beckons."

Without argument, Kellie allowed her husband to help her mount her stallion, and as Savage mounted his own steed, Kellie remembered her earlier inquiry. "What is in the leather bags, Blakely?"

"One of the bags holds the gold that was sent to pay the salaries of the soldiers stationed in Charleston."

"And the other?" Kellie questioned, now struck by the gravity of the crime they had committed against the Crown.

"The other holds stamps."

"Stamps? They were bringing more stamps into Charleston? But I thought that after the Sons of Liberty threatened Elroy Beeking, the governor put the stamps aboard ship."

"That he did, sweet. But the stamps have to get to Charleston somehow, and the British thought that by sending them overland from Wilmington there would be a better chance of them arriving without incident. They did not count on the contacts and spies the cause now employs throughout the colonies."

"So that is why the governor and those men with him seemed so surprised when you ordered the driver to throw down the bags?"

"Exactly. And I can well imagine Governor

Mansfield's anger at this moment at being out-smarted by his sworn enemy."

"What will you do with the gold and stamps?" Kellie asked.

"Why, tomorrow I will go into town and deliver them to my contact."

"But isn't that dangerous?" Kellie said fearfully.

"Nay, my love. Who would suspect Blakely Savage to have the Crown's gold and stamps hidden in his carriage? The British will think the Falcon wise enough to rid himself of his ill-gotten gains this very night."

Kellie nodded her head thoughtfully. "I will go with you, then, to town tomorrow," she stated.

"Kellie," Savage sighed with exasperation.

"I will not get in the way of your business, Blakely. Besides, I wish to visit Marie. I have not seen her since we married, and I thought I would invite her out to Savage Hall. Perhaps we can arrange a small dinner party. I will invite my cousin, Vern, too."

All Blakely could do was moan. He knew there would be no keeping her from going to town with him upon the morrow.

Blakely Savage, bedecked in his frivolous garb, and his beautiful golden-haired bride, were an uncommon sight in town. The pair descended from the Savage carriage, and Lord Savage, with his high-toned voice and dandy ways, presented his arm for his wife to take, as he helped her to the sidewalk and then proceeded to escort her to the tavern.

Kellie smiled with pleasure as her husband greeted passersby, nodding his bewigged head at a group of ladies out doing their afternoon shopping. Kellie watched the ladies stare after them from across the street, where they had hurriedly gathered into a tight circle with Emily Winthrop, their fans flying wildly about their faces as they speculated about the unlikely couple.

"I do believe we have caused a stir, my love," Savage whispered as he bent his head to Kellie, and she burst out with laughter, causing those viewing them to look all the harder.

Marie approached the pair as they stepped through the front door of the tavern. "Kellie, I am so glad that you came by! Can I get you both a table?" The pixyish girl looked to her dear friend with a wide grin and then her gaze settled upon Blakely Savage.

"My wife will indeed be in need of a private table," Lord Savage responded in his high-pitched tone. "I have some matters to attend to, and thought she would be more comfortable here at the tavern."

"Oh, yes, sir," Marie agreed. "There is little business here this afternoon, so I will keep her company."

Kellie watched her friend as she reacted as most everyone else in Charleston did to Blakely Savage. He held a title, and this fact alone seemed to set him apart. The inhabitants of the town may think him vain and flippant, she thought, but all seemed to go out of their way to do his bidding.

After seeing that his young bride was comfortably seated at a small table in a corner near the warm hearth, Savage, with a bow to the two women, left the tavern to see about his own affairs.

After placing two mugs of warm cider upon the table, Marie sat down across from her friend. "Kellie, why did you not tell me of your plans to marry? I was so surprised when Vern came to the tavern the evening after your wedding and told me the news. I did not know that you even knew Blakely Savage!" Over the past weeks, Marie had thought often of paying a visit to Savage Hall, but had not wished to intrude upon the newly married couple. Now that her friend was at the tavern, she was hard pressed to keep her curiosity to herself.

"It was all very sudden, I confess." Kellie had always been able to tell Marie everything, but she could not confide even in her dear friend the fact that it was not Blakely Savage she had wed, but the Falcon. She could not tell *anyone* about her husband's true identity. "It is enough to say that Blakely was in need of a wife, and I realized quite suddenly, with my Aunt Rose now at Moss Rose, that my father was no longer in need of my attentions and that I could begin my own life."

"But, Kellie, of all the men throughout the colonies, you decided upon Lord Savage? Why, you could have had any man you wished. I still do not understand." The wide brown eyes beseeched her friend.

"It is pointless to state all of my reasons. It is enough to say that Blakely Savage is a kind and generous man and we are well suited."

"Well suited?" Marie could not believe her ears. "You and Lord Savage are the most unlikely couple I have ever known!"

A small giggle escaped Kellie's mouth. "We have shared many pleasant conversations," she offered.

"Pleasant conversations? But what of the patriots? Everyone knows where Lord Savage's sympathies lie! Will you be able to quietly sit by and listen to him and his friends as they uphold a King who's only thought is to drain the colonies, without regard to the injury inflicted? There is little thought in England about their subjects across the seas. They see only riches to be gained from our sweat and labor. And the small portion they do not take from the fruit of our labor, they devour with their taxes. Will you be able to still your tongue, Kellie, when the subject of our worthy Sovereign arises?" Marie felt somehow betrayed by her friend's marriage to a man that all in Charleston considered a Tory.

"My husband knows of my loyalties," Kellie stated coolly, her anger pricked by the knowledge that so many thought her husband a callous man.

"And does he know of the help you gave to the patriots? Does he know of the Falcon?" Marie asked, wanting to find out how much Kellie had confided in her husband. It could mean the life of those she had been involved with, if he were to report their actions to the British; one of those lives could well be her own.

"I have told Blakely about none of these affairs," she truthfully stated. There had been no need for her to tell her husband; he had learned everything as the Falcon. "And of course he has heard of the Falcon, as has everyone else in Charleston," Kellie added, resenting the fact that she was being questioned in such a manner, and by her closest friend.

"I did not mean has he heard of the Falcon. Does he know of your involvement with him?" As Marie watched Kellie's features lightly flush, she knew she had been correct in her belief that her friend and the Falcon had been involved with one another for more than the sake of the cause. Over the past weeks, ever since hearing about Kellie's marriage to Blakely Savage, Marie had been at a loss to find a reason for her friend's casting such a bold and dashing man aside in order to wed a man like Lord Savage.

It was strange, Kellie mused inwardly, that hearing her friend talk about the Falcon could still make her tremble slightly and feel a bit breathless. "There was nothing that my husband should know about the Falcon and myself." For a moment Kellie remembered the night past, and the secluded canopy of trees where she had been held in the arms of the man they were speaking about, and her face blushed the hotter for her thoughts.

Marie was no fool. She easily glimpsed Kellie's reaction to her mentioning the Falcon. But she would push the subject no further. Her friend had made her choice; she would be the one living with all that powder and silk. Marie could do no more than warn her to have a care for what she told Lord Savage. "I wish you all the happiness in the world then, Kellie," she said at last.

Kellie had planned to ask Marie to Savage Hall, but now she thought better of it. She would give her friend a bit longer to adjust to the fact that she was now married to Lord Savage. "Has anything happened here in town over the past weeks? Were those young men taken to serve in the Crown's navy?"

"It would appear that the names of the men on the governor's list came to naught. When officers were sent to their houses, they had all left Charleston, their families swearing not to know their whereabouts."

Kellie smiled with relief. "Thank God. It is better they are gone for a time from family and friends than risking their lives on those inhuman ships."

She thought of Emory Savage and only wished that he had been able to escape the clutches of the Crown's navy.

"There is talk that the governor has appointed a new stamp master."

"I thought the stamps were aboard ship and anchored off the coast?" Kellie said.

"A large portion of the stamps are kept aboard ship, but not a day passes that Governor Mansfield does not have one of his officers on duty selling them. The officers have been so threatened by the local gentry and the rowdier, younger men of town, that they have appealed to be spared the duty. There is talk that the ladies, shall we call them *light skirts* for a better word, have even joined the cause, refusing the favors of those officers who have had a hand in the selling of the stamps."

Kellie could well imagine how quickly any censure from the ladies of the street had taken effect. "Who has been appointed, then, for the foul duty?" She knew it could not be Elroy Beeking, for the Sons of Liberty had put true fear into him for having the stamps at his house.

"I heard talk that it is Sampson Spires, the town printer. And rumor has it that his own wife has threatened to leave town if he takes the unpopular job. Why, already their friends are not talking to them and snubbing her on the streets. But Governor Mansfield has pumped Sampson up with promise of a sizable salary, and the high prestige that he will gain in England. He has been heard to say that if Martha deserted him, he would fare better without her constant complaints."

It all seemed so unbelievable to Kellie. Would there never be an end to British willfulness?

Glancing toward the doors of the tavern, Marie saw Blakely Savage returning and quickly offered Kellie one last piece of information. "They say that the ranks of the Sons of Liberty are swelling daily. Many of the shopkeepers and landowners have joined the campaign. Martha Spires may indeed be leaving town shortly, but her husband may well be at her side."

Kellie took her leave of Marie shortly after Savage's arrival, for the couple were to ride out to the Fishers that afternoon. Kellie set about telling her husband all that Marie had told her as soon as they climbed into the carriage.

"Much of what Marie told you is true." Savage settled himself upon the seat opposite Kellie. "The resistance to the stamp tax and to British tyranny in general is spreading like wildfire. Men such as John Morin Scott and William Livingston from New York, John Hancock from Boston, and William Allen of Philadelphia, all of high regard and standing, are in league with groups like the Sons of Liberty and helping to direct and organize the resistance. The mobs under their direction are running the stamp masters out of town and burning the stamps and the places where they are housed.

It is not only in Charleston that this warfare over rights and liberties is being waged, but throughout the colonies, and much of our success is due to the British themselves."

Kellie looked at him wide-eyed.

"The colonial provinces are finding it easier to gather information and to report on events taking place in their own townships, and thus are better able to coordinate resistance to the mother country by use of the post office. By making it possible for the rapid delivery of mail, the British have opened the doors wide for the colonies to create a united action."

"Do you think, then, that the Sons of Liberty will run the Spires out of Charleston if Sampson goes along with the governor and becomes the new stamp master?"

"There is little doubt in my mind. These stamps are a taxation that cannot be borne. If the resistance to such outrages is not kept up, the future of the colonies is bleak."

"It will be the Spires's own friends and neighbors who will denounce them."

"It is a fact that if the people should perceive one of their own townspeople and a trusted friend willingly agreeing to stand over them with his hand held tightly about the lash of tyranny, then Spires will soon be facing an unruly mob of men and women made up of people he has called his friends." Blakely's features held little sympathy for one that would turn his back on his own countrymen.

Kellie would have spoken further upon the subject, but her attention was pulled outside of the carriage window as she heard the shouts of several of Mab and Molly Fisher's children and saw them running alongside the vehicle. "I am so glad we thought to pay them a visit today." Kellie's eyes misted over as she looked toward the rustic cabin they were approaching. "The food supplies we brought for them will be well appreciated."

"I made sure that a small portion of the gold from last night's raid will see that the children all have a warm coat for the winter ahead, and there will be plenty of food to fill their bellies." Savage reached over and took Kellie's hand in his own.

Smiling up at her husband, Kellie bestowed upon him a most generous kiss.

Giggles broke through the magical spell that had momentarily settled over the couple. Savage broke away first and, seeing the audience they had attracted, his high-pitched voice was full of laughter. "This will have to wait until later!"

The children stood back in awe as Savage helped his bride down from the carriage.

The pair were greeted warmly by Mab and Molly Fisher. " 'Tis a pleasure, to be sure, that ye have come fur a visit," welcomed Mab as he shook Lord Savage's hand. "Me Molly here just set a pot of root tea to boiling. Would ye be caring to join us fur a cup?"

Kellie smiled at the couple's willingness to share with guests the small bounty that they had to offer.

"Indeed, a warm cup of tea would be most welcomed," Savage said, and with a nod of his head directed the driver to unload the supplies they had brought from Savage Hall. "Your Mrs. may find a tin of Irish tea in one of those boxes."

Molly and the children delightedly converged upon the carriage.

"We appreciate yur thinking of us, me Lord, but charity be a bitter tab to swallow all the same." Mab watched with a sinking heart the happy smiles of his family quickly disappear. Each and every one of them knew how hard he worked just so they could survive, and they also knew that Mab Fisher never asked for or looked for a handout.

"Charity, my good man? I should say not!" Lord Savage had expected no less of Mab. "Savage Hall will be in need of shellfish for its dinner parties. I will be expecting some of the boys to call upon occasion."

Weighing the offer over in his mind, Mab slowly nodded his head. As though on cue, the noise and laughter started up once again, as the two eldest boys carried the boxes into the cabin.

"Mistress Kellie," Molly called, but then quickly amended, *"Lady Savage,* would ye care to come inside and warm yerself?"

"It's *Kellie,* please, Molly," Kellie said. "And yes,

242

I would love to come in." In fact, Kellie was as excited as the children as she entered the cabin and watched the tempting assortment of food being pulled from the boxes. A large wrapped smoked ham, slabs of bacon, flour, sugar, tea, jams, jellies, even a fresh baked pie were all spread out upon the large rough-hewn table. A jar of peppermint candy discovered at the bottom of the box brought a round of squeals from the children.

"Now, Bethany, ye go over before the hearth and give each child one piece and then set the jar on the shelf." Molly handed the jar of candy to a young girl of about ten years with a long wheat-colored braid down her back.

Kellie watched as the younger children hurried to obey their mother, sitting before the hearth with their eyes wide and hands outstretched waiting for the treats.

Molly hurriedly set about fixing the tea, placing her precious chipped teacups out for the adults' use. Her gaze fell on Tommy, her eldest son, and he smiled toward her in understanding, for there were only four cups. "That be all right, Ma, I don't be wanting any tea."

Molly smiled upon him with a sigh of thankfulness, leaving Kellie with little doubt that Molly would have willingly given her own cup to her son if he had desired.

As the men joined the ladies to partake of the tea and delicacies, Savage's eyes roamed over the meager appointments of the small cabin. Kellie easily read her own thoughts in their silver depths. *Why was it that there were so many with so much and these good people had so little?* "Mab, you know, with the winter months setting in, I could be using some help at Savage Hall. If you and the two boys would like to work, I would welcome your assistance," Savage said.

"I would be liking a job, sir," piped up Tommy Fisher, who jumped up from the crudely fashioned chair he had been sitting in.

Mab looked sharply at his oldest son. "Ye has to be looking over Tommy here, yer Lordship. It peers as how he sees himself in love, and I be a'fearing he's got himself betwixt a rock and a hard place."

"It be more liking to a hard spot and a boulder," the young man mumbled.

Both Lord Savage and Kellie looked toward Tommy questioningly. "Well, tell me all, young man," Savage encouraged.

"It would peer, sir, that me and Lisa Bricken be wanting to get ourselves married up, but without a job and no coins, we can't be buying the stamp duty for the marriage license. I been trying to find a job, but there just ain't no work to be found."

"And where will you and Mistress Bricken be residing after the wedding?" Savage questioned as he wondered if the young man intended to bring another person into the already cramped living space.

"Pa said he would help me build a cabin down

near the valley." Tommy's eyes filled with hope for the dreams that he and his lovely little Lisa had shared together in secret moments. Lord Savage watched as Mab Fisher's gaze fell to the floor. The boy's father, Savage knew, had no illusions of what the future held in store.

"Listen, Tommy," Savage said after a moment's reflection. "There *is* a job at Savage Hall that is yours if you want it."

"I will do anything, sir," the young man said excitedly.

"Right now there is only my man Thomas in charge of the house and the gardens at Savage Hall. There is a greenhouse that needs care, along with the front yards of the estate. If you think you can handle the greenhouse and the yards, the job is yours." Before Tommy could accept, Savage added, "Your hours will be rather long, Tommy, so I think perhaps you and your bride would be better suited in the cottage that resides on my property. It is comfortable, and affords enough privacy, certainly, for newlyweds."

Amid the smiles, the shouting about the cabin, and the shaking of hands at the table, Savage felt his entire being warmed by the small hand that rested on his thigh. Any more good deeds on his part and he would be hard pressed to control the woman, he thought with an inward grin.

Before leaving the warmth and cheer of the Fisher's cabin, Savage pulled out his purse and advanced Tommy Fisher the coins that he and Lisa Bricken would need to say their vows. Obtaining a promise from Tommy that he and his bride would be at Savage Hall the following day to start their duties and set up house, Kellie and Lord Savage climbed into their carriage and started on their way home.

"You were wonderful back there, Blakely," Kellie said softly as her warm gaze engaged her husband's across the space of the carriage.

Not able to tolerate the distance that separated them any longer, Savage eased his form next to his wife's. "They are good people. They deserve a chance to improve their lives. My only fear now is that we will be overrun with little Fishers at Savage Hall." Blakely took her hand and squeezed it fondly against his thigh.

Kellie smiled. "They would certainly bring some life to that old stone mansion," she ventured.

"I was thinking that a couple of the younger boys look to be almost of an age to become cabin boys, and with Mab's love of the sea, perhaps he would consider signing aboard one of my ships." Savage's mind was busy making plans for the family's future.

"You know, Blakely, you have told me so little about your affairs at sea. Oh, I have seen the ledgers that show your losses and gains from voyages, but I know little else." Kellie peered up at him through thick lashes.

"Tell me what you would care to know, my love. The number of ships? The cargo that we transport? Will there be silks for your gowns and ribbons for your hair?"

"Tell me about your smuggler ship," Kellie stated, not in the least interested in silks and ribbons.

Savage sighed with some exasperation. "What do you wish to know?"

"How often do you sail this ship? Do you have it hidden near Charleston? What do you smuggle?" And lastly, "When can I go with you on one of your ventures?"

Blakely had known she would get around to this last question. The woman seemed to look for trouble he told himself. "To your first question, Kellie, the ship is sailed as often as the need arises. And yes, she is hidden in Charleston. The ship's holds are filled with goods that are mostly heavily taxed. Brought in from the islands, the goods are distributed throughout the colonies at a reasonable price. Spices, teas, coffee, wines, fine laces and silks, almost every item you can imagine. And in return, we smuggle out of the colonies cotton, wood, sugar, rice, or whatever commodity the planters wish to sell for a fair profit." Before going on he heaved a large sigh, "To your last question, madam, I wish to make clear a few things before I give you my answer. Smuggling is a risky business. Far more dangerous, even, than holding up a coach or outwitting the British on the back of a fast horse. There is nowhere to hide on the sea. If the British come upon you and you are caught, it can mean imprisonment or death." Daring to hope that she would be sensible, he ended softly, "Under no circumstances will I allow you aboard that ship."

Kellie saw the firmness of his jaw. She knew she had to proceed with care. She placed her hand lightly upon his chest and coaxed, "Could I not just *see* the ship, Blakely? What harm could there be in that?" If she could just find out where the ship was hidden she could ready a plan she would use when Savage announced he was going to sea without her. For in her heart, she knew the day would come when he would demand that she stay at Savage Hall while he embarked on one of his dangerous smuggling missions.

"Your wheedling will do you little good in this matter, Kellie. If I showed you the ship, I could never trust you not to try to board her. I tell you again, I will not expose you to such dangers." He could remember saying these same words only a night past when the headstrong woman had desired to go with him on his raid as the Falcon. He now knew that the only way of saving her from her own rash impetuousness was by being more clever than she.

"I cannot believe that you would not share everything with me, Blakely. I am your wife, after all. Do I not deserve some consideration?" She made a small pout, her mind already at work. If he thought that he could conceal the hiding place of his ship from her, he would find he had set himself no easy task. She would watch him closely and await her chance. What harm could there be for her to share in some of the adventures of racing across the seas with a ship full of contraband?

"It is because of the fact that you are my wife and deserve every consideration that I do not tell you more about the ship." Savage bent his head and kissed her pouting lips. "I love you dearly, Kellie," he whispered, and she responded by wrapping her arms about his neck. For the moment, Savage believed that he had won.

The following morning, Sampson Spires began his duties as stamp master, and that evening, shortly after dark, the Spires's printing shop was set afire. As the British troops were dispatched to quell the flames, the Sons of Liberty, along with a large number of the townspeople of Charleston, went into the streets to gather before the house of Sampson and Martha Spires.

Torches were held high; the two-story, white-washed house was thoroughly illuminated. Martha Spires's frightened face could be seen gazing down with horror upon the mayhem in her front yard.

"Come on out, Spires!" A large, burly man with a torch in one hand and a rope fashioned into a noose in the other, shouted toward the house, and a wild chorus of voices took up the call for the stamp master to show himself.

The house was silent as a frightened Sampson and Martha Spires took cover in the central part of the house, seeking shelter in the formal dining room and waiting for the help Governor Mansfield assured them would come the moment they faced any danger.

As the couple heard the windowpanes breaking and the persistent thud of a battering ram at the front door, Sampson Spires realized a bit belatedly that help would not arrive in time to save him from facing the unruly mob.

With shouts of encouragement from those standing about the front portal, the door was forced open, and stomping feet could be heard infiltrating the house. Martha Spires could be heard to cry, "This is all your fault, Sampson! You and those damn stamps have brought about our downfall!"

As men and women gathered within the space of the dining room, they witnessed Martha weeping bitter tears into the hem of her apron, and Sampson now confronted by those he had called neighbors for the past twelve years. He pleaded for his life. Oh, why had he not listened to Martha to begin with? Governor Mansfield had made the job of stamp master sound so appealing. Every doubt that Sampson had voiced, Mansfield had so easily explained away, making it appear such a great honor to be a stamp master. "Listen, my friends, there has been a terrible mistake," he cried out as he was faced with the outrage of his neighbors and those he had worked beside for years. He would forthwith relinquish the job of stamp master, he thought frantically, if only they would give him a chance to explain!

"No one here is your friend, Stamp Master!" An angry voice shouted, setting Martha Spires to weeping all the harder.

No pity was to be found for them. The outrage the mob had suffered at the hands of the British had hardened their hearts. At the moment, Sampson Spires represented the Crown and all its oppression.

"Villain! You son of a foul, deceitful mongrel!" Oliver Skinner, the blacksmith, shouted and lunged toward Sampson, grabbing hold of his shirt collar and thrusting him toward the doorway and into the arms of his accusers. "My own family is doing without because of England's taxes and the fact that a man can't be using currency any longer! The Crown's gold is scarce for a man needing to pay for a horse's shoeing or a wagon wheel's repair!"

"This is none of my fault!" Sampson cried in defense as Martha whimpered softly where she stood. "My own print shop has suffered greatly."

"And to make up for your losses, you take the side of the devil!" A buxom, gray-haired woman yelled loudly and many echoed her sentiments.

"You won't be a'needing to worry yerself about yer print shop after this night!" Zack Hemsley declared, as he and several men began to drag the stamp master to the front door.

Sampson Spires moaned despairingly as he realized that his world was falling down about his head. His print shop, he held no doubt, was destroyed; if he were lucky enough, he would be driven from his home. If not, he would be made to pay a price with his life for his own greed for gold and England's approval.

Being dragged to the street, his hands were tied behind his back and about his neck was hung a sign that read, TRAITOR TO HIS OWN — THE STAMP MASTER.

Two men on horseback appeared on the street, and these Sampson recognized as men he had raised a mug of ale with at the tavern. Without a word, both tossed ropes about his body and began to lead him out of the town.

Martha faced the group alone, but the townspeople knew of her opposition to her husband's position as stamp master, so none in the gathering looked upon her with ill intent. "What have you done with my husband?" she cried.

"He is being run out of Charleston, Mistress Spires. Ye must not fear for yerself though, for we all be knowing of yer loyalty." Zack Hemsley had returned to the dining room and offered this assurance to Martha Spires.

"My loyalty is also to the man I have been wed to these thirty years!" Martha exclaimed and straightening her spine, she pressed down her apron with nervous hands and started past the group about her. Proceeding to the carriage house and accepting no help from those around her, she hitched up the horse to the small carriage and climbed aboard the vehicle, starting off in the direction she knew they had taken her husband. She had a sister who lived in Georgia. She and Sampson would go to her, she told herself, as the bent and trudging figure of her husband came into view just outside of town.

Miles away, in Pennsylvania, another brave lady was acting in defense of her husband's actions. Mrs. Benjamin Franklin, having been warned to flee the wrath of unruly mobs in Philadelphia, prepared to withstand a siege against her home with all the arms and ammunition afforded her, and with the help of a few friends.

Having failed to prevent the passage of the Stamp Act, Benjamin Franklin advised his countrymen to make the best of the situation and not rise up against British authority; he had even obtained for several of his friends the job of stamp master. It was his belief that the colonies needed the security and protection of England in order to survive.

The mobs were set against Franklin and his

friends, and on this date it was well for Mr. Franklin that he was in England, and the Atlantic was between him and those who had had enough of British tyranny.

Chapter Eight

The news of the Spires's expulsion from Charleston was brought to Savage Hall by Tommy Fisher. His new bride's father had been a member of the group that had forced Sampson from his home. The next morning Tommy had told Thomas, who had relayed the information to Savage.

"I think that I will go into town this afternoon to visit with the seamstress, Mrs. Peabody," Kellie announced after hearing about the events of the night past. Perhaps there would be a minute to see Marie and get the details from her friend. Marie's position at the tavern kept her informed of everything that was happening in the area.

"I would go along with you, but there are a few things I must attend to," Savage said as he sipped his coffee, his mind already on the business of the day.

Kellie smiled sweetly and with some relief. If her

husband was with her, Marie would be uneasy and unwilling to speak freely. "I also have things to see to this morning," she said as she finished her breakfast and started to rise from the table.

"And what business is so important, my love?" Savage questioned. Rising to capture her about the waist, he held her against him for a long moment.

"I thought I would visit Lisa Fisher and make sure all is well at the cottage. Perhaps there are a few things here at the hall that would be useful to the couple."

Savage kissed her on the tip of her nose. "You are truly a good and charitable woman, Kellie Savage."

"Why, thank you, my lord." She stood on tiptoe and pressed her lips to his. "I also heard that Tommy's wife is a fine hand with a needle. I thought perhaps she would care to do some work for me."

Savage grinned. "Have a good day then, my sweet. My thoughts will be with you." When his wife was busy seeing to the care of his home and retainers he felt relaxed and at ease. It was the side of her that went in search of adventure that drove him to distraction.

After a farewell kiss, Kellie left the hall and started down the path that led to the cottage. She wondered for a moment what her husband would be about this day. Perhaps she should have questioned him, she thought, but as she approached the cottage and Lisa Fisher met her at the door, she forgot her concerns and for a time enjoyed the company of the other woman.

Lisa was a lively young woman who was thoroughly in love with her new husband. She spoke of little else besides Tommy, his new job, and their plans for the future. Kellie listened to all she had to say, gave some advice where she thought it wise, and generally delighted in the new bride's obvious joy.

After gaining assurance that Lisa would be more than willing to do any sewing that was needed at Savage Hall, Kellie left the cottage with the promise that she would return often.

It was nearing the noon hour when Kellie made her way back to the hall, and with plans for the afternoon ahead, she started through the front hallway toward the great room and up the stairs to her chamber. As she passed the study, she heard her husband talking with Thomas.

Hurrying up the stairs, Kellie quickly changed into a warm velvet gown. She would say goodbye to Blakely and then go to town before it got much later. Late afternoon usually found the tavern busy, and Marie with little time to herself.

Entering the study, Kellie was surprised to find Thomas on his way out, and the room empty. "Where is Blakely?" she asked.

"Lord Savage has not returned from his business." The manservant averted his dark gaze and continued toward the door.

"But I heard the two of you in here a short time ago when I returned from the cottage," Kellie insisted.

"You must have been mistaken, my lady. I have been in here alone, straightening up the master's desk."

Kellie looked toward the desk, noticing that nothing was changed from how it had appeared the day before. When her gaze shifted back to Thomas, he quickly nodded his head and left the room.

He was indeed a strange little man, Kellie thought. Looking about the study one last time, she decided that she must have been mistaken about her husband being at the hall. Perhaps Thomas talked to himself. She had no doubt that the man had some strange habits. But she could have sworn she had heard Savage's voice!

The tavern was as yet not busy and Marie had some time to spare her friend. She proceeded to tell Kellie all she had heard about the Spires's print shop being set afire and the couple's leaving Charleston.

"They say that the Spires's entire stock of wine was taken from the house and used to toast the victory over the stamp master." Marie laughed happily, but quickly lowered her voice after her father glanced sternly across the common room at her. "Papa fears that the day's business is suffering because of the free wine last eve. But I say that some celebrating was in order."

Kellie agreed with her friend, feeling strongly that a show of union against the Stamp Act had to be made.

"Vern came by the tavern last eve. We are going for a carriage ride this afternoon," Marie volunteered when the subject of the Spires and the Sons of Liberty was exhausted. Soft lights shone in her brown eyes as she looked to Kellie.

"That is wonderful." Kellie smiled, knowing how much Marie cared about her cousin. "Have you two been seeing much of each other?" She wondered how far their relationship had progressed. Over the past weeks, Kellie had been so concerned with her own affairs, she had found little time to think of Marie or Vern.

"He has been coming to the tavern often in the last weeks and we have gotten to know each other better." Marie grinned in her good-natured way.

"I have only been to Moss Rose a few times since my marriage, and Vern is always away. I will have to make a point of seeing him soon. After all, I cannot allow my cousin to see my best friend without finding out all the little tidbits that I can."

Marie on impulse hugged Kellie tightly. "Isn't it marvelous? It seems that I have waited forever for Vern to notice me."

It was marvelous, Kellie agreed. She only hoped that her friend was not courting disaster. Her cousin could be much the lady's man and had broken many hearts over the years. She would not look kindly upon him if he added Marie to his long list of conquests.

A short time later, Kellie was walking down the sidewalk toward the dressmakers shop when she spied Elroy Beeking making his way across the street in her direction. She quickened her steps with the hopes of reaching Mrs. Peabody's shop before he could approach her.

Luck was not with her, though, for she had taken only a few more steps when Elroy stood before her, a twisted smile pasted upon his thin lips.

"Mistress." He gave her a curt bow, his bespectacled eyes taking in her gown and lovely features with a single glance. "Should I now call you, Lady Savage?" he added in a taunting tone.

"Whatever pleases you, Master Beeking," Kellie said curtly.

"I believe, then, that *mistress* suits you well," Beeking stated.

"If you will please excuse me, I was on my way to Mrs. Peabody's dress shop." Kellie started to step around him.

"I will only keep you a minute," he said, maneuvering to block her path. "I wish to know if you are willing to admit your mistake, and if you are now ready to become my wife."

Kellie had at first thought she had not heard him correctly. "Whatever are you saying?" she asked.

"You said yourself at Savage Hall that Lord Savage was but a friend to you. I have allowed you time to realize your mistake in marrying that overdressed dandy, and to recognize your need for a real man."

"And you see yourself as this *real man* who would take my husband's place?" Her tone became somewhat sharper as she thought how ill-advised his latest proposal was. If he knew of the Blakely Savage that shared her bed each night at Savage Hall, he would not be quite so presumptuous.

"Aye, mistress, I can show you all that a man can give you, all that this fop you call husband cannot." His smile turned into a calculating leer. "We can leave Charleston at the end of next week. There is a ship bound for London; once there, you will get an annulment and we will be wed, as we should have been to begin with."

Kellie had had about as much as she could stand of the odious man. "Master Beeking, you must be mad! Do you think that I would leave my husband to flee with the one who forced me to wed in the first place? I have found much happiness and protection at Savage Hall as the wife of Lord Savage. I tell you now, I do not intend to give up either my husband or his protection!" Kellie's eyes glistened with ire.

"You will be mine!" Beeking seethed between clenched teeth, his hand reaching out to grab hold of her. As Kellie stepped out of his reach, a gentleman passed on the sidewalk and tipped his tricorn hat. Beeking remembered where he was; slowly he drew his arm back to his side. "Think upon my words, mistress. The ship leaves Charleston at the close of next week."

"There is no need to think over such an outrageous proposal. You will do well to look to another for affection. For you will never receive any from me!" With these words Kellie pulled her skirts back and pointedly stepped around him, stomping down the sidewalk and into the dress shop.

"One way or another you will become my wife!" Elroy Beeking swore under his breath as he watched her retreat. Over the past weeks he had become obsessed with the idea of gaining Kellie as his own. Now that she was wed to Blakely Savage, he told himself, all he would have to do was show her what a real man could give her and she would willingly become his wife. He held to this thought, for it was his only connection with sanity. "She will be mine. She will be mine," he murmured over and over like a person possessed.

262

It took Kellie much less time to calm her anger, and in minutes the humor of the situation presented itself. Elroy Beeking would certainly give up his insane delusions after this latest encounter, she thought. The nerve of the unattractive man claiming superiority over her husband! She laughed to herself as she examined a bolt of silk material that would be perfect for one of Lord Savage's suits.

As Mrs. Peabody approached the young woman she saw the small smile flitting over her lips. "You are looking well this fine day, Lady Savage," she greeted as she offered her services.

Roses! They were everywhere, beautifully arranged bouquets placed all over the room. Single long-stemmed beauties had been strewn upon the silken coverlet of the bed and deep, red, velvety petals were scattered across the carpet. The sweet-smelling fragrance saturated the air and filled Kellie's senses as she entered the bedchamber.

With widened eyes, she gazed about the room. A dim fire glowed in the hearth and before it sat a brass tub with steam rising from the water. Candles on two small tables flickered sensuously over the gleaming brass tub and lent a warm, golden hue to the bathwater.

Kelllie stepped farther into the room, taking in a bottle of champagne and two crystal glasses resting on a table near the bed.

And then Blakely Savage was suddenly behind her, softly kissing the back of her neck.

"Blakely, however did you arrange all this?" Kellie exclaimed as Savage pulled her back against his broad chest.

"I wished this evening to be special, so while you were in town, I was busy here in our chambers. The roses are from the greenhouse. Tommy was delighted to cut them when I told him of my plans for a most romantic evening."

Kellie turned about in his arms. "So this is why you would not allow me upstairs to change before dinner?" She laughed. "You are the most wonderful husband." She sighed before their lips joined in a tantalizing promise of what the evening held in store.

With a sigh of pent-up passion, Blakely broke away from the embrace. "Let me get us a glass of champagne, my sweet."

"You seem to have thought of everything." Kellie eyed the sheer red nightgown that was delicately laid out at the foot of the bed.

"This is your night to be pampered." Savage's voice had the ability to physically caress her; his words stole over her entire body and left her trembling.

He brought her a glass of champagne and after she had taken but a single sip, he took the glass from her hand and set it down on the table near the tub. "If you will allow me, I would deem it an honor to play the part of lady's maid this night." He turned her about and started to unbutton the row of tiny glass buttons that ran down the back of her gown.

Kellie delighted in his attentions and the seductive spell he had cast upon her.

Slowly the gown slipped to the floor, her petticoats and underclothing following to make a silken puddle about her ankles.

Kellie turned in his arms, putting her lips to his, eager for his touch. With a deep laugh Savage lifted her naked form, his arm easing beneath her knees as he carried her to the tub.

"We have the whole night before us, love. Let us enjoy each moment," he said, setting her in the warm water.

"You even put rose petals in the water!" Kellie exclaimed, luxuriating in the silken depths that circled her body.

Savage handed her the glass of champagne and then, pulling the stopper from a crystal vile of rose-scented bath oil, he poured a small amount into the tub.

Kellie's eyes followed his every movement. Earlier he had taken off his wig and washed the powder from his face, and now he began to pull off his jacket and shirt. When his back was to her, Kellie marveled at the muscles that rippled across his shoulders. She took a deep drink of her champagne, her body shivering; she was intoxicated by the very sight of him. She wondered if, in the years ahead, the mere sight of him would still have this overpowering effect on her.

Turning around, Blakely moved to the dressing table and gathered some hairpins from the tabletop. Regaining the side of the tub and bending down, with gentle hands he gathered the mass of golden curls hanging over the rim of the tub and fashioned the lengths at the crown of her head. For a lingering moment his hand caressed the nape of her neck. Kellie leaned longingly into his touch.

Savage then reached over her, took up a soft sponge and soap, and gently began to wash her.

As Savage lathered her foot and slowly, sensuously roamed up her leg, Kellie surrendered herself completely to his attentions. Sipping from her glass, she felt as liquid as the water surrounding her.

"You have the most beautiful legs," Savage murmured, breaking the spell of silence and timelessness that had settled over his wife. Rinsing the creamy soap from one leg, his lips lightly pressed kisses upon the sole of her foot.

This was more than Kellie could take; but before she could reach out for him, he set the one foot down and picked up the other and tenderly began the same ministrations.

When he was finished, Savage's silver gaze rose up to his wife's face. She was positively angelic, he thought, her eyes closed and her head leaning back. "Let me refill your glass," he said huskily, rising and walking to the bedside.

"I forgot to ask you, Blakely," Kellie murmured, "what you did today."

Blakely returned with her glass full and, taking up the sponge, he began to lather her arms and neck and breasts. "I did little this day but think of you, of this moment," Savage replied.

Her heart fluttered wildly beneath his hands. As he rinsed the soap off of her, his mouth followed the path that his hands had taken, and desire for him filled her senses. Her fingers laced through the dark strands of hair on his chest as she drew him to her breasts. As his mouth and tongue sampled one delicious, moist mound and then the other, moans of pleasure filled the chamber.

"I have a gift for you." Savage's lips rose to her's and for a full moment he drank of the rare ambrosia of her champagne-sweetened mouth.

Kellie cared only at this moment for his touch, for the soul-shattering feelings he stirred within her body. The last thing she desired was for him to release her.

A soft, throaty chuckle filled her ears as Savage disentangled her fingers from his hair. He heard her groan of dismay and his fingertips softly outlined her fragile jawline. "As with all things of priceless value, my heart, our passion should be savored, should be prolonged to its fullest."

"But I do not wish to prolong it, Blakely," she said pleadingly, and would have risen up out of the water and forced her attentions upon him, but for his strong hands upon her shoulders.

Her needs were much as his own, Savage knew, but desiring the night to be one to remember, he kissed her forehead lightly and in a deeper tone reminded, "I have a gift for you and I wish to view you wearing it now." With his words he drew a slim box from the table by the tub.

As he opened the velvet box, Kellie gasped at its contents. "It is beautiful!" she exclaimed as her eyes devoured the ruby and emerald necklace, that glittered on the black velvet.

"The emeralds are the color of your eyes when you are lost to passion, and the rubies are for the fire that burns beneath the surface of your soul." He fastened the golden clasp behind her neck and then sat back to look at her. His silver eyes took in the priceless gems resting above the smooth swells of her breasts. "Never before have I beheld such beauty," he breathed. He stood, gently lifting her from the tub and placing her on her feet before the hearth. "Let me dry you, sweet." He took a large, fleecy towel and, before the heat of the fire, he

268

lovingly went over every inch of her body.

Kellie felt afire; each touch set her to quiver with longing until she thought she would surely die from her need of him.

Savage also felt that he was at the limits of his control. As he let her hair fall about her waist and gently drew the brush through the strands, he felt his breath growing ragged, his blood racing fiercely through his veins. Her scent, her softness, her beauty surrounded him like a magic elixir. "Wait here for a moment," he said as he crossed to the end of the bed and picked up the nightgown.

As he turned back to her, her radiance assaulted him. Her naked beauty was beyond description. Firm, high breasts, a slim waist and hips, and shapely, long legs. Her pale, golden hair cascaded over her creamy shoulders like a sea nymph's. Her eyes were the same deep green as the jewels about her throat, her lips were roses.

He again approached her and drew the sheer red gown over her head. So attired, Kellie was glorious. The paleness of her tresses and the flashing of the stones about her neck, the gown that fit over her body as though it were a second skin.

Savage reached out and drew her close to him. They held each other tightly for a long moment, then he pulled away and brought her to their bed.

He laid her among the roses, his hands lovingly caressing her silken flesh and golden curls. The moment had been claimed for them, he knew. It was perfect, crystalline, priceless, and eternal.

Their eyes never strayed, they remained locked in a joining that held them forever. The outside world was lost to them all that remained was their heartbeats, their breathless anticipation, their incredible love.

Savage brought her gown up to her waist, but Kellie could not wait for him to disrobe her; she captured his hands in hers.

Their fingers entwined as though no single portion of their bodies could be without the other's touch. Their bodies slowly moved together until they were as one. In their steadily quickening rhythm they were dependent; they determined each other in a rapid rise toward culmination, thrust upon thrust. Kellie softly cried her husband's name into his mouth and he breathed back hers, and they exploded together in a blaze of heavenly white light.

What words spoken could capture such a moment? Slowly their limbs stilled and their heartbeats slowed, they lay silently in each others arms until sleep overcame them, each knowing that without speaking them, they had laid bare the most tender secrets of their hearts.

As Savage awoke in the early hours of the morning and heard the north wind blowing against the hall, he drew his wife closer into his embrace.

The woman, he knew, had changed his life forever. She had touched the innermost portions of his soul. He had never known love until he met her, and now knew that it was something he could little live without. *Love,* the mere word had never held such meaning to him before.

"What are you thinking, my lord?" Kellie softly questioned as she awoke to her husband's faraway look of wonder.

"I was thinking that the wind whispers your name . . . the breeze carries your scent, and that you hold my heart." Savage held her to his chest.

"I am pleased with your thoughts then. I love you," Kellie murmured and fell back to sleep.

The day was spent inside the walls of Savage Hall. The first winter snows had begun to fall but as Kellie and Savage spent most of the morning hours in their chamber, the outside world was powerless to undo them. They shared their morning meal while sitting closely together on the large oak bed. As the morning wore on, Savage sat in a comfortable chair before the hearth and read aloud from a book of sonnets as Kellie sat on a small stool at his feet.

"There are a few things I must talk to Thomas about," he said. He bent down and placed a light kiss upon her brow. "I will not be long."

"I think, then, that I will finish going over the ledgers in your study. I did not finish them the other day." She was curious to know what he was up to, but reasoned that in his own time he would confide in her.

A short time later as Kellie sat in the study behind the large oak desk, Savage entered with a tray in his hand containing bread, fruit, and slices of cold meat. "I thought you might share a bite with me." He put the tray upon the desk and arranged small plates for both of them.

"You are so good to me, Blakely." Kellie smiled as she set the ledgers aside, glad for the moment's reprieve.

"Have you found anything interesting in those pages, my love?" Savage sat in a comfortable, red leather chair near the desk. In the past, Blakely had little inclination to go over his books regularly, so it was with pleasure that he left the matter in her hands.

Kellie grinned. "I admit they are a far cry from the ledgers at Moss Rose. But I do love a good challenge."

"Indeed, my love. I have already found that you are a woman who accomplishes whatever you set your mind to."

Again Kellie glimpsed the intent look upon his features as he looked at her.

"How did your visit go with the seamstress yesterday?" he questioned before she could question him. "I hope you ordered at least a dozen gowns for yourself."

"Well, truthfully, I ordered little for myself, but I did find the most beautiful aqua silk. The moment I saw it, I thought how splendid it would look upon you. I am having Mrs. Peabody fashion you the most elaborate suit. The vest will be just a shade lighter, with tiny love knots sewn down the front panels." Looking at her husband as he sat casually in his dark trousers, a loose fitting white shirt covering his broad shoulders, his dark hair resting upon his open collar, it was hard to imagine that he was the same man who bedecked himself in frivolous silks and satins.

"Ah, love knots, how appropriate. I hope your seamstress was not shocked by your order?"

"I think Mrs. Peabody rather enjoyed the total outlandishness of the outfit I described. I am sure she will outdo herself." She took a deep breath and then added, "I also went by the tavern and saw Marie." She left out telling him about her meeting with Elroy Beeking. There was little sense in recounting the incident; it would only cause Savage to become angry, and she wanted nothing to spoil his mood.

"And how is your friend, Marie? Did she fill you in on all that happened to the Spires?"

Kellie realized that her husband knew her better

than she imagined. A light flush touched her cheeks as she nodded her head. "She also told me that my cousin has been coming to see her at the tavern."

"Your cousin is a smart man, then. Miss Darring is a very attractive and intelligent young woman."

Kellie felt no jealousy over the compliment her husband paid her friend. She felt only admiration for him. How many men with his wealth and position would believe that her cousin was wise in courting a tavern keeper's daughter? Leaving her chair, Kellie made her way around the desk and sat gingerly down upon her husband's lap. She wrapped her arms about his neck. "Have I told you today that I love you, my lord?"

"Not nearly enough times." He tasted greedily of the petal-soft lips that she willingly offered him. With their release, Savage gently rubbed her arms, his sterling eyes looking deeply into her face, with serious intent. "I have put off telling you this, sweet, for fear of your reaction. But I can put it off no longer."

"What is it, Blakely? You seem so serious." *At last,* she thought. Whatever had been on his mind this day, he was finally going to share with her.

Serious indeed, he thought to himself. If Kellie were any other woman, he would worry little over what he was about to say; but knowing his wife as

274

he did, he dreaded her reaction to his words. "Now, Kellie, you must remember what we have talked about in the past. My main concern as your husband is your safety."

Kellie remained quietly upon his lap, waiting for him to finish.

"The thing is, Kellie," he continued, drawing a deep breath, "I am going to have to leave Savage Hall for a couple of days." There, he had gotten it out. Now he would have to deal with her questions and requests.

"Where are you going?" Kellie asked calmly, surprising her husband by her even tone.

"It is business, love. I leave tomorrow evening and I will return as soon as possible." Perhaps this was going to be easier than he had expected, he thought.

"Is there something afoot with the British? Is it in the disguise of the Falcon that you shall be leaving the hall?" She still spoke calmly.

"It is not as you think. But yes, there is a matter that the Falcon must attend to."

"This has something to do with the smuggler ship, does it not, Blakely?" Her eyes looked deeply into his and his hesitation told her all.

"You must learn to trust me, Kellie. We cannot go through this every time I have to leave Savage Hall."

"You are going off on that ship!" Kellie jumped

from his lap, her jade eyes flashing with excitement. "I want to go with you! You cannot leave me behind!"

It had been too good to be true, Savage realized as, standing before him, Kellie half begged and half demanded to be taken along. His only satisfaction was in the fact that she did not know where the ship was. "We have already discussed this, Kellie. My answer is the same. You will never step foot aboard that ship. It would be too dangerous."

"You cannot leave me here alone!" Kellie declared.

"You are perfectly safe here at Savage Hall. Thomas will be with you. He would protect you with his life. You must know that I would never leave you, if I held doubts over your safety."

Kellie knew she needed a new angle. "Blakely, please, I *want* to go with you. I promise I will not get in the way. I will do whatever you say. I can be of help, I am sure."

With a sigh, Savage pulled her back into his lap. "Sweet, if it were anything else, I would not deny you. But I would never be able to forgive myself if something were to happen to you, so I am forced to say again that you must stay here at the hall." Before she could say anything else, he bent his head and covered her mouth with his lips.

The power the man had over her once again worked its magic. Wrapped in his embrace, his lips over hers, she could no longer fight him. His objections were voiced because of his need to protect her—how could she fault him when his motives were so unselfish?

As their lips broke away, Kellie sighed and laid her head against her husband's chest. He was not going to leave until tomorrow night. There was still a chance that she could find out where the ship was hidden. She would bide her time, for surely he would have to make certain that all was ready aboard ship, and when he did, she would follow him.

Savage's hands gently smoothed back her golden curls. At last, she was being sensible, he thought to himself. If not for the fact that he would be meeting some important people in Wilmington, he would not be going himself upon this venture.

That evening after dressing for dinner, Kellie went downstairs in search of her husband. Passing the study and finding no one there, she started toward the back of the house. Only the kitchen help were about, so Kellie started back to the great room. She would await Savage there; he was more than likely giving instructions to Thomas.

It was with some surprise, then, that she found Savage exiting the study. "I was looking for you," she said, confused to find him where, only a few short minutes ago, he was nowhere to be found.

"I was looking for you too, my love." Savage laughed as he led her into the great room and brought her to a chair before the warm hearth. "Would you care for a glass of wine before dinner, sweet?" When she shook her head, he poured himself a small goblet of brandy and stood before the large stone fireplace.

"It would seem, Blakely, that you somehow got your pant-leg wet while you were looking for me." Kellie noticed as he stood before her that his trouser's leg was damp, and her curiosity was piqued.

"Oh, that," Savage said, casually brushing his leg. "I was out at the stables. One of the mares is foaling and I did not think to wear my boots. Did you finish with the books?"

Her husband's causal attitude about the matter appeased her. "There is just one more ledger that I wish to go over and then all will be set to right."

"I do not wish for you to spend all your time closed up in my study poring over those books. Perhaps you could go over to Moss Rose and visit your father and aunt for a day?

Before she could answer, Thomas stepped into the great room and announced that dinner was ready to be served. "Yes, perhaps I will go out to Moss Rose while you are away," Kellie stated as her husband took her arm and led her into the dining room.

Her answer seemed to relieve him and put him at ease for the rest of the evening. After the couple finished their dinner they retired early to their chamber, both wishing to recapture the incredible joy they had shared the night before.

The following morning Kellie awoke to find Savage's side of the bed empty. After dressing and going downstairs, Thomas informed her that her husband had gone into town.

"Would you care for your breakfast in the dining room?" he questioned as Kellie stood before the servant in indecision as she wondered what her husband could be about. She was positive his leavetaking so early had to do with the smuggler ship.

"Why, no, Thomas, I think I will eat in the study." There was little else for her to do except try to occupy herself.

"Would you not prefer another room, madam? There is no fire set up in the fireplace. Perhaps the great room would be more comfortable?"

Kellie smiled upon the little man; she thought how she had misjudged him. She still felt that he was a bit strange, but since she had been at the hall he had made every effort to see to her comfort. "A fire will have to be built up in the study anyway, Thomas. I plan to finish the ledgers today and with Blakely away there is little else to do."

"I could bring the books to your chamber, madam," Thomas offered. "It would be an easy matter and your room is already warm."

Was there a reason that he did not wish her to go into the study? Kellie wondered. "No, Thomas, I will take my breakfast in the study, so please start a fire." She turned about and started back down the hallway toward the study. She certainly was not going to stand and argue with a servant over where she would eat her breakfast!

Within moments, Thomas had started a roaring fire within the grate. After this task was completed, he puttered about the room, his mood sullen. Kellie eyed him suspiciously, distracted from the work she had set for herself.

"Your breakfast will be in shortly, madam," he mumbled, and left the room.

As she nibbled thoughtfully upon the food that was brought to her, her eyes traveled about the confines of the room. Why would Thomas object to her working in the study this morning? Was there a reason or was his agitation just another one of the manservant's strange quirks? She remembered the day before when she had found him coming out of the study and had thought him talking to himself. She had thought the incident strange, especially when she had expected to find her husband within the room with him.

As the morning wore on, Kellie could not keep her mind on the work before her. Again and again, she pulled up her head and looked about the room.

With a final sigh, she gave up her pretext of working on the ledgers. Not knowing what she was looking for, only believing that there was something amiss, she slowly began to pace about the room.

Her green eyes went over everything one more time. Standing before the bookcase, she studied the rows and rows of expensively bound books. With little thought to what she was doing, she reached out her hand and went over the oak casing, now and then her glance going back to the books.

As she was about to turn away, something caught her attention. On the second shelf in the left-hand corner, two of the books were pulled out a bit farther than the others. This in itself would not have struck her as odd except for the fact that Thomas was meticulous when it came to the upkeep of her husband's small sanctuary.

With nervous hands, she slowly pulled the two volumes out of the case. Her heart began to beat rapidly when she discovered that, behind the books, a small lever had been concealed.

She slowly pressed the lever back toward the casing. Nothing happened. She wondered what the lever could be for. Resignedly, she pulled it back toward herself and gasped as the bookcase began

281

to move.

When it came to a stop, she looked behind the case. Her heart hammered in her chest when she discovered that a dark passageway lay beyond. Only cold air greeted her as she stood at the entrance in wonder.

Hurriedly, she pushed the case back in place and put the books exactly as they had been.

Going back to the desk, excitement bubbling up within her, Kellie clasped her hands tightly together. What could be in the secret passageway? Did it hold her husband's smuggled goods? Had the ruby and emerald necklace been hidden in that cold, stone secret place and were there other wonderful treasures hiding away until Savage thought to share them with her? All these questions assaulted her as she debated what she should do next.

Shortly Thomas entered the room to gather her breakfast tray, and with his entrance she busily went about studying the ledger before her. Kellie spied the little man as he started out of the room, noticing how his eyes shifted to the bookcase for a moment before he exited.

Slamming shut the ledger, Kellie could have shouted out her indignation. So her husband and his servant did not wish her to know about the secret passageway! What other secrets were they keeping from her? Getting to her feet, she quickly came to a decision.

Leaving the study, she made her way out to the kitchen. Seeing Thomas, she smiled sweetly. "Thomas, I am going to my chamber. Please tell Blakely when he returns to the hall that I am resting."

"Yes, madam." He seemed pleased with her announcement.

Kellie quickly made her way up the stairs to her bedchamber. She went directly to her wardrobe and pulled out her dark cloak.

Waiting only a few minutes in case Thomas decided to go back into the study for anything, she quietly went downstairs.

Thomas was nowhere in sight. With a sigh of pent-up emotion, she slipped into the study and hurriedly went over to the bookcase.

The two books that earlier had been out of place had been neatly pushed back where they belonged. Thomas had indeed returned to the room after she had vacated it, Kellie thought.

The passageway was not quite what she had expected. She had thought to find a room off of the narrow tunnel full of smuggled spoils. What she found instead was a narrow, dark hallway. Following it, she found another passageway leading off to her right. As she followed on, she realized that she was making her way toward the back portion of the house; perhaps she was somewhere beneath the great room.

It was dark and damp and as a chill touched her, she drew her cloak tightly about herself.

As the hallway eventually came to its terminus, Kellie could dimly make out steps which led downward. With hesitant steps she followed them down, her hand held against the chilled stone wall to steady her progress.

As her steps slowly led her down the winding stairway, she glimpsed dim light beyond.

Cautiously, Kellie continued, until the sound of lapping water and male voices came to her ears. What met Kellie's eyes at the end of the stairs astounded her.

The stairs opened out into a huge cave, a huge basin, really, accessed by higher ground that surrounded it. Rising out of the water rather ominously was a ship. Kellie watched several men hurrying about as they loaded barrels and crates onto the deck.

Hearing her husband's strong voice yelling orders to those loading the goods, Kellie pressed herself tightly against the cold wall.

The smuggler ship! It was right beneath her home! She could not believe her eyes, but with the burning torches on the cave walls illuminating it, there could be no mistaking what she saw.

Thank God no one had seen her, she thought, as she backed up a few steps and then turned, fleeing up the steps as quickly as she was able with the little lighting afforded her.

She was out of breath by the time she went through the bookcase and reached the safety of the study. She still had to gain her bedchamber without being seen, she told herself. If Thomas or one of the other servants saw her now they would surely report to Savage the fact that she was seen in his study with her cloak on and her features showing the excitement of discovery.

With cautious steps she left the study, making sure no one was about. She rushed up the stairs and shut her chamber door, letting out her breath as she leaned heavily against the portal.

For a few minutes she stood where she was and relived the moments she had spent in the secret passageway. Finally regaining her composure, she put her cloak away and went to the hearth to warm her chilled limbs.

So, the smuggler ship was right beneath her nose! she thought. What would she do with this information? She sat down in a chair, her mind flying in every direction.

It was obvious that her husband had no intention of taking her along with him on his journey. It was also apparent to her that he did not wish for her to know anything about the secret passageway or his smuggler's cave. He had even gone so far as to have Thomas cover for him and watch over her while she was working on the ledgers in his study.

No matter his tactics, she swore to herself, she would find a way to be on that ship when it left the cave tomorrow evening. Once they were out to sea, she thought, Savage would not risk bringing her back to Savage Hall. He would be forced to keep her along.

When Savage returned he found Kellie sitting before the hearth and, with a loving smile directed toward her, he questioned, "Did you have a good day, love?" Entering the room, he began to pull off his wig and jacket. "Did you finish the ledgers?"

"Yes," she murmured, telling herself that she would finish them as soon as they returned to Savage Hall.

"Are you not feeling well?" He looked across the room at her as he changed into another shirt, and noticed her flushed cheeks and quiet manner. "Thomas told me that you came upstairs earlier in the day. I would have awoken you before I left, but you were sleeping so peaceably, I did not wish to disturb you."

She could well imagine that Thomas had told him her every movement! "I am fine, Blakely. Come and tell me about your day in town." She would teach the man that she was not one that could be easily misled! As he washed the powder from his face, she wondered where he had changed his outfit; for surely he had not spent the day in that damp cave in his satin jacket and wig.

"There is little to tell, sweet." He came to her side looking handsome and refreshed with his hair hanging loose and his shirt unbuttoned halfway down the front. "I went into town to check on a ship that arrived yesterday. You will find some more additions for those books when the full inventory is finished. I think we made a fair profit even though we are taxed so heavily."

Kellie went along with him, for she did not wish to give herself away. She remembered his words of warning the night she had defied him in the robbing of the carriage. She dared not let him suspect that she knew anything about the smuggler's cave for the time being. "I am pleased that everything went well," she remarked, trying to show some enthusiasm for the story he had concocted for her benefit.

"I thought we could have dinner downstairs. Thomas is setting up a small table in the great room before the fireplace," Blakely offered, still wondering at her curious mood. She was probably still upset about not being allowed to go with him. But there was little help for it. As soon as he returned he would make it up to her and then all would be back to normal. He had found a pair of diamond hair combs this morning in one of the crates they had been loading aboard ship, and he had put them aside as a gift for her. Already he joyfully anticipated his homecoming.

Dinner was a pleasant affair. Kellie was an easy target for her husband's masculine charm and as the table and dishes were cleared away, they sat closely together before the hearth and watched the amber flames.

"I talked to your cousin today, and he will be taking my ship, the one that made port yesterday, back to England at the end of next month. His own ship is in need of some repairs, so while he is away it will be scraped and repainted."

Kellie wondered at the nerve of her husband. Did he not know that his story could be easily disputed? How could he have seen her cousin when he had been right here beneath Savage Hall throughout the day? "Did Vern say anything about Marie?" she asked, wanting to see just how far he would go with the story.

"No, I am afraid he did not mention her. Though I should have thought to question him for you." He laughed, drawing her closer.

Even when he lied to her, he was irresistible, Kellie thought, and with pleasure responded to his closeness, her small hand tracing patterns on his thigh.

"Thomas mentioned that one of the Fisher boys came by today with a bushel of clams and said that his father and older brother would be by the

288

hall next week about that job I offered them," Blakely commented, appearing well relaxed as he stretched his legs out toward the hearth.

"I am glad that you were so generous with them, Blakely. With the snows setting in, it will be hard for Mab to fish and to make a living for his family."

"If the rest of them are as hardworking as Tommy, I will be the fortunate one for the offer."

Kellie had noticed the flowers that Tommy brought each day to the hall and, remembering the roses in their chamber, she smiled in agreement.

Savage took in her bewitching smile. He admired the fine beauty of her features and the delicate way her hair was swept up from her face. He bent his head toward her and gently held her lips beneath his own. "I did not know how pleasant marriage could be until you came into my life." He spoke softly against her cheek as he caressed her silky flesh with his mouth.

Kellie had never dreamed that any couple could share such wonderful closeness, but without having the words to express her feelings, she kissed him in return.

As the kiss awoke a deeper passion, Savage pulled Kellie into his arms. She wrapped her arms about his neck, and he carried her up the stairs to the privacy of their chamber.

The next morning, Kellie again awoke to find her husband gone from their bed, but this morning she did not hurry downstairs in search of him. Instead she snuggled deeper into the warmth of the covers. Of course there would be much for him to do in preparation for his departure this eve, she thought, as she closed her eyes and drifted back to sleep.

For most of the day Kellie stayed in her chamber, going over every aspect of her plan time and again. Twice she went to her wardrobe and made sure that her dark trousers and boots were within reach. She had gone through her husband's clothes and had found a warm, dark knit sweater that she planned to borrow, and at the back of his wardrobe she had spied a woolen seaman's jacket and cap. She knew that it would be fiercely cold at sea. She had to be prepared; especially since she would have to hide herself somewhere on the ship until she thought it safe to make her presence known. She planned to take every precaution.

Thomas seemed more than pleased with her desire to stay in her chamber. He brought up her meals on a tray and had tea and little cakes sent up in the afternoon.

Kellie had pretended to be reading whenever she heard steps in the hallway, and some small sense of satisfaction filled her each time Thomas left the room, for she was not only going to outsmart her husband and prove to him that she was more than capable of being at his side, but she would also be proving this to his manservant.

It was shortly before dark when Savage entered the bedchamber, his mood jovial but hurried as he came to Kellie and swept her up into his arms and kissed her soundly before releasing her. "I have missed you, my heart. I dread being away from you for even a short time." He held her tightly to his chest, leaving Kellie with little doubt of his words.

This statement sent Kellie's spirits soaring. All day the one part of her plan that kept plaguing her with anxiety was her husband's inevitable anger when he discovered her. "I will miss you too, Blakely," she murmured softly in return.

"I have but a small time to share dinner with you. The ship and men are awaiting me and we must leave with the tide." Blakely went to his wardrobe and started to change his clothes.

Kellie sat in the chair before the hearth and watched him. He must feel more at ease in speaking of his leavetaking now that the moment was so close, she thought.

Savage, dressed as the Falcon, stood before her. "Come, sweet." He stretched out his hand. "Thomas will have our meal ready and there are a few things I must see to before I can leave."

Taking the hand offered her, Kellie complied with

his wishes in a pleasant manner. "Be sure that you take a warm coat, Blakely," she reminded him lovingly.

"Aye, it is damnably cold outside this hall." He placed a light kiss upon her lips before going back to his wardrobe and pulling forth his cloak. "I have a jacket aboard ship; this will do until I get there."

Over dinner, Kellie nervously watched her husband as he consumed the food before him.

"Thomas will see to all your needs while I am away," he said as he finished eating, came around the table, and lifted her from her seat. "Perhaps you can spend more time with Lisa Fisher. I am sure she would be glad of the company." He worried over her, though he reminded himself that he would be gone only a couple of days.

Kellie did not speak but nodded her head, hoping to keep him at ease. Inside she was a bundle of nerves, as she knew that the time was almost at hand for her husband to leave and for her to change her clothing and somehow get aboard the ship.

"I will say my farewell now, my love. I must go to the stables and see that the boys make sure the horses are kept warm. The snow is falling harder outside and I want no problems while I am away."

"I understand," Kellie said lightly, relieved that he was not returning to their chamber. She prayed that she would have enough time to change her clothes and get through the secret passageway before he came back to the hall.

The kiss that the couple shared was warm and generous, meant to last them throughout their days of separation. With a sigh, Savage pulled himself away. "I love you, my heart. You shall be in my thoughts day and night until I once again hold you in my arms."

Kellie felt a pang of guilt at his words; the thought settled over her that the time would be shorter than he expected before she would once again be in his arms. "I love you too," she said softly, and he kissed her once more before leaving the dining room. She waited for only a moment before turning, and hurried down the hallway and up the stairs to her chamber.

She could only hope that Savage did not come back upstairs for anything, she told herself, as she pulled the gown off her body and pulled on her trousers and sweater. She pinned her hair upon her head and secured the knit cap over her curls.

Pulling on the seaman's jacket, she took a quick glance in the mirror before leaving the room. No one would ever be able to tell by a single glance that she was a woman. If observed she would easily pass for a boy.

Feeling her every limb shaking, but determined to keep her resolve, Kellie cautiously and with quiet steps made her way back down the stairs and into the study.

She knew her need to be quick, for if she were caught now Savage would surely lock her in her chamber. She went to the bookcase and pulled the lever. The casing moved as easily as it had before. With some apprehension, for she did not know if her husband had already gone through the bookcase, she slipped into the passageway. Pushing the case back into place, she stood for a moment and tried to adjust her eyes to the darkness.

Taking a deep breath, and with her heart beating a rapid tattoo in her chest, she started down the hallway. It seemed forever before she reached the stairs. But as she heard the sound of the water lapping against the flooring of the cave and the voices of those about the ship, she knew that her moment of courage was at hand. She had to try and get aboard ship without being seen. This would be the most difficult part of her plan.

As she reached the bottom step and the dim light of the torches revealed the ship, she surveyed the interior of the cave. There were few men on the outside of the ship; most were already within, apparently waiting for Savage's return. She had to make her way to the other side of the cave where the ship was tied. Knowing that at any moment Savage could come down the steps, she slowly began to cover the short distance that would bring her to the ship, staying as close to the cave walls as possible with the hope that the shadows would conceal her if any were to look in her direction. Soon the ship's tall side was looming above her.

"The cap'n is coming!"

She heard the shout called from the ship and her eyes frantically searched for a way to get aboard. The only means she saw other than the makeshift gangplank that stretched from the ship to the cave floor, was a rope that hung from the ship's side.

Without another thought, for time was dear to her, she ran from the wall of the cave and jumped the few feet that was between the cave floor and the ship, her hands clutching the rope. Instantly she began to pull herself upward. Savage's anger would be full-blown if he were to catch her now, she thought, and scurried all the quicker up the rope.

Almost within reach of the top side of the ship, Kellie held to the rope as though her life depended upon it as she heard her husband's deep voice. "Make ready, lads. The tide is with us and if we wish to get this tub out of the cave, we had best set about it."

His footsteps thudded over the gangplank and soon Kellie heard the scraping of the large vessel as it was released from its moorings.

Thank God she was toward the back end of the ship! she thought, and as she held her position she could only pray that none of the crew pulled up the rope she was dangling from. With her hand clutching to the side railing she waited with bated breath for the moment she could swing her body up and over to the deck.

Fear gripped her as she looked down and saw nothing but the water below. She would have to take a chance, she thought, as she pulled her eyes from the dark depths below her. Not knowing who might be about, she heaved her weight upward and with her breath caught in her throat, she peered over the side.

Fortune was with her. The men were busy with their tasks and no one was at hand. She quietly scampered over the railing and for a fraction of a second attempted to gain her bearings and her footing aboard the swaying decks, as she searched around for some form of shelter in which to hide.

Her husband ran a tidy ship, she soon discovered. There was little above deck to hinder the crew in the running of the vessel. The only thing she saw as a possible hiding place was the longboat that was secured in place at the very back of the ship.

Hurrying over to the smaller boat, she climbed on to the railing and looked over the side. There was a small tarpaulin thrown in the back end. Without hesitation, Kellie climbed within and pulled the canvas over her body.

Only a moment passed before she heard footsteps running past her and, her location undisclosed, Kellie was able to breathe with some relief. She was safe for the time being. If no one discovered her before then, she would wait until morning and then face her husband's wrath.

Chapter Nine

Kellie could not have imagined the extent of her husband's anger. Her body trembled as she was brought up before him.

"What the hell? How did you get here?" Savage shouted, his silver-gray eyes taking in the two men and the woman between them with a mixture of rage and disbelief.

Kellie's knit cap had fallen off when two burly crewmen had hauled her out of the longboat and dragged her across the deck. At this moment she looked for all the world like a wild creature, her hair tangled about her body and her aquamarine eyes staring frightened from her beautiful, pale face.

Kellie summoned up her courage, wanting to explain everything to her husband in an attempt to mollify his anger, but before she could open her mouth, he glared down upon her and asked in a chilling tone, "How did you find the cave?" Not giving her a moment to reply, he grabbed her by the shoulder and spun her about, pushing her before him in the direction of the captain's cabin below.

The entire crew gathered on deck to see what the commotion was all about. The crew was made up mostly of men who had spent their lives in the Charleston area and, as they saw the mass of golden curls falling over the frail shoulders of the little stowaway, they hid their grins with the knowledge that their captain had gotten more than he'd bargained for.

"She be a handful for the cap'n, that's the truth," one man laughed to another as the couple disappeared below.

"Mistress Kellie be a handful for any man," the other returned.

Slamming the cabin door with a resonant thud, Savage stared at the silent figure of his wife, his fists held tightly to his sides.

"Did you give no thought to your actions, madam? Do you not know that at this very moment your life is in danger? This ship's hull is full of molasses from the French West Indies. We go to Wilmington and from there the shipment will be sent northward. Do you have any idea what would happen if we were captured by the British with a ship full of untaxed molasses? We would all be hung from the tallest mast of our own ship, and woman be damned, you would be shown no mercy!" Savage knew it was far too late to turn the ship around and take her back to Savage Hall. He would be forced to keep her with him through whatever danger befell them.

Kellie knew of the Sugar Act that the British had put into effect the year before, in 1764. She also knew with what determination the British men-of-war combed the sea looking for lawbreakers. But if her life was now in danger, her husband's was also, and she was resolved to be at his side if he were to be brought down. "I would be with you if you were captured." Her words were spoken so softly he had to strain to hear them.

Savage was at a total loss as to what he should do as he looked into her sea-green eyes. "I would imagine, then, that you thought over the fact that you not only put your own life at risk, but the lives of my entire crew?" As her gaze faltered he added, "How can I make a decision if we are attacked without first considering your safety? Do I stand and fight if the choice is forced upon me or do I turn and flee with little hope of escape?"

Kellie's gaze fell to the floor. Her only consideration had been her desire not to be left behind at Savage Hall. Why did he have to make her feel so guilty, when all she wanted was to be at his side? "I did not think of that," she admitted in a low tone. "I only wanted to be with you."

"At least you gave some thought to wearing warm clothing."

Kellie nodded her head as she watched his features soften slightly; she hoped that the worst of his anger had passed.

What was he to do with the woman? Savage asked himself. He should have put more weight in the fact that she had been too docile for the past couple of days. But it was far too late now for any thoughts about what action he should have taken. She was aboard his smuggling ship and he had no alternative but to deal with the fact. "Since you took it upon yourself to steal aboard ship, we shall make the best of it. Do not dare leave this cabin!" With these words he turned around and stormed out of the cabin, closing the door firmly behind him.

Kellie slumped upon the bed. All her strength seemed to depart with her husband.

Nothing had gone as she had planned. She had wanted to approach her husband of her own accord. But the lulling motion of the ship and the dark cover of the tarpaulin had caused her to sleep through the break of day. A crewman had discovered her in the longboat and she had found herself being dragged by two large brutes to stand as any common stowaway before her husband and his entire crew.

If only she had wakened earlier, she could have made her way down the companionway to the captain's cabin and in private announced her presence to her husband. She had wished to put him on the defensive for leaving her behind and in so doing make her offense seem a small one.

But everything had happened so quickly! She had been unprepared to face Savage when she had been so roughly pulled up before his cold, argent eyes.

Kellie's own anger began to surface as she beat her small fists upon the pillow. How dare her husband make her feel guilty for having boarded his ship, when all she wanted to do was be at his side and assured that he came to no harm? He had spoken as though the entire fate of his crew hung upon her actions. "Well, drat the lot of them!" she exclaimed as her indignation fueled her determination. If her husband was the commander of this vessel, he would make the wisest decision for its safety if attacked. What difference did it make if she were aboard?!

Pacing about the small quarters, Kellie recounted every insult, real or imaginary, that she had borne over the past weeks. Her husband had lied to her. He had enlisted the help of his manservant to watch her movements, and he had concealed the truth from her about the secret passageway and the smuggler's cave.

She had been the one who had been played falsely! And now here she was after all he had put her through, commanded to stay below in his cabin! "I should say not!" she declared as she stomped to the door in a high rage. She had not gone through all that she had just to be locked away out of sight!

She would face Savage while she was fully in charge of her faculties and she would face him before his men. She would tell him in no uncertain terms that she had as much right as he did to fight the British!

Making her way up on deck, some of her nerve deserted her as she glimpsed her husband standing alone, his back to her and his hands tightly gripping the ship's rail as he stared out to sea. She could well imagine the thoughts that were going through his mind. All concerning her, she knew, and none of them pleasant.

Not wishing to come up against his anger, the crew had retreated to different areas of the ship and were occupying themselves with their duties.

Swallowing the lump that had settled in her throat, Kellie slowly approached her husband. "Blakely," she said.

Savage acted as though he had not heard her. He held his gaze upon the blue-green depths of the water, his manner unyielding. He was not surprised that she approached him, for after everything that had happened could he expect that this woman would obey him and stay in his cabin?

"You must allow me to explain, Blakely." She

tried again to penetrate his dark mood. "I could not stay behind at Savage Hall and remain uncertain of your fate. I would rather be taken prisoner at your side than be safe at home. I could not live a day without you. I would rather *die* at your side than go on alone, knowing I would never again know the love that we have shared." Kellie had intended to demand her rights and to force him to see her capabilities, but his manner had once again forced her to take a different route. She had never meant to hurt him, but something in the set of his shoulders told her that that was exactly what she had done.

"It is no game that we are about, Kellie. This fight with the British is a matter of life and death."

"Do I not have as much right to fight the British, even if it means risking my life for the cause?"

"Go on, Blakely, tell her that she is right."

Swinging about in surprise upon hearing the familiar voice, Kellie gasped in disbelief. "Vern!"

"In the flesh, dear cuz." His blue eyes were full of merriment. "It must be in the blood, this desire to dance with danger."

"*You* are part of this crew?"

"First mate, Kellie. Don't look so surprised! Smuggling is a lucrative business, and your husband is an expert when it comes to outsmarting the British."

Kellie looked incredulously from her cousin to

304

her husband. "Then you know that Blakely is the Falcon? You knew when we married that I was not simply marrying the lord of Savage Hall?" She turned to her husband. "You kept from me that my cousin knew everything about your life? That he is in fact a party to your affairs?"

Savage could sense her anger beginning to stir and quickly set out to soothe her. "I was going to tell you everything, sweet."

"When?" Kellie demanded, her crystal green eyes searing both men. They had been in league to betray her! she fumed.

"It would not have been much longer. I was awaiting the right moment." He knew that she would not be easily pacified. Sighing deeply, he confessed. "I feared that if you knew of your cousin's connections with the Falcon, you would set out to persuade him to reveal more than I wished you to know of my enterprise."

"You mean you thought that I would somehow get Vern to tell me about the cave beneath the hall?" Kellie questioned. As her husband nodded sheepishly, a satisfied smile came over her lips. "I needed no help, my lord, in finding the passageway behind the bookcase. You will find that I am a woman who will allow no secrets in her marriage."

"I have learned as much." Savage drew her to his side. Much of his anger had dissipated with Vern Fielding's disclosure. "I realize now that much of my time has been wasted in my scheming to protect you. You will have your way no matter what I say."

"I could have told you that long ago, Blakely," Vern said laughingly.

"Only in certain matters," Kellie said with a grin. "But be forewarned, husband. Secrets intrigue me, and I can find no rest until I ferret them out."

Savage had indeed been warned, and had learned a hard lesson. He should have locked her in their room at Savage Hall until he was far from Charleston, he told himself.

But it was too late to take any action now, he thought. Kellie was aboard his ship, and now she had learned that her cousin was involved in his illicit activities. There were indeed few secrets that she had not discovered. The woman could drive him to total distraction, but he was powerless to sustain his anger when he looked upon her. She somehow broke down all of his defenses with her soft green eyes.

"Well, I see that you two have come to an understanding. I had best be about my work," Vern said as he winked at his cousin and strode away.

Savage turned to face his wife. "Once again, madam, you have won your way." He pulled the collar of her jacket up tighter around her neck. "I ask only that you abide by my orders while aboard this ship."

Thinking that he was again going to order her below to his cabin, Kellie firmly tilted her chin.

Glimpsing the mutiny cross over her features, Savage stated, "I mean that, if the occasion warrants, you must obey my orders without question."

Kellie's green eyes sparkled with delight. "Of course, Blakely. After all, you are the captain. Whatever you say, I will comply," she said.

Aye, he was the captain. Or was he? he wondered as he looked down at this minx of a woman. He wondered if *ever* a man could claim to have authority over a woman such as she.

Kellie went at her will about the ship for the rest of the day. Several of the men who made up the crew she knew by name, for they lived in the Charleston area, and as she made her way to the galley, she was greeted by Jeffery Stark and Ned Bowlings, who had been assigned to the position of cooks. She was delighted to find both young men hale and hardy in their new seafaring life.

The two young men invited her to sit with them at their small worktable. Ned Bowlings poured her a cup of tea, and they plied her with questions about home and family. Her heart went out to them as they asked her of their mothers, but she knew their strong commitment to the cause, and that not for a moment did either young man hold

307

any regrets for the part they played the night they and the Sons of Liberty had laid siege to Elroy Beeking's house. The fierce desire for freedom that she heard in the young men's voices was not strange to Kellie, for she had heard it in her own husband's voice, and now she felt it deep within her heart.

Shortly after dark, their supper was served in the captain's cabin. Savage and Kellie sat alone at a small table near the desk; Savage announced that they would shortly be approaching their destination.

Kellie gave him her full attention. "Where are we bound?" she asked.

"We will put in along the Wilmington coast. There, our contact will meet us and the ship will be unloaded. After our arrival, I will have to leave the ship for a short time."

"Why? Where will you go?" Kellie asked.

"There is a meeting scheduled for tonight with some very important men. It will not take long."

"May I go along, Blakely? I will not be in the way, I promise." Kellie readied herself for a fight.

To her total surprise Savage smiled upon her. "I gather that if I refuse, you will follow me anyway?"

Kellie had the good grace to blush at this statement, but as he slowly nodded his dark head in consent, she jumped from her seat and wrapped her arms about her husband's neck.

"My compliance in this matter does not mean I will lightly give in to all your demands while we are away. I only take you with me tonight because it would be as dangerous for you to stay on the ship. At least with you at my side, I will be able to see that you are well protected."

Kellie could care less about his reasons for taking her. All she cared about at this moment was the fact that she was not to be left behind. She was sure that in time he would realize that she was not a woman whose only purpose in life was to see to her husband's home and do his bidding.

There came then a loud knock on the door and as it opened an excited Ned Bowlings stepped within. Glimpsing Kellie's arms about her husband's neck, he stammered out an apology. "I'm sorry to interrupt Captain, but land has been sighted and Master Fielding thought you should be told."

Kellie began to step away to alleviate the young man's embarrassment, but with a slight movement Savage put his hand about her waist and stilled her actions. "Tell Mr. Fielding to carry on, Ned," he instructed.

"Yes, sir," came the reply, and the cabin door was swiftly shut.

Savage moved to pull his bride down upon his lap, but Kellie pushed against his chest, her excitement high with the prospect of the evening ahead. "Should you not go above deck? If land has been sighted, we must be almost to Wilmington."

"Your cousin is more than capable. He knows where to take the ship."

"But—" Kellie insisted, not wanting to miss a moment of the action on deck. She was so excited, she could barely keep still. As she started to persuade him that his services were surely needed on deck, his mouth covered hers in a branding kiss.

"That will have to do until we return," he said laughingly as she squirmed in his lap. He rose and set her to her feet in front of him. "Fetch your jacket, sweet, and bundle up warm. Though the snow is no longer falling, it is still dreadfully cold."

Kellie hurried to do as instructed, and within seconds was following her husband out of the cabin.

The crew were all assembled above decks as the lights of Wilmington came into view. There was much activity about the ship as the crew readied the vessel for landing. Kellie noticed that the men made very little noise.

"We will sail up the coastline for a short time and hope that there are no British ships prowling about this night." Beside her Savage spoke in hushed tones and Kellie realized the need for silence. A small noise could carry for a far distance on a quiet night at sea. Their dark sails would lend them protective cover if there were any British ships in the area, but excessive noise would surely give them away.

Kellie stood at the railing of the smuggler's ship as the town of Wilmington slowly passed by in the distance. They traveled only a short way down the coast before receiving their signal—torchlight wavering over the water. The boat turned into a small waterway that led to a secluded cove. The crew swiftly secured the ship to a dock where several men stood about waiting to help with the unloading of the untaxed goods.

"Come, love, we must be quick. A carriage awaits us." Savage approached her at the railing with Vern at his side.

Kellie did not hesitate, but quickly hurried between the two men over the rough planking between ship and dock and followed Savage's lead as they pushed through some underbrush and came to a clearing where driver and carriage awaited.

About a mile from where they had docked, the driver pulled up before a modest farmhouse. "You are expected inside, sir," a tall, lanky black man informed Savage as he opened the carriage door and allowed the occupants to step to the ground.

Upon the first knock at the front portal, the door was eased open and a gray-haired and fully bearded man peered out, his quick look about the front of the house gaining for him the assurance he desired. He stepped back and permitted the group to enter. Without comment, he started to the back of the house and entered a room that was used as a library. Books lined every wall and were stacked upon a small desk in the corner and on the only table in the room. The lighting in the room was dim, a lantern set amid the clutter of the desk giving out a yellowish hue.

Savage entered after the elderly gentleman. A large man with sandy brown hair who looked to be in his midforties stepped from his chair before the desk and held out his hand in greeting. "I see you made it, Blakely. I trust you had no problems?" His voice seemed to boom in Kellie's ears after the quiet of the evening.

Savage grinned good-naturedly at the man. "Aye, Christopher, all went well with the trip from Charleston. I trust your news is as good?"

"And who have we here?" the man asked, ignoring Savage's question.

"This is my wife, Kellie," Savage stated with some pride as he watched his bride approach the large man unintimidated. "Kellie, this is Christopher Gadsden. I believe you already know John Vern Fielding." He motioned toward Vern.

"Yes, John Vern and I have already met," Gadsden said, his gaze holding upon Kellie. "I have heard much of you, mistress."

Kellie had recognized Gadsden's name as being linked with the Sons of Liberty. She had no doubt that this man knew of all her exploits as a courier for the cause.

Clearing his throat, the gray-haried man now sitting behind the desk stated, "Our women are playing a major role in the fight for liberty in the colonies. There is a group calling itself the Daughters of Liberty. Young women are refusing suitors who are not willing to resist the despised Stamp Act. We welcome help from any direction," he said smilingly.

Kellie looked admiringly toward the wise, old man.

"Why do you gentlemen not take a seat? And you also, my dear?" the older man invited. "I am known as William Kraemer around these parts. I have invested much time and energy in this country that England would sift dry, so let us get down to business."

Gadsden chuckled. "Old William here would like to see the repeal of the Stamp Act and the removal of the British from the colonies in one fell swoop."

The man behind the desk smiled. "Aye, then I would know contentment."

"You may yet have a little wait for that," Gadsden remarked before turning his attention toward Savage. "I have only recently returned to the area.

313

As you know, James Otis proposed in the Massachusetts House of Representatives that an intercolonial congress be summoned so that all the provinces might act in concert against the Stamp Act. His plan having been adopted, the colonies were invited to send delegates to a congress that was held in New York."

"And did all the colonies respond?" Vern questioned.

"Nay, a few did not. But the Stamp Act Congress brought home to the British the fact that our resistance to parliamentary taxation is by no means confined to the lower classes in the colonies nor to the colonial seaports," Gadsden responded.

"The members who did attend were by far some of the most distinguished men in the colonies. This fact alone had to force England to take notice," William Kraemer added.

"I was of the opinion that the congress should ignore England's Parliament and petition King George himself to repeal the Stamp Act. After all, we colonists are not recognized by Parliament as having rights, and have in truth been insulted by the refusal of the House of Commons to accept any petitions from the colonial assemblies against the Stamp Act," Gadsden said heatedly.

Savage slowly nodded his head. "And did they listen to you?"

"Only a few. In the end, the congress drew up an

address to the King, a memorial to the lords, and a petition to the House of Commons, which only serves to show our dependence upon Parliament as well as King George III. Though the congress did acknowledge that we of the American colonies owe all due subordination to Parliament, at least a doctrine of no taxation without representation was put forth."

"So what now?" Savage questioned insistently. "Do we sit back and abide unfair taxation until we receive a yeah or nay from our lords across the sea?"

"That is exactly why we are here this night, my friend." Gadsden grinned, reaching over to pat Savage on the shoulder as though to impart some patience. "You have ever been a man to be counted on and we, the cause, are still in need of your help. The Sons of Liberty in the northern colonies are attempting to create a military alliance to prevent the landing of British regulars if the appeal is rejected and England attempts to further enforce the Stamp Act. In Connecticut, Colonel Putnam has declared that ten thousand men will spring to arms in that fair province alone if the need arises. We are ready at last to fight; there are those who claim that they will fight up to their knees in blood if necessary. Even in Philadelphia, the stronghold of the Quakers, war and bloodshed are being regarded as inevitable if the British government calls

315

upon the Army to break our resistance to their tyranny. We shall purge the colonies of these stamps and stamp masters alike, and we shall demand that the seaports open and the courts do business without the damnable things."

"I see," Savage stated.

"The final means that the colonists will employ to achieve their ends is economic pressure," Kraemer said. "The colonial merchants will countermand their orders for British goods, and will proclaim to their creditors that dark days are ahead for all if the Stamp Act is not repealed immediately. There will be a boycotting of British goods the likes of which England has never seen."

"With such a threat Britain is faced with ruin," Vern said absently. "Surely the merchants and manufacturers will clamour to the King to make haste for a repeal."

"That is exactly what we are hoping for," Kraemer stated and Christopher Gadsden nodded his head in agreement. "We colonial Americans have enough gall to risk our own ruin to bring about England's downfall."

Kellie looked around her and realized that those in the room held a religious fervor for the land known as the American colonies. They would do all in their power to fight off the tyranny of England's greed.

"It is agreed, then. We will step up our fight in

the Charleston area. The Sons of Liberty have already been given instructions and are ready to see to it that the newspaper be printed without the stamps and that ships be loaded and unloaded on the docks," Gadsden declared. "Your help in past days has been greatly appreciated, but now is the time we must stand firm and be ready to do whatever we need to, to ensure that England takes our message to heart."

"The cause can certainly count on any help I can give." Savage rose from his chair and Kellie and Vern followed suit. "My ship should be unloaded and ready to set sail. I will be in touch with you soon, Christopher." Savage held out his hand.

"We can only pray that our plans will grant us the desired effects and we will all be able to celebrate soon," William Kraemer offered amid the farewells.

As Savage had anticipated, the ship was unloaded by the time they returned. Wagons piled with barrels of molasses and crates and boxes stacked high were pulling away from the dock.

"Let's be getting underway, lads," Vern shouted as the three boarded ship.

In a short time the vessel was once again sailing back down the Wilmington coastline. Kellie stood against the railing and reveled in the peaceful sur-

rounds as the crew once again employed a caution-
ary silence.

As they made their way out to sea, Savage went
to his wife's side after being assured that Vern had
set their course and had everything under control.
"It is beautiful," he murmured as he took in the
view that had captivated his wife. The moonlight
glowed down upon the phosphoric shimmer of the
waves formed by the wake of the ship. Showers of
salt spray sparkled like diamonds cascading upon
the dark depths of the sea. "Before we were wed,
on nights like this I would be reminded of you.
Your golden hair gleams as though phosphorescent
when it hangs free down your back."

Kellie leaned against her husband, for the moment content to feel his closeness and succumb to
the husky seduction of his voice. "You truly
thought of me?" she whispered.

"From that very day when you came to Savage
Hall to enlist my help in freeing your cousin from
the guardhouse, I thought of only you. You
plagued my dreams until at last I made you my
own." Blakely sighed upon inhaling her sweet rose
scent.

"And now what thoughts plague you, my lord?"

"Thoughts of the most incredible, most beautiful
woman I have ever known. Each waking moment I
am consumed by the image of her smiling face."

Kellie was delighted; he always made her feel so

remarkably alive.

Thousands of stars twinkled against the backdrop of a dark velvet sky as the pair marveled at the panoramic splendor. They were a world unto themselves; a unity that would allow no intrusion.

As the hour was late and the crew, but for a small watch, had gone below to get some much-needed rest, Savage ventured softly, "The cabin would be much warmer, love. Why do we not retire for the night? I know you must be tired after your cramped night's sleep in the longboat." His voice held a trace of humor that was not lost on Kellie.

"One night's ill sleep will be worth the price of having your arms around me this night," Kellie replied, not in the least disturbed by the reminder of her misadventures. She would stow away all over again in a minute, she told herself.

"Come, then, let us seek the warmth of our bed." Savage wrapped his arm about her shoulders and the pair retreated to their cabin.

Inside, Savage helped Kellie out of her jacket. The heat of the small wood-burning stove made of the cramped quarters a cozy lair for the lovers.

Savage put out the tallow candle hanging in the lantern above his desk; the one near the bed he allowed to remain lit as it was the only light in the cabin. "Come to me," he whispered caressingly, and without a word Kellie crossed the room to him.

Skillfully, the pair undressed each other. A large

breath escaped Savage's lungs as his wife stood naked before him. When he saw her thus, it was always as though for the first time. Her beauty captivated him; her touch left him intoxicated.

Very tenderly, Kellie's hand began to stroke his massive chest. Her fingertips played wantonly over his hard, flat nipples and, with the most delicate touch imaginable, fluttered lightly over his rib cage.

Her fingers lingered at the small indent in his belly and then slowly roamed downward over the firm molding of his hips. Her eyes glowed as though sparkling emeralds as her hands traveled ever lower.

Blakely could but gasp as her hands encircled his pulsating hardness. He breathlessly withstood her enticing assault upon the locus of his desire.

At last, unable to bear any more, Savage groaned aloud. "Let us go to bed," he said pleadingly.

As the pair reached the side of the bed, Kellie gently pushed against her husband's chest until he lay flat on his back. "*I* would make love to *you* this night," she whispered.

Savage had to force himself not to roll her on her back and put an end to this torturous play; as she placed her luscious body atop him, he could only clamp his teeth together to prevent himself from emitting an animallike groan.

Not fully aware of the effect her enchanting ministrations was having on him, Kellie rose above him and captured his throbbing lance in her warm, moist sheath.

For a moment she stilled. He filled her so completely it took her breath away. And then slowly Kellie began to move. The long, golden strands of her hair showered over Blakely's body and over the bed.

As her head bent and she captured her husband's lips beneath her own, her body began to move to an inner primitive beat. Her undulating movements grew more and more urgent and they clutched tightly to each other. When the storm of their passions peaked, they were both sent spiraling to unimaginable heights. Savage's body rose up to meet hers in one final rapturous convulsion, and Kellie cried aloud as she was hurled toward the zenith of utter fulfillment.

What claim could words hold when such feelings were shared? What small whisper could express more than their hearts had already proclaimed? They slept. Their limbs twined, their breaths mingled upon each other's cheeks, their heartbeats pounded softly against each other's chest. They were as one upon the darkness of the sea.

In the early hours of the morning Kellie's sleep

was intruded upon by the sounds of pounding feet overhead. Forgetting for the moment where she was, she turned over to reach for her husband. All that met her searching hand was the cold bed and an empty pillow. Instantly her eyes opened and she looked fearfully to the lantern swinging recklessly over the desk.

Climbing out of bed, she stumbled over to the chair where Savage had thrown her clothes the night before. The steady rocking motion of the ship forced her to return to the bed and sit upon its side to dress.

Kellie had never been aboard a ship in foul weather, but she had heard wretched tales. With a determined breath, she started for the door, her hands reaching out to anything for support, to keep herself from being thrown to the floor.

As she reached the end of the companionway, the force of the wind sent rain and sleet showering over Kellie; she clutched to the side of the ship. The incessant downpour stung her skin, blinded her, and left her gasping for breath.

Kellie rubbed at her eyes in an attempt to look for her husband. The crew was hurrying about to secure the sails and rigging. The wind howled and the darkness seemed to increase and Savage was not in sight.

A rope had been tied about the inner portion of the ship and to this Kellie clung as she groped past the companionway. The ship was being hurled every which way in the waves, and sea water was washing over the wood decking. Kellie wanted to reach the helm of the ship; she thought she would find Blakely there. Instead, she found Vern with a strap lashed about his waist; he had taken the wheel from the helmsman.

The moment her cousin set eyes upon her, he began to shout for her to get below, but Kellie could understand little of what he was saying. "Where is Blakely?" she called above the commotion, but all she gained was a mouthful of rainwater. Her cousin urgently directed her back the way she had come.

As a large wave jostled the ship to and fro, Kellie held to the rope for dear life. As it momentarily righted itself she wiped the rain and sleet from her face and eyes in her attempt to seek out her husband once again. Where could he be? There was desperation in her movements as she left the helm. Had Savage been hurt or washed overboard? Her mind recoiled at the horror of such thoughts. Fighting against the gusting wind, she tried to make her way back along the deck. As she saw two crewmen reinforcing the longboat, she yelled to them, hoping they could tell her the whereabouts of the captain, but the noise of the storm overwhelmed her shouts and the men kept to their work.

Letting go of the guide rope, Kellie started across

the deck. Surely *someone* knew where Savage was, she reasoned, as with faltering steps she started toward the longboat. Halfway across the deck another wave battered the ship, throwing Kellie to the wood deck and with a whoosh sweeping her toward the side railing. Her hands clutched out to no avail for anything to stop her from being washed overboard. *I am going to drown,* she thought, and a terrified scream broke from her mouth. The churning water held her in its grip and sucked her fiercely toward the side of the ship.

It all happened so quickly; one moment she was being swept to her death and the next a strong hand had encircled her wrist. Savage dragged her to her feet, holding her tightly against his chest as the water completed its journey back to the raging sea without its victim.

"What the hell are you doing out on deck?" he shouted at her when he regained enough of his composure to speak. The terror he had felt when he had heard her scream and saw her being washed toward the side of the ship had caused his heart to stop in his chest.

"You are all right," she wept, her hand caressing his handsome face and her own body flooding with relief.

"Of course, I am all right." Now Savage began to feel his anger replacing his earlier fear. Would this woman never learn? he asked himself.

"I thought something had happened to you when I came on deck and could not find you." Kellie was trembling from the cold and her teeth were chattering so much that Savage could barely make out her words.

Fearing for her health, Savage lifted her into his arms and carried her back to the cabin. Helping her to pull off her sodden clothes, he ordered her back to bed. "I want you to stay right here." He pulled the covers up beneath her chin.

"But the storm! You cannot go back out there!" Fear for his safety filled her emerald eyes.

"The storm will pass soon, and you may, too, if you take sick from this foul weather!"

His attempt at humor pacified her. "You will be safe?"

"Aye, my sweet. I have faced much worse storms at sea. We will hold with the wind with a minimum of sail and shall ride this out, I promise." Lightly he caressed her soft cheek. Once again he marveled at her behavior. The danger she placed herself in seemed not to affect her; her thoughts were always of him.

"Will you return soon?" Kellie questioned, her hand clutching his forearm.

Placing a light kiss upon her forehead, he murmured, "I will be back before you know it. Do not try to light a fire in the stove. Stay right here and rest." Savage straightened, and within seconds headed out of the cabin door to once again face the elements.

Kellie pulled the covers tightly about herself. She had been foolish, she berated herself, and she had almost paid the price with her life. If Savage had not come upon the scene when he had, she would be at this very moment lying in her grave at the bottom of the sea. A fierce trembling took hold of her. She should have realized long ago that Savage was capable of taking care of himself without her help; the storm had only brought the point home once again.

Eventually the chill left Kellie's body and a warm lassitude settled over her entire form. Even though she had almost paid the ultimate price for her folly, her last thoughts before a fretful sleep overtook her were for her husband's safety.

It was late afternoon when the storm finally passed and Blakely returned to the cabin bearing a tray of food and hot tea he had gotten from the galley.

"Is the storm over?" Kellie questioned and sat up beneath the covers, pulling a pillow up behind her back.

"Aye, love, it is over, and we shall be arriving at Savage Hall shortly after dark. I brought you something to eat." Setting the tray down, Savage started a fire in the small wood stove to break the chill in the cabin.

"I will be glad to get home," Kellie murmured as she bit into a piece of bread.

Savage changed out of his sodden clothing and returned to the side of the bed. He could well imagine her desire for the comfort of home. After all she had been through, she would have much to remember about her trip aboard his ship. Spending her first night in the cramped confinement of the longboat beneath a piece of canvas, and then being dragged to stand before him as though a common criminal, and on top of all else being almost swept overboard! He would not remind her of any of this, he told himself. She had been put through enough as it was. "I, too, will be glad to get home, my love." He sat down beside her and partook of the meal he had prepared.

"I was thinking of all that Christopher Gadsden and William Kraemer were saying. Do you think that their plan to force the ports and courts to carry on their everyday business transactions without the stamps will work in Charleston? Governor Mansfield will use all the force within his power to stop such a movement." Kellie wanted more than anything to get her mind off her own misadventures.

"Those in Charleston have had enough of the Stamp Act. What happened to the Spires proves

327

this. Over half the town turned out to chase out of town one of their own who had become a stamp master. Our strength now lies in numbers and unity. The British militia under Governor Mansfield's direction is not strong enough to enforce England's dictates if we stand together. The only way the stamps will be sold is if the British bring in more redcoats."

"Do you think England will do that?" Kellie could not imagine the British lightly giving up the revenue they were gaining from the stamp tax.

"If the merchants are threatened with ruin, Britain will quickly see the error of its ways. I fear that if King George does not take a different view of the situation soon, there will indeed be much bloodshed." Blakely Savage was a man with an eye toward the future. He held strong beliefs that if the time was not yet right for the colonists to take up arms, then one day soon it would be, if not over the Stamp Act, then over the colonists' desire to rule themselves. One way or another, blood would be spilled upon this fair land.

Savage took only a short time to eat before readying himself to go back on deck. He promised Kellie he would return soon and bring her clothes from the cabin boy to replace her damp apparel. He soon left Kellie to her own thoughts.

Kellie felt an inner surging of excitement over the events that were taking place in the colonies. At last some headway would be made against the Stamp Act. She looked forward with great anticipation to the days ahead. She would do all she could to ensure the repeal of the Stamp Act, and she would somehow try to make Savage believe that she could help him in his crusade as the Falcon.

It was late that evening that the ship sailed into the cave beneath Savage Hall. With the assurance that Vern would see to the securing of the ship, Savage led Kellie over the gangplank and the pair made their way up the steps leading to the secret passageway and into the study.

Thomas had fallen asleep as he awaited his master in the study. As the bookcase creaked open, he jumped to his feet. His eyes fell upon Kellie standing at his master's side and relief flooded his tired features. "My lady, we have been searching for you since yesterday morn. The servants have been out of their minds with worry." He did not mention his own worry over her whereabouts or the fact that he had dreaded facing his master with the news of his wife's disappearance.

"Kellie went with me, Thomas. I am sorry if we caused you concern." Blakely did not say that his wife had stowed aboard his ship without his knowledge.

"Then is it safe to say that there is no longer

329

need of secrecy in the hall?" Thomas assumed that Savage had told his bride everything about his affairs, since he had seen with his own eyes her stepping through the opened bookcase.

With the nodding of his master's head, Thomas sighed aloud, and Kellie realized that the manservant had in truth been under pressure to keep her from discovering Savage's secret cave.

"No more secrets are necessary, Thomas," she offered and received a smile from the little man.

"That pleases me greatly, my lady. If you will both excuse me now, I will see to your bathwater. A warm fire has already been started in your chamber." Thomas did not wait to be dismissed, but turned about and started to the kitchen to hurry the boys upstairs with the water that was being warmed in anticipation of the master's arrival.

Until this very moment Kellie had felt uncomfortable in Thomas's presence, but this night she had glimpsed warmth in the little man. The strain of keeping her husband's secrets must have kept Thomas at a distance. She hoped that now they could have a better relationship. After all, her husband found the man invaluable, and Kellie had found in the past that it was much easier for a household to run smoothly when she got on well with the servants.

"Come, sweet. I have a yearning for the comfort of our chamber." Savage settled his arm about her shoulder and the pair made their way upstairs to the pleasant surroundings of their bedchamber.

After a relaxing bath and a shared meal, the couple retired to the large oak bed. Their lovemaking was an affirmation of their commitment to each other. Each touch was a caress of surrender; each kiss was a sharing of their souls. Soft whispers of adoration were borne in the air as Kellie was swept beyond the shadows of reality in the embrace of the one she loved.

Chapter Ten

The downstairs portion of the governor's house was dimly lit. The only sign of life came from the study, where the governor and three other gentlemen were holding a meeting. They were discussing a plan to quash the surge of radicalism that had been sweeping over the Charleston area.

"You have the stamps with you now, Captain, and your men will be on the docks first thing in the morning. With your help we should be able to force this town into submission once and for all!" Governor Mansfield was outraged. The whole of Charleston appeared to be in defiance of the Crown. Under threats to their lives, those who ran the docks, newspapers, and courts were doing so in defiance of the Stamp Act. Tomorrow would be the first step in his plan to bring order back to the rebellious town. Captain Sutterfield's entire crew would be on the docks with clubs in hand to enforce the law that these malcontents were so willfully defying. With the aid of the military, Governor Mansfield felt assured that the British would once again gain the upper hand over the colonial rabble.

"The stamps are in these pouches," Captain Sutterfield said, placing two leather bags on the desk before him. "And my men have been instructed this evening as to their duty tomorrow." Captain Sutterfield was a strong advocate for the Crown. He ran a tight ship, demanding strict obedience from all under his command. He felt that the English colonies should be run in a like manner. If the Crown's dictates were disobeyed concerning the Stamp Act, there was no telling what law the colonists would think to disregard next.

"Once the docks are brought back to order, the courts and printing presses will follow suit," Colonel Burch stated as he sat back confidently in his chair.

"You and your lieutenant here are to make sure your men are stationed along the docks to reinforce Captain Sutterfield's men. I want no mistakes made. Arrest any who resist your authority." Governor Mansfield looked upon the colonel and his first lieutenant with serious intent.

"The men under my command are more than ready for such action, sir," Colonel Burch stated in a strong voice, as every complaint he had heard over the past weeks from the men in his command came to mind. There had been insults hurled at them, as well as threats. Something had to be done quickly to show the populace of Charleston who they owed their loyalty to.

Governor Mansfield drank deeply from his brandy goblet and for a moment indulged himself with his visions of taking command of Charleston once again. Everything was working out just as he had planned. "Well, gentlemen, I do believe that —"

"I say, this is a charming setting, isn't it?" As a new voice interrupted the governor, the men lifted their eyes to see the dark figure of the Falcon step boldly into the room, his gun leveled.

"What the hell are you doing here, you bloody bastard?" Governor Mansfield leapt to his feet as all eyes held upon the intruder.

"Why, Governor, I was dismayed not to receive an invitation. I reasoned that it must have been an oversight."

"Get out of my house!" The Governor's face flooded with the fury that took hold of him.

"Not so fast, Governor. And you, gentlemen, just relax," the Falcon calmly directed as Colonel Burch reached for the sword at his side.

"Alex!" the governor shouted loudly toward the open door.

"If you are summoning the gent who tried to detain me in the hallway earlier, I am afraid he will be of little assistance to you now."

"What have you done to him, you vile cur?"

"He is in the kitchen. I assure you he's quite

comfortable." The Falcon grinned at the governor.

"What do you want here?" Captain Sutterfield questioned as he glared up at the one who had evaded him for two long years.

"Why, Captain, if I had known you would be here, I would have brought you a bottle of my fine French wine." The Falcon turned toward the one who questioned him, not able to resist the temptation to prick the man with his humor.

"Smuggled wine, no doubt," Captain Sutterfield snarled.

"Smuggled or untaxed, however you would term it, Captain." The Falcon laughed aloud. "But now to the point, gentlemen." He stepped farther into the study. "I believe you have something here that I am very interested in. If you do not mind, I will just relieve you of these." With one hand the Falcon kept the gun turned upon the men and with the other he hefted the leather pouches from the desk.

Both officers rose instantly to their feet.

"Easy now, men, let us not be foolhardy. Your lives are surely worth more than the contents of these pouches." A hard glint filled the Falcon's eyes as his lips thinned and his jaw muscle throbbed with the seriousness of his statement.

Slowly the officers lowered back into their chairs beside the governor as they wisely heeded the warning given.

"That is better, gentlemen. And now, I am afraid I must depart your pleasant company. Perhaps you can hatch another scheme to occupy your time." The Falcon started to the door.

"You will not get away with this! You will be chased down and hanged this very night!" Governor Mansfield sputtered in impotent rage.

The Falcon gave a smart salute in the governor's direction. "I can only say that I have heard these words before, Governor, and as upon many other occasions, I will indeed heed your warnings." With this he exited the room.

"After him!" Governor Mansfield screamed at the officers, and without thought the two men started to rush out of the study door with their swords drawn.

Instantly the colonel and lieutenant jumped back into the study; the Falcon had fired a shot over their heads. The bullet lodged over the portal.

"Get after him!" Governor Mansfield shouted once again as he pushed his way in front of Captain Sutterfield. "He will get away with the stamps!"

"But, Governor, he is firing at us," Colonel Burch declared in a ragged breath. He fully agreed with the Falcon that his life was worth far more than a couple of pouches of stamps.

"You fools! He has only one pistol and is not about to take the time to reload!" Governor Mansfield rushed through the doorway and ran as fast as his heavy bulk would allow down the hallway and toward the back of the house.

"Get on your horses and get after him! I want those stamps back tonight!" Governor Mansfield directed his orders at the two officers and watched as they started back to the front of the house to gain their mounts.

"He went through the back door," the servant said weakly as the gag was pulled from his mouth.

The officers mounted their horses and started galloping down the road leading out of Charleston after their prey. Colonel Burch shouted to the first lieutenant to gather some soldiers to aid in the chase and meet him at the crossroads.

Immediately acting upon the order, the lieutenant turned his horse in the direction of the military barracks.

Colonel Burch pushed his horse to a faster pace in the hopes of heading off the Falcon.

Savage had hurried through the Governor's back door and rounded the carriage house, where he was met by Kellie, who he had earlier demanded stay hidden with the horses and await his return.

"Did you get the stamps?" Kellie questioned anxiously.

Savage nodded his dark head and quickly secured the pouches to his saddle. Going to his wife's side he gave her a hand up onto the back of her stallion. "We had best hurry. Every redcoat in Charleston will soon be looking for us."

Dressed in her own dark apparel and large-brimmed hat, Kellie looked much like a boy as she sat on the back of her large horse. In ready agreement she kicked the beast's sides and raced through the Charleston streets behind her husband.

"We will avoid the main road into Charleston and head for the side road leading to the coast," Blakely called over his shoulder and headed in the direction that led to the side road, his silver gaze searching out any sign of danger.

As they reached the coast near the Fisher cabin, Kellie sighed with much relief. Their venture was successful. The stamps would not be sold tomorrow as the British had planned. Kellie felt sheer jubilation course through her. Once again, the patriots had struck a blow at English injustice.

The couple did not relax their pace until they were at Savage Hall. "Take the pouches and put them behind the bookcase in the study," Savage instructed as he helped her from her horse. "I will take care of them later, but for now we had best retire as quickly as possible to our chamber. The militia may make a house-to-house search for the Falcon and the stamps, so we must be prepared."

Kellie hurried into the house and as her husband

requested, put the stamps behind the bookcase and then made her way upstairs. The fear that the British were searching the houses throughout Charleston spurred her as she pulled off her dark clothes and hid them in the back of her wardrobe. She pulled on a gown and robe and sat down at her dressing table to quickly brush out her long hair. She anxiously awaited her husband.

It was only a short wait. Savage entered the chamber and hurriedly changed out of his dark clothes. He took from his bureau a long white nightshirt that boasted a wealth of embroidered flowers down the front, puffed sleeves, and a high, stiff collar, and pulled it over his large frame.

Kellie watched as Savage pulled his wig over his dark hair and began to powder his face. "What is so amusing?" Blakely questioned as he turned toward Kellie and saw the grin on her face.

"It is just that I have never seen you in a nightshirt." Kellie burst out laughing as she took in the figure of her husband in his outrageous attire.

"Why, madam, you dare to sit there and ridicule your husband?"

"Never that, my love." Kellie went to his side and wrapped her arms about his neck. "For, you see, I know what lies beneath all this disguise."

"Fie on you, mistress!" Blakely grinned. "I do believe that your designs upon this frilly nightshirt are not very respectable."

A knock upon the door interrupted them. Thomas entered with the announcement that there was an officer downstairs waiting to talk with Lord Savage.

"See him to the front parlor and tell him I will be down shortly," Savage instructed and Thomas set out to do as he was bid.

Pulling on the dressing robe that matched his nightshirt, Savage started to the chamber door. "I should only be a few minutes, love. He will want to look about the grounds and the stables."

"But if he looks in the stable, he will see the horses!" Panic shot through Kellie as she envisioned the soldiers finding their horses damp and tired from their nightly ride.

"I awoke one of the stable boys before coming to the house and told him to take the stallions out to the back pasture beyond the stable. The lad should have returned and will be back in his bed by now." Savage saw that her uneasiness remained. "This is not the first time the redcoats have come to Savage Hall in search of the Falcon. It is but a routine search in the area. Do not read any more into it."

"I will go with you," Kellie stated and tightened her robe about her body. She thought to hide her pistol in the folds of her robe, but she knew Savage would not allow this. Her greatest fear was that her husband would be found out and captured by the British. There was no possible way she was going to sit by in their bedchamber when he was being threatened with discovery downstairs.

There was little time for argument, and by the determined look upon his wife's face, Blakely knew that if he denied her, an argument would surely ensue. "Come then, let us not keep the officer waiting any longer than necessary." Savage surprised Kellie by giving in so easily to her wishes.

As the couple went down the hallway to the front parlor, Kellie spied Thomas lingering about and knew he was ready to give assistance if the need should arise.

Colonel Burch stood tall and unyielding with his helmet in hand before the hearth as Kellie and Savage entered the room. His eyes took in the lord of the hall's flamboyant night attire and the gracious form of his wife. "I beg your pardon, Lord Savage, for seeking you out at this time of the night. But we have had another incident with this fellow known as the Falcon, and my orders are to search the area. I hate to put you out, but my men must examine the grounds about Savage Hall."

"Will there never be an end to this rebel's misdeeds?" Lord Savage's high, whining voice questioned and then with an exaggerated movement he brought his hand up to cover a large yawn. "Does this Falcon villain not realize that there are people who are in need of their rest? One would think he would limit his lawless deeds to the daylight hours

341

for the sake of those who wish to live a normal life. Do you not agree, my dear?" Savage's gaze went to his wife.

"Indeed, my lord, this Falcon must be a very unsavory character."

The colonel sighed. There was no understanding the nobility, he thought to himself. They were an indulgent lot with positively outlandish ideas. Desiring that the Falcon keep his robberies to the daylight hours, so that the lord could get his sleep! When he told his men this one, he would surely get some laughs and more than likely a mug or two at the tavern. "Again, I am sorry to disturb you, Lord Savage. I only thought it best to advise you that the search for the Falcon included your property."

"I fully understand. Indeed you have your duty to uphold whether day or night." Savage waved his arm to indicate his consent, and the full, puffy sleeve of his night robe flapped about.

"Good evening, then, Lord Savage, Lady Savage." Colonel Burch quickly made his way out of the room, his high-heeled boots clicking against the wood floor as he saw himself out the front door.

Kellie could have doubled up with laughter. It had all been so easy; her husband was a superb actor. She had seen the look of unease upon the colonel's face and knew he would be quite happy to be out of their presence and back outside with his men. "No one would ever be able to guess that you are the Falcon." She grinned up at her husband.

"That is the whole idea, sweet." Savage grinned back. "Now if you are ready, let us seek out that sleep I professed to be in need of."

"Will you keep on your nightshirt?" Kellie wantonly drew her eyes over his form in a teasing manner.

"Now that you mention it, the idea does hold some interesting possibilities."

Kellie reached out and fluffed the material of the nightshirt and robe, her hand lingering over Savage's broad chest. "I have ever loved a good game of hide and seek, my lord," she said, then laughed as she turned about and fled the study, squealing as Savage followed closely in pursuit.

Charleston, like the other provinces in the colonies, was in a state of total unrest. The Sons of Liberty's ranks had swelled to a large number and even those who had not sided with the patriots before were fighting the British against the Stamp Act. The ports were daily patrolled to ensure that ships were loaded and unloaded in disregard of the hated stamps. The Charleston Daily Press sang the praises of the Sons of Liberty and those who stood against British tyranny; each afternoon the latest news about the protest against unfair taxation was

343

circulated throughout town. Even the doors to the courthouse were opened wide and licenses were bought and cases heard without a stamp being purchased.

The British were frustrated time and again in their attempts to bring about order and to enforce the stamp taxation. The stamps had been burned or stolen, stamp masters' lives were threatened, and any who tried to sell the stamps were beaten and run out of town. Even the children were to be seen throwing rotten vegetables and stones at the red-coated soldiers as they made their way through the Charleston streets; and the women who had previously enjoyed the soldiers' favors now shunned them as though they were plagued with the pox.

The pressure against the Stamp Act was on, and the one to feel the brunt of the patriots' handiwork was Governor Mansfield himself. He took the latest resistance to authority as a personal insult. He had come to this province to exert the full weight of British control, but he was beset with problems at every hand. He did not have enough troops to enforce the Stamp Act and, as if this were not enough, the Falcon was tormenting and eluding the British at every turn. Even those who Mansfield had relied upon since coming to Charleston seemed to flee his side. Captain Sutterfield would not leave his ship for fear that the Falcon and some of his smugglers would venture to steal aboard and take over his vessel. And Elroy Beeking more and more kept himself locked in his house, taking every threat made against him to heart; he claimed that he would as soon as possible be leaving for England.

Governor Mansfield himself secretly desired nothing more than to return to his mother land, but his pride would not allow him to turn tail and flee. The barbarian colonists would not have the last laugh, he swore adamantly to himself. He would only leave Charleston when his pride and honor had been vindicated.

Elroy Beeking's thoughts were not of honor or pride. This night as he sat alone in a corner of the tavern, his glance went nervously about the large common room. He hoped his presence went unnoticed by the local customers. He had not wanted to hold the meeting here in the tavern; but the pair of unsavory characters he had met along the docks this morning had insisted, and Beeking had at last relented.

From the corner of his eye, he watched as the pair made their way to his table. "Sit down, gentlemen," he said to the two unwashed and unkempt men.

"It surely be our pleasure, gov'na," the one who was obviously the leader of the pair answered and pulled out a chair. The other followed.

"Let's get right to business." Beeking had little

desire to stay in the pair's company any longer than necessary.

"Now hold up just a little bit," the same one spoke out. "We done come all this way from the docks, and Cal here has gotten hisself a mighty thirst."

Beeking could see that he was not going to get anywhere until he bought the man a drink. With a sigh, he motioned for the serving girl to take their order. This was his last chance to obtain what he most desired. He could not entrust the task to just anyone; surely not anyone respectable. "Here is the note you are to deliver to Savage Hall tomorrow morning. Be certain that only the lady of the house sees it; entrust it to no other, and then await me at the fork in the road leading into Charleston." Beeking would give them more information after they had been served their drinks. Men such as these two, he knew, would agree to almost anything with the promise of a few coins and a drink in their bellies.

"We ain't got no horses, gov'na. How you specting we be getting all the way to Savage Hall and back into town?" The one Beeking did not know by name took the note and shoved it into his filthy shirt.

"Go to the stable in the morning. There will be two horses ready for you," he instructed. He had seen to everything. In a few days he would have all he had been dreaming about for so long right within his grasp.

Savage had left Savage Hall early to attend to some business in town and Kellie, with little else to do, had decided to spend the morning in the study going over the ledgers she had told her husband she had already finished setting into order.

The small room was warmed by the blazing fire in the fireplace and Kellie pored over the books with the hopes of finishing before her husband returned. This afternoon Savage had promised they would go for a ride to Moss Rose, and Kellie eagerly anticipated the outing. It had been some time since they had visited her father and Aunt Rose and she was looking forward to spending the afternoon in their company.

As she shut the last ledger, she heard a loud knocking on the front door.

Usually Thomas answered any summons by visitors, but this morning as the pounding continued, Kellie supposed Thomas to be busy in the back of the house. Leaving the book upon the desk, she hurriedly went down the hallway to the front foyer and opened the door, wondering as she did so who could be so persistent.

As she peered out upon the front step, an untidy little man stomped about in the cold and slouched

347

down in his large coat. "Ye be the mistress of this here house?" he questioned and as she nodded her head, he drew forth a rumpled piece of paper from inside his clothes. "This be fur ye then." He turned about and Kellie watched as he awkwardly proceeded to mount a frail-appearing beast that barely passed for a horse.

The poor man, Kellie thought, as she watched him ride down the lane from Savage Hall. If he had waited just a moment, she would have gone inside the hall and found him a few coins for his trouble.

Shivering from the cold wind as she shut the door, Kellie looked down at the dirty, rumpled piece of paper in her hand. Going into the study, she sat down in a chair near the hearth and slowly opened the note.

A worried frown crossed her brow as she began to read.

COME QUICKLY FOR MY LIFE MAY DEPEND UPON IT. TELL NO ONE, NOT EVEN LORD SAVAGE, OF THIS NOTE. I WILL AWAIT YOU AT THE TAVERN.

YOUR FRIEND,

MARIE

As she reread the note, Kellie imagined the urgency of the writer. Marie usually had a very neat handwriting but the words scribbled upon this piece of parchment were scarcely legible. Marie surely must be in trouble, she thought. Without a second thought, she hurried up to her chamber.

She knew that time was of the essence. She hurriedly changed into a warm riding habit and pulled on her fur-lined boots. If Savage had been home she would have told him about the note. His concern would be as great as hers if Marie were in trouble because of her rebel activities.

For a moment she thought to pen her husband a note, but upon reflection considered that she would perhaps find him coming from town on his way back to the hall. Taking with her her warmest cloak, she rushed outside to the stable.

In a short time Kellie was on her horse and racing down the lane from Savage Hall.

Perhaps the British had found out that Marie was a courier for the patriots. She could already be in the guardhouse! The thought made Kellie push her mount to a faster pace.

As she neared the fork in the road that led into town, Kellie saw the same disheveled little man who had brought the message to Savage Hall riding toward her. She saw that there was another man at his side, and as she drew closer, she found him to be as ill-appearing as the messenger. Thinking that perhaps they had come from Marie, she slowed her pace. The one who had come to the house waved a piece of paper in his hand, and Kellie halted and awaited their approach.

"I be back on me way to bring ye this, mistress," the man called as the pair drew in their mounts on both sides of her.

Kellie reached out for the message and as she did so, the little man dropped the piece of parchment at her horse's feet. "I be right sorry about that, mistress, but ye had best fetch that note, fur the lady that sent it seemed awful upset."

Kellie was too eager to get to the bottom of Marie's request to be put out by the man's clumsiness. She dismounted and bent down. She fumbled with the note, oblivious to the actions of the two men, who were making an effort to dismount unnoticed. As Kellie opened the note and saw that the paper was blank, she looked up to see both men on foot and moving toward her menacingly. "What is going on here? There is no message on this paper!" she exclaimed.

"Now, is that a fact?" the one man asked as he took hold of her arm. As she tried to pull away, the other took hold of her other arm.

"Take your hands off of me!" Kellie shouted as she twisted frantically in their grasp.

"Make no trouble, mistress, and ye won't be hurt," the messenger said as he pulled a piece of rope from his jacket pocket and started to tie it about her wrist.

"What do you want? Why are you doing this?"

350

Kellie cried.

"Ye be finding out everything soon enough. Now just let us do our job." He tied the other wrist amid Kellie's desperate attempts to free herself.

Within minutes Kellie was tied and gagged and thrown across the saddle of her horse. The two men mounted their horses and led her stallion into the woods near the edge of town.

Kellie was powerless to do anything. She had been tricked into believing that Marie had needed her help, and had been abducted by ruthless men. She neither knew the reason for their actions nor their present intent. Her only thoughts were of escape.

The two led Kellie's horse deep into the woods, and then started down a track that Kellie assumed would take them along the coast. Frantically her eyes roamed the area as she twisted her neck to gain a view. Where were they taking her? she wondered as the coastline came into view and they veered back toward town.

"That gent said everything would be waiting for us along here somewhere."

"Yeah, Cal, it won't be long now until we're done with this job and can get out of this town. There ain't a thing here fur the likes of us."

"But Albert, ye said that we could take some of the coins and have one big night of it before we head down South. Ye ain't furgetting are ye?"

"Naw, I ain't furgetting. As soon as we deliver the woman and get our due, we'll head fur the tavern."

This seemed to satisfy the one called Cal, but in no fashion was Kellie's mind put at ease. Who would have hired two vagrants such as these to abduct her? And what could anyone wish to gain by holding her prisoner? Her mind went over all manner of horrible thoughts. Was she to be held for ransom? Did this man who they said had hired them think to gain some vast wealth from her husband for her return? Or was there another reason for her abduction? Had the British found out that Savage was in truth the Falcon, and were they going to hold her until he gave himself up for her release? She tried to call out to the two men who were leading her horse, but the gag in her mouth prevented all but a strangled moan. If she could only speak to them, she would try to convince them to return her to Savage Hall. If their interest was only in money, she would offer to pay them double what they had been promised.

Eventually the pair halted before an old, worn-looking wagon that was pulled by an even older-looking horse. "This be it, Cal, just like the boss said. All we got to do is load her up and take her to the ship."

Paying close attention to everything that was said, Kellie was struck with terror when the one called Albert said they were taking her to a ship. With all the strength she could muster, she tried to fling herself from the back of her horse. If she could get to the ground, perhaps she could run into the woods and hide somewhere until they gave up searching for her. But her attempt at freedom proved fruitless. As she landed on the ground, Albert was upon her quick as a cat. He held her firmly by the arm and dragged her to the wagon, not giving her a moment to catch her breath from the fall.

In a frenzy, Kellie tried to push against him. Her feet, which were untied, kicked out at his shins; but as Cal added his strength to subdue her, all she was capable of was an attempt to beseech them through her gagged lips.

"I think she be wanting to tell us someting," Cal said to Albert as they picked her up and tossed her into the back of the wagon.

"We ain't removing that gag. She be a fighter and the first chance she gets she would be screaming fur help. Remember what that gent said, she be a smart one and right tricky," Albert claimed as he climbed into the back of the wagon. Pulling out another piece of rope, he began to tie her feet together. "We being paid more coins than we done seen over the whole of this year. And I ain't about to take no chances of letting her get away from us."

Cal nodded his head in agreement and climbed into the back with his companion. He pulled out a piece of canvas from the back of the wagon and pulled it over Kellie's form. "That should do it. No one will be seeing her."

As darkness surrounded her, Kellie fought her constraints, but all she gained for her efforts was total exhaustion. She bucked and twisted, pulling at the ropes, all to no avail. She soon lay panting beneath her gag, unable to move.

The docks were busy at this time of the afternoon. Albert pulled the wagon close to the ship that was docked near the wharf. "This looks like the one the boss told us to take the lady aboard." He squinted at the name boldly printed on the large vessel's side, but he was not able to read. "Cal, go on over there and ask that fellow if this here be the ship we're looking fur. I hate to be taking the lady aboard the wrong ship."

"Yeah, that fancy gent sure would be mad if that happened." Cal grinned widely, as he climbed down from the carriage seat and went over to the man his friend had pointed out. He was gone only long enough to ask the desired question and returned, nodding his head. "That be the ship! *The Wind Mistress.*"

"Then let's get going. Keep her wrapped in that canvas, and try not to let her move about. We ain't wanting anybody to know what we're bringing aboard, cep'n the çap'n. He is suppose to have a cabin all ready fur her."

Over the past four years Cal had followed Albert's directions without question, and in this matter he was of no different mind.

The pair quickly set about their task. They wrapped their kidnapped victim up as tightly as possible, and then gathered her in their arms and started to carry her the several feet down the dock to the ship.

Wriggling and kicking out as much as her tied legs would allow, Kellie fought for release as she felt herself being smothered under the dark, stifling material of the canvas. Muffled noises reached her abductor's ears.

"Keep her still!" Albert warned as he tried to get a better grip on their curiously shaped baggage.

"She be worse than trying to hold on to a wiggling snake!" Cal declared as he also tried to control her movements.

"Let's just hurry and get her aboard," Albert said in a louder tone, for he feared that at any moment she would spill out upon the dock. He began to hurry Cal across the wood planking from dock to deck.

Captain Stephen Barret met the two men as they stepped aboard his ship. "Can I help you?" His eyes went over the pair of disreputable-appearing men and the canvas-covered object they held between them.

"Ye be the cap'n of this here ship?" Albert questioned, and seeing the captain's neatly combed, sandy-red head nod in the affirmative, Albert continued. "We got this bundle to deliver to ye."

For a moment Captain Barret appeared at a loss, but then he noticed the canvas moving in the men's grip and heard a slight, muffled protest coming from within. Slowly he nodded his head. This must be the woman he had agreed to harbor aboard his ship, he thought. Though at first he had been against holding a woman against her will, what had changed his mind was the flash of gold that had been set down on his desk by Elroy Beeking. "Bring the delivery along," he ordered in a clipped manner and started across the deck to the companionway.

Albert and Cal were only too glad to hurry after him; their arms were aching from their struggle to keep the woman hidden beneath the canvas.

Captain Barret opened a cabin door and waited as the men revealed to him his new cargo. He was taken aback by what met his eyes. Even in her disheveled state, with her hands tied behind her back and the gag tied about her mouth, the woman was beautiful. "You are sure there is no mistake? This is the right woman?" he questioned the men as they held Kellie upright by the arms.

"She be the one, Cap'n," Albert answered for the

pair.

Stephen Barret shook his head perplexedly. He had expected a much different sort to be the future bride of the thin, bespectacled man who had approached him with this plan. This woman, looking up at him with her wide, sparkling green eyes, her soft, golden hair falling down over her shoulders, absolutely took his breath away.

"Well, she be all yours now, Cap'n. We were told to bring her aboard your ship and then report back to the fancy gent who hired us." Albert hoped there would be no arguing about this. All he wanted to do now was to get his money and for him and Cal to get on with their own plans for the future.

This was fine with the captain of *The Wind Mistress*. Something inside him rebelled at the sight of the two filthy creatures touching the woman standing between them. "I will take care of things from here on out," he said stiffly.

"Ye best keep a watch on her, Cap'n." The two released their charge and without a backward glance they left the cabin.

For a full moment Captain Barret and Kellie stared at one another. Kellie scrutinized him in an attempt to determine what sort of treatment she could expect from him, and he was still captivated and a bit unsettled by her incredible beauty.

"Well," he cleared his throat, "I see no more

357

need for your constraints." He started toward her, then hesitated. After a moment's reflection, he went to the cabin door and locked it, tucking the key in his pocket.

Kellie felt all of her renewed hope of escaping draining away. Her mind had been quickly formulating a plan of running out the door as soon as she was untied; now she would have to conceive of another way to gain her freedom. Perhaps she could convince the man that she had been abducted against her will and beseech him for her release. After all, she thought, he was a captain of a ship; he must hold some code of honor toward women.

The captain of *The Wind Mistress* began to untie the rope knotted about her ankles. His hands began to tremble as his fingers lightly brushed over the smooth pale skin of her legs. He hurried to finish the task. He then untied her wrists, admiring the slim beauty of her hands. He stepped back a few feet as she immediately reached up to remove the gag herself.

All the outrage that had been building up in Kellie, and which she had been powerless to vent, now came spewing forth vehemently. "How dare you heartless people treat me so wretchedly! You will all pay and pay dearly for the abuse I have suffered! If you do not release me this very moment, I will see you charged with abduction!" Out of breath, she glared at the captain as she rubbed her aching wrists.

Captain Barret was impressed. If he had thought her beautiful earlier, he now believed he was in the presence of perfection. Her cheeks were flushed with her anger, her lips slightly swollen and pink from the gag, and her lovely green eyes were deep jade jewels that sparked with fury beneath her lush lashes. "I am sorry for all you have been put through, madam," he said calmly. "I can only assure you that your treatment from here on out will be civil."

"Civil?" Kellie was amazed at his comment. I am now going to be treated with civility? I am lured away from my home, tied, gagged, thrown over my horse's back, wrapped in a piece of smelly canvas, and brought aboard this ship for God knows what reason, and now I can expect to be treated in a more *civil* fashion? I want none of your civility! I demand to be released!"

Captain Barret had been cautioned by Elroy Beeking that she would put up a fight and use all manner of threats, but he also remembered the man's insisting that his actions were in the woman's best interest. He had said that her life was at risk if she remained in Charleston, and that the captain must not give in to her demands for release. Even setting the gold he had been given aside, the captain knew that it would be less than honorable if

359

he allowed her to return to the dire fate that Beeking had outlined to him. "I am afraid that your release is impossible at this time, madam. You will find this cabin comfortable and your meals pleasing; more than that I cannot promise."

"But why? Why have I been brought aboard this ship? Who is this man that the other two were working for, and who gained your aid in this horrible plot against me?" Kellie demanded in a firm voice. If she were not going to be released, she demanded to know who it was that had arranged for her abduction. She had to know if it were the British trying to bait her husband. But the more she had thought of the idea of the British being behind her kidnapping, the less it had made sense. Surely they would have sent out soldiers to bring her to face her jailer. And this ship! The British would have taken her to the guardhouse or to one of the British naval vessels in the area if they feared her husband would rescue her before they could capture him.

Captain Barret felt some sympathy for the spirited young woman standing before him. Any other woman would have been reduced to tears over the ordeal. But heeding the warnings that he had been given by Elroy Beeking about keeping his identity a secret until they put to sea, he knew he was not at liberty to answer her questions. "I can only assure you that the gentleman who arranged passage for you holds your best interests at heart."

"How can you say this?" Kellie demanded. "I have been taken from my home and my husband and brought to this ship for some insane reason that you will not reveal. How can you declare that this is in my best interests?"

Captain Barret began to feel rather uneasy. The woman before him did not appear to be a victim of abuse, as he had been told. But what mattered was the fact that he had already been paid a handsome price to hold her aboard *The Wind Mistress*. The gold would go toward the purchase of his second ship. It was far too late in the game to back out now. "There is little more I can tell you, madam. We are about to finish loading our cargo and shortly will anchor off the coast. Late tomorrow evening we shall set sail." He turned around and started toward the cabin door, feeling rather ill at ease.

Fear gripped hold of Kellie with his words. "Captain, where is it that your ship is bound?" she forced herself to ask.

Captain Barret blanched when he heard the fear in her voice. "We sail for London, madam." With this he unlocked the door and left the room.

London. The word echoed in her mind. Running to the door, she tried the knob. She knew that any legitimate exit would be barred her, but she would exhaust every possibility. The door held firm as she kicked and pounded upon the wood, her voice calling out for someone to let her out of the cabin. "You will regret this, Captain," she shouted loudly against the door. "My husband will come after me, and when he does you will all pay." She slumped to the floor in exhaustion.

What was she to do? she asked herself over and over as she sat with her back against the door, her eyes traveling about the cabin. She could not give up. She had to get off this ship before it left Charleston!

Chapter Eleven

Savage arrived at Savage Hall shortly after the noon hour. He had given the morning over to business, and had anticipated spending the rest of the day with his bride. He smiled to himself as he entered the hall. He would never have imagined himself so eagerly seeking out a woman's company, but with each passing day he seemed drawn closer to Kellie. If he was not near her, his thoughts were constantly filled with her image. Many of his male friends complained of boredom with their wives, but he had found the marriage state to be utterly fulfilling. Kellie was exciting, clever, and intelligent. What more could any man ask for?

Not finding Kellie downstairs or in their chamber, Savage sought out Thomas. He questioned his manservant as he stepped into the warm, fragrant-smelling interior of the kitchen where the cook was baking bread and Thomas was inspecting the work of two servants who were polishing silver.

"She was in your study earlier this morning, my lord, but I have not seen her since. Would you like me to search out the hall for her?" Thomas held little concern for his master's wife's whereabouts. He had found over the past months that the new lady of the hall kept herself busy. She was more than likely at some task in one of the downstairs rooms.

"Nay, I have already looked. Perhaps she went to the cottage to visit Lisa Fisher." As Savage turned about to leave the kitchen, one of the stable boys met him at the open door.

"Lord Savage, the lady's horse came back to the stable alone." The teenage boy's features plainly showed his concern.

"My wife went out riding?" Savage asked in confusion. Why would she have left the hall without him? he wondered. They had planned to go together to Moss Rose as soon as he returned from town.

"Yes, sir. She had me saddle her stallion earlier, and she seemed in quite a hurry too, sir."

"Did she say where she was going?"

"No, sir. She just asked me to ready her horse and I gave her a hand up in the saddle." The boy's anxiousness increased in view of his master's frown of worry.

"Saddle a horse and head toward Moss Rose; perhaps she was thrown between here and there. Have the groomsman and stable boys search out the area around the hall." Savage was already rushng through the kitchen and starting back upstairs. Perhaps Kellie had left him a note. There must have been a reason for her sudden leavetaking! Surely she would have known that he would be worried when he came back to the hall and found her gone.

Looking over the dressing table and bureau, he did not find any kind of message. Wondering if he had overlooked something on his desk when he was in the study, he started back out of the room. As he crossed the carpet, something caught his eye. A piece of rumpled paper lay near the wardrobe.

Scanning it, he quickly left the room and hurried out to the stables. He would need the carriage readied for his trip back to town. Perhaps Kellie was still at the tavern. Her horse must have gotten untied, and returned back to the stables where it knew it would find warmth and food.

The note he clutched in his hand indicated that Marie was in enormous trouble, but uppermost in Savage's mind was his concern for his wife.

Hindered somewhat by the bulk of his satin jacket, Savage hitched up the vehicle and was quickly on the road leading into town.

There were only a few patrons in the tavern when Savage went through the front double doors. He spotted Marie near the hearth, where she was busy feeding more wood into the blazing fire.

"Where is Kellie?" he demanded, not mincing

words.

"What?" Marie straightened and stared at him confusedly. "Did Kellie come to the tavern today?"

"You know that she would come here after receiving your note. I only want to make sure she is unharmed. Her horse returned to Savage Hall without her."

"I don't know what you're talking about," Marie replied. "What note?"

"This note." Savage pulled the creased piece of parchment from his jacket pocket and handed it to Marie. "I found it after her horse returned to the stable."

"But I didn't send this!" Marie declared as she looked up with wide eyes into Lord Savage's face. "What does this mean?"

Savage felt as though the wind had been knocked out of him. "You are sure you did not send this note out to Savage Hall?" Even as he asked he knew the truth. Kellie had been lured away from the hall for some reason, and by someone who had signed Marie's name to a fraudulent note.

Marie shook her head. Tears brimmed in her eyes as she confirmed her earlier statement. "I never saw that message before! But who would have written it and forged my name, and why?"

"I am not sure," Savage said, "but I will soon find out!"

"Perhaps we should go to the authorities. If her

horse came back to Savage Hall, she must be in trouble!"

Savage's hand reached out and took hold of her arm. "No, Marie. I will take care of this. There is no need to go to anyone else."

Marie looked at the fancy-dressed and bewigged lord in horror. How was *he* going to find Kellie? Everyone knew him to be a helpless dandy. "But we have to find her!" Marie implored. "Though you are her husband, there are those who are better able to handle such matters."

"Trust me. There are some people I know who owe me a favor. They will find out where Kellie is and help me to regain her." Savage wasn't about to trust the British in Charleston when at this moment he wasn't even sure that they were not involved in his wife's disappearance. No, he would have his own men seek out the information he needed, and he would handle this in his own way.

Something in his voice reassured Marie. As she gazed into his powdered features she was surprised to see a hard glint in his silver eyes that spoke of strength and determination. Slowly she nodded her head. She would give him some time, but he had better find out something soon, or she would make her own contacts. If she had to, she would have the Sons of Liberty and the British looking for her friend at the same time!

"I will send you word as soon as I find out anything." Savage did not wait for her reply but was soon out of the tavern and heading back to Savage Hall.

Kellie lay upon the cot in the cabin and moaned softly. She had been ill since yesterday evening. She had felt a queasiness in her stomach after *The Wind Mistress* had left the dock and anchored off the coast. She had been able to disregard these feelings, though, as her anger over her abduction had kept her in a constant state of rage. It was not until the cabin boy brought her a supper tray in the late afternoon hours, and she glanced down at its contents, that the full force of her illness hit. With but one thought, she fled across the cabin to the washbasin.

After a night and a day of misery, again her supper tray lay untouched. She had suspected over the past few weeks that she was pregnant; now without doubt she knew her suspicions to be true. She had not even gotten the chance to tell her husband, she cried into her pillow, and for the first time in her life she felt totally without hope.

As the first night of her captivity had given way to daylight and then darkness had slowly encroached again, she had seen no one but the cabin boy who came and went with her meals. Feeling weak and spent from staggering to the basin, slowly her hope of rescue had begun to drain away.

Would Savage ever know that he was to be a father? Her tears slipped down her cheeks. She had not seen the captain since yesterday morning, and if she could believe him, *The Wind Mistress* would be setting sail sometime this evening.

For a moment she thought of her father and Aunt Rose and cousin Vern. Would she ever again see their loving faces? Again her thoughts went to her husband. How could she go on living without his love? The fear of the unknown gripped her.

Who was the madman who had brought her to this ship, and why was she being taken to London? And what would happen to her and the child she was carrying once they reached their destination? Her head ached with questions, but no answers could be found.

The message that Savage had been anxiously awaiting came early the morning following Kellie's disappearance. Setting his entire crew to the task of combing Charleston's taverns, inns, and waterfront for any information that might lead them to his wife, Savage had remained at Savage Hall unable to sleep or eat as he prayed that word would come from some direction that would advise him of his wife's whereabouts. This morning, at last, word had been brought to him.

While questioning an old man along the docks, one of his men had been told about a strange sight the man had viewed the morning previous. He had seen two men carrying a canvas-covered item aboard the ship called *The Wind Mistress*. What had drawn the old man's attention was the fact that he had seen the canvas moving and had heard strange, muffled noises coming from the baggage.

"It must have been Kellie!" Vern jumped to his feet with the news brought to them by an out-of-breath middle-aged man, who stood nervously in the study wringing his hat in his hands.

"I be of the same mind, sir," the crewman stated. "That fellow swore that the two men were on the ship but a short time and left the docks seeming mighty pleased with themselves and without the canvas baggage."

"Is *The Wind Mistress* still docked?" Savage questioned anxiously.

"Aye, Captain. She be anchored off a bit in the harbor. But she's supposed to set sail sometime tonight."

"When the men report back today, have them remain in the cave. Ready the ship to sail as soon as the sun sets this evening."

As soon as the crewman left the study to carry out his orders, Vern turned to Savage. "You cannot mean to sail up to the Charleston docks? Why, the British will blow your ship out of the water." Vern had been at Savage Hall since being summoned by Savage the previous night, and he more than anyone else had witnessed the torture that his cousin's husband was going through without knowing where his wife was or how to go about rescuing her; but at this moment Vern wondered if Savage was in possession of his faculties.

"There is no other choice! If *The Wind Mistress* plans to leave Charleston this evening, we will need my ship to give chase."

"And if she is still in the harbor when we arrive?"

"We will anchor down the coastline and approach her in the longboat."

Vern saw Savage's reasoning. It rankled that his cousin could be aboard the ship against her will and unprotected. "Why do we not go now and board her and demand the captain allow us to search his ship? We could gather men together to force the issue."

"We cannot afford to rush into this without thinking the situation out first." Savage rose from his desk and paced about the room. "We still do not know who took her. The British could well have a hand in this. It could be a trap in which they think to catch the Falcon. After all, our marriage was brought about with the accusation that Kellie was a courier. We can only trust that she has thus far been unharmed and will remain so until

371

we can rescue her."

"You think it possible, then, that the governor and Elroy Beeking are responsible for this?"

"I am not sure, but we will find out!" Savage's tone left little doubt in Vern's mind that the ones who kidnapped Kellie would pay dearly for their deeds.

The Wind Mistress rested in the harbor, her decks lit as Captain Barret relaxed in his cabin and waited for the rest of his crew to return from their last night ashore. They would set sail after midnight and by then his last passenger would have been brought to the ship in the longboat.

There was much that the captain wanted to discuss with Mr. Beeking, and most of it concerned the young woman who was locked in a cabin aboard his ship.

The cabin boy had reported to him after each trip to her room and his news each time was not good. The young woman was ill. He hoped it was just seasickness, which perhaps would pass in a few days, but still, it went against the grain to be witness to her harsh treatment.

Aye, he would demand some answers and if they were not satisfactory, he had already made up his mind to return the gentleman's purse of gold and take the woman back into Charleston.

These were Stephen Barret's thoughts as he reclined in his favorite chair with a glass of wine in his hand, when suddenly his cabin door was thrust open wide and several strange men burst in and circled about him. "What is this?" he shouted, jumping to his feet. "Who are you men?" His ship was being taken over, he thought with mounting horror, as Vern and three other crewmen stood around him with pistols aimed.

"Sit back down, Captain," Vern demanded in a tone that left no room for argument.

"Where are my men, and how did you board my ship?" Captain Barret said as he eased his body back into the chair.

"Your men are being held and unharmed, as you had best hope my cousin is." Vern held his finger on the trigger of the pistol that was pointed straight at the captain's chest.

"Your cousin?" Stephen Barret questioned.

"The woman who was brought aboard your ship yesterday."

"But I was led to believe that her life was in danger from her husband. I was not told her family lived in the area and was able to protect her." Captain Barret defended himself as he witnessed the raw anger on the younger man's face. He had known from the start that the woman would be trouble.

"Your cabin boy is taking her husband to her

this minute, and I forewarn you, Captain, if she is harmed in any way, *you* will be the one who is in danger for his life, when you face the one who has the honor of being her husband."

As the cabin boy opened the door and stood back to make room for the large man dressed all in black, Savage boldly stepped into the small room. Instantly his eyes went to the bed. He saw Kellie lying pale against a dark blanket thrown over the cot, and rushed to her side.

Bending down he pulled her into his arms. "Kellie, are you all right?" His voice caught in his throat.

Kellie had finally drifted off into a deep sleep and as she felt the arms about her and her husband calling out her name, her eyes opened slowly and she threw her arms about his neck. "Blakely, is it truly you?" She thought perhaps she was caught up in a dream, but feeling his strong arms wrapped around her, she knew the moment was real. Weeping upon his chest in sheer relief, she cried, "I thought you would not be able to find me! I thought I would never see you again!"

Savage clutched her tightly to him as he felt his chest filling with fury. Always his wife had been fearless in the face of danger. Her obvious distress brought out all of his protective instincts. "You are safe now, my love. There is no more need for tears." He gently wiped at the moisture on her cheeks. "We must hurry, now. The rest of the crew will be coming back soon to the ship, and I wish to be gone before they arrive." It had been easy for his men to overpower the few sailors aboard *The Wind Mistress,* but he would rather not take any more chances while his wife was aboard the ship.

With a gentle hand, Savage started to help Kellie up from the cot. With the movement, Kellie felt her stomach turn in rebellion. She groaned and her hand quickly covered her mouth as she ran to the washbasin.

"The lady has been like this since yesterday, sir. I am glad you came for her," the small cabin boy offered as he watched the couple from the doorway.

Going to her, Savage gently held her shoulders, offering her the little comfort that he could. As she straightened, he dampened the cloth lying by the pitcher and wiped her brow. "You will be well as soon as I get you home." He would send for a doctor as soon as they reached Savage Hall, he thought. Feeling her trembling under his hands, he lifted her into his arms.

Placing her arms around his strong shoulders, Kellie shut her eyes as she allowed her husband to take charge.

"Go to your captain's cabin and tell my men to meet me at the longboat," Savage ordered as he

375

swept past the cabin boy and hurried out on deck. The most important thing at this moment was to get Kellie to Savage Hall. He would deal with the villains who had kidnapped her at another time. His retribution would be known another day, he swore, as he climbed down into the longboat with his precious cargo.

In a short time those of Savage's smuggler crew who had boarded *The Wind Mistress* were in the longboat and rowing the craft back toward the smuggler ship.

Vern had taken only a moment to hug his cousin fiercely to him before taking up one of the oars. His single glance toward Savage as he had stepped away from Kellie implied that he had learned much while in the presence of Captain Barret.

After settling Kellie in the bed in his cabin and being assured that she was resting comfortably, Savage slipped from the room in search of Vern. "What did you find out?" he questioned as soon as he saw him.

Leaving the helm to another man standing at his side, Vern joined Savage at the ship's rail. "It is as you thought, Blakely. Elroy Beeking planned the whole affair. He paid the captain of *The Wind Mistress* handsomely for his help. You had best be cautious, for the British may have gotten wind of your identity as the Falcon. Captain Barret claims to have no knowledge of Beeking's plans for Kellie other than what he was told. And according to him, that was little enough. He thought Kellie in some sort of danger from you, and Beeking was needing passage to London for the both of them to keep her safe." Little of this made sense to Vern, but knowing Elroy Beeking was involved gave him reason to hold concern for Savage and the crewmen of this ship. Many lives would be in jeopardy if the British had discovered Savage's involvement with the patriots and his smuggling operation.

Thoughtfully Savage went over all that Vern had related, but something did not seem quite right. If the British had been the ones who had arranged Kellie's abduction, why were there no guards aboard *The Wind Mistress?* And why had the trap not been sprung that would have proven his downfall the moment he stepped aboard ship? He remembered too well the times that Elroy Beeking had sought to gain Kellie for his own and the feeling persisted that this again was another such ploy. He would look into the matter himself and if his feelings were proven correct, he would settle the matter with Beeking once and for all. He had almost lost Kellie once; he would not do so again.

"Is Kellie all right?" Vern asked.

"She has been ill since yesterday. As soon as we reach Savage Hall I will send for the doctor."

"Is there anything I can do to help?"

"Nay, there is nothing to be done. She is resting

377

now. I hope that it is but a touch of seasickness."

"Kellie, seasick?" Vern questioned with disbelief. "I have never known my cousin to be affected by such afflictions. I cannot remember a day that she has been ill!"

Vern's words did not help to put Savage's mind at ease. Not lingering overlong on deck, he hurried back to the cabin. Gingerly he sat down on the side of the bed and silently watched his wife, who appeared to be asleep.

"I had hoped that you would be back soon," she whispered softly.

A small smile flitted about Savage's lips. So much for thinking her asleep, he told himself. "Are you feeling better, love?" He gently caressed her pale cheek. "When we reach the hall, I will send for Dr. Thomson."

"But there is no need for a doctor, Blakely." Kellie sat up a little against the pillows.

Looking down at her skeptically, Savage shook his dark head. "I will hear no argument, Kellie. I must be assured that you are well."

"But, Blakely, I already know what is wrong with me." Kellie's green eyes seemed to sparkle as she looked into her husband's handsome face and viewed his confusion. She was already feeling somewhat better with the disappearance of the fear and tension of the past two days. Now she could feel some excitement for the news she was about to

378

impart to her husband.

Savage was not sure of her thoughts as she looked at him thus, but ventured softly, "I am sure that your illness is due to the motion of the ship. The water has been rather choppy, but I still insist that you see the doctor."

"You think me to be seasick?" Kellie began to laugh and Savage looked upon her confusedly. "It is not the sea that has caused my upset, my lord, though I do confess it has added to it a small bit." Her radiant smile never left her face as she added, "We are going to have a baby."

For a full moment Savage stared at her as though he had not understood her words. "A baby?" he at last got out, and when she nodded her head, her meaning dawned on him and a large smile slowly came over his face. "Are you sure?" He reached out and gently held her by the upper arms. "A baby?" he marveled.

Nodding her head once again to assure him that indeed there was little doubt, Kellie delighted in the pleasure she viewed on her husband's face. "I would have told you sooner, for I have suspected for the last few weeks, but I wanted to wait until the right moment."

"The right moment?" Savage laughed.

"I guess this is as good a time as any," Kellie said, smiling in return.

"Anytime, such wondrous news is welcomed." He

still could not believe she was going to have his baby. Bending over her, he covered her lips with his own and kissed her tenderly.

Touching her fingertips lightly to his chin, Kellie murmured softly, "I was not sure I would ever get to tell you. *The Wind Mistress* was to leave for London tonight."

"I would have come for you no matter where you were taken. Never doubt my love. No time or place will ever keep us separated." Again Savage thought of Elroy Beeking and in his darkest thoughts, he swore that one day vengeance would be his.

Elroy Beeking was livid when he arrived at *The Wind Mistress* and found that Kellie had been rescued. All of his dreams of power and wealth were dashed once again, only this time he had been so close!

Captain Barret's anger was little compared to Beeking's own. The captain was a fool, he told himself. The man had not even put up a fight to keep the woman aboard ship. He had allowed a group of men to steal aboard his vessel and overpower him and his men. His features held bitter scorn for the captain's incompetence as the man returned to him the purse of gold that was to be payment for passage for himself and Kellie Savage.

There would always be another ship sailing for

London, Beeking told himself as he was rowed back to the dock. Kellie Savage had slipped out of his grasp this time, but there would be another opportunity, he would see to that. He would not return to his family and London as he had left them. Kellie would be at his side and he would still claim all the power and prestige that her wealth would bestow upon him!

It was after midnight when he returned to the dark house that he had thought he was leaving behind forever. As he fumbled with the key in the front door, a note fell at his feet. Retrieving the piece of paper, he glanced around the dark front stoop as though expecting someone to attack him at any moment.

Securing the lock back as he entered, Beeking lit a lantern and hastily scanned the message: YOUR TIME IS DRAWING TO A CLOSE, BRITISH TYRANT! LEAVE CHARLESTON NOW OR ALL YOU VALUE WILL BE BURNED AROUND YOUR HEAD!

The note was unsigned, but Beeking could well imagine who had tacked the message on his door. The Sons of Liberty over the past weeks had been threatening him and other British loyalists, but they had not, since setting siege to his house, ventured to be so bold.

The rest of the night Beeking lay awake listening for any noise which might signal the rebellious band of ruffians returning to his house to carry out their threats. He also thought of Kellie Savage. Her beauty was conjured in his mind; her image constant. Over and over again he imagined the many ways he would make her pay for all he had been put through in his attempts to make her his own. "One day soon, my beauty, one day soon," he swore to the empty bedchamber. "You will be at my mercy and there will be no one to protect you!" His eyes shone with a strange light in the darkened chamber as he savored the image of Kellie standing helpless before him.

The following day Beeking ventured to the governor's house with the request that he be allowed to move to safer quarters, near the military barracks.

Colonel Burch was leaving the governor's study just as Beeking arrived, and seeing the agitated manner of Governor Mansfield, Beeking questioned, "Is there something the matter, Governor? You look a bit disturbed this morning." Beeking was more than pleased that he no longer held the position of governor in this thankless colony. The entire populace had turned out to be a rebellious lot. With the added aggravation of the Sons of Liberty and the Falcon running about the countryside out of control, he indeed did not envy the heavyset man who looked drawn and tired.

"Colonel Burch just reported that his men captured one of those patriots, who they also believe has information about the Falcon and his smugglers." Governor Mansfield wiped at his forehead with a linen handkerchief.

"This could be a lucky break," Beeking stated. "Have they questioned the fellow about what he knows about the Falcon?"

"This traitor had the nerve to point the finger at one of our own!" Governor Mansfield stated heatedly. "The cad dared believe that we would consider a fine, British servant to be a traitor on his word alone!"

"Who is the one that this traitor would point a finger at, Governor?" Beeking would decide for himself how valid the information was.

"It is totally ridiculous! Who would believe that Blakely Savage is the Falcon?" The Governor would have laughed if the situation was not so humorless. The whole matter was but another thorn in his side.

"Blakely Savage?" Beeking stared back at the governor in amazement. "Why the bloke cannot even sit a horse, he is so clumsy!" Beeking's thoughts filled with the image of Lord Savage in all of his puff and finery and a laugh escaped his mouth. Stretching out his skinny frame in the chair before the desk, Beeking pulled off his glasses and wiped at the lenses. "Blakely Savage, the Falcon?"

"I told you it was a ridiculous story, concocted no doubt to throw us off the trail of the real Falcon."

Elroy Beeking thoughtfully nodded his periwigged head and began to formulate a plan. "Do you intend to check out this information?" The humor was now gone from his voice and his gaze was serious as he looked across to the governor.

"Check it out? Why, it is but a farce!" Governor Mansfield was somewhat surprised by Beeking's question.

"But, it is true that there needs to be only an accusation for an arrest to be made."

"You would have Lord Savage arrested?" One thick, gray brow rose over a dark, piercing eye as Governor Mansfield considered Beeking carefully.

"This could be the answer to both our problems," Beeking explained. "You would be able to return to London with your head held up, with everyone thinking that you had sent the traitor known as the Falcon to stand trial; and at the same time Savage would be out of the way and Kellie Savage would be once again free."

"No one would ever believe Savage to be the Falcon!" Governor Mansfield again wiped at his brow as he mulled over all that Beeking was saying.

"None would *have* to believe it. A judge would have the final say; you would be doing what your duty demands."

For a full minute Governor Mansfield did not speak as he thought over what the other man was saying, his hand absently thumbing through the

384

pages of a book that was lying upon his desk. "There would have to be more proof." The governor knew that he would be severely reprimanded by taking such strong actions against a titled lord upon only the word of a criminal.

"Then let us get this proof. I am sure we shall find a piece of black clothing such as the Falcon might wear or a bottle or two of untaxed wine, if we search Savage Hall."

Governor Mansfield began to consider the merits of Beeking's plan. It would certainly solve a lot of his problems. He decided that it was perhaps an opportunity he could not afford to pass up. "We will have to take along some of Colonel Burch's troops to conduct the search and make the arrest. I will also pen a note to Captain Sutterfield to begin to ready his ship for the voyage to England. I intend not to stay a moment longer than necessary in this heathen country. If Savage is arrested, I will be heading homeward tomorrow, if the captain is willing."

This sounded good to Beeking. He also would be aboard Captain Sutterfield's ship, only he would have Kellie Savage as his guest. With Savage out of the way and none to say him nay, he would at last have all that he wanted. What a stroke of luck the arrest of this patriot would be, he told himself. "I will be needing a few soldiers to clear out my belongings from my house. The Sons of Liberty have left me a threatening note, and I thought I would move into the barracks until I leave Charleston." He had almost forgotten the reason for his visit.

"Perhaps your time in the barracks will be quite short indeed." Governor Mansfield rose from his chair. "Let us be about this search of Savage Hall. The sooner we have done with this affair the sooner we can begin to live as civilized gentlemen once again. Once I am shed of these troublesome colonists, I swear, I will be content to sit before my great hearth in my townhouse in London for the rest of my days."

It was not until the late hours of the afternoon that Governor Mansfield could set the plans into motion. With Colonel Burch and a dozen of his men, he started out to Savage Hall to obtain the proof that was needed to declare Blakely Savage the Falcon and to make an arrest.

As the group started out of town, a lone horseman also made his way, but along the coast to Savage Hall, avoiding the main roads.

The patriot who had been captured by the British had been only recently inducted into the smuggler's band. When the man had disappeared shortly after Kellie's rescue from *The Wind Mistress*, Vern had instructed two of his men to make a search of the town and then to linger around the guardhouse in case the man was arrested.

One of the men Vern had sent to Charleston had already returned to Savage Hall with the news of their companion's arrest; the other was riding hellbent from Charleston to warn that the governor and his men were on their way to search the hall.

This news was received by Savage, Kellie, and Vern as they convened in Savage's study to go over the events of the day before. As the man hurriedly announced that the governor and his men were en route to Savage Hall, Kellie could only stare at him in horror. All her fears were being realized. Her husband would be arrested as the Falcon and hanged for treason!

"You have to leave the hall," Kellie exclaimed, grabbing her husband's arm in a frantic attempt to make him take immediate action. "They will be here soon! You cannot be here when they arrive!"

"I will not leave you." Savage wrapped his arm around her shoulder in an attempt to calm her. If the British were coming to the hall to arrest him, there was a fair chance that they would arrest Kellie too, he thought. If he ran now, he would have to take her with him.

"They will be looking for some kind of proof, Blakely," Vern said. "Perhaps I can lead them away from the hall."

"How will you be able to lead them away?" Kellie asked.

387

Savage had followed Vern's line of reasoning and immediately sprang into action. "Kellie, go and get me the Falcon's clothes from my wardrobe. Vern will take the black stallion and ride through town and draw the soldiers' attention. It should not take long for word to come back to the hall that the Falcon has been sighted. With any luck, the governor and his soldiers will be heading back to town before the afternoon has elapsed."

Kellie knew that time was of the essence, and hurried from the study. She was gone only a few minutes before returning with the black clothing of the Falcon. "You will be careful?" she asked her cousin. She would have refused to allow him to take such a risk if she saw any other way out of the situation. All in the small room knew that many lives would be in jeopardy if Savage Hall were to be searched thoroughly.

Vern kissed his cousin's brow and hurried out of the room. Kellie turned to her husband with wide eyes that bespoke her fear.

"Come, love, let us go into the parlor. I will have Thomas bring us some tea," Savage said in an assuring tone. "All will work out fine. Even if the British search the hall, they would have to find the secret passageway to find the cave and the ship."

His confidence helped to put Kellie at ease. Of course the British would not be able to find the lever in the bookcase that opened into the secret passageway. She herself had only found it after careful study of the room and with a lot of luck. "Do you believe that the man the soldiers arrested confessed that you are the Falcon?" she asked, unable to keep the tremor out of her voice.

"If he did, he would have to have been under a lot of pressure. He is a good man. Vern will see that he is freed from the guardhouse."

Kellie was amazed at her husband's answer. Any other man, she was sure, would be condemning the imprisoned patriot. Her courage was bolstered by her husband's brave demeanor and good intentions.

Savage was not as confident as he appeared to be that everything would work out well. He could only hope that the plan for Vern to lead the British away from the hall before they discovered anything would work. If worst came to worst, he would take his wife and those who depended on him and flee Charleston. Even if he were arrested, he held little doubt that his men would arrange for his release, but with Kellie carrying his child, Savage was loath to leave the life he had found in the colonies.

Kellie and Savage were sitting on the settee in the front parlor when a loud knock sounded at the front door.

Bidding the governor and Colonel Burch to wait in the foyer, Thomas announced their presence to Lord Savage.

"Why, send our good governor into the parlor,

Thomas, where he can be warmed." Savage's high-toned voice carried out to the foyer.

As Thomas showed the two men into the parlor, they were met with the comfortable picture of the lord and lady sitting on the small settee before the warm hearth.

"We are sorry to disturb you, Lord Savage," Governor Mansfield began. Now that he was at Savage Hall, he wondered how he had ever allowed Beeking to talk him into conducting a search for the Falcon here. Standing before Lord Savage, he realized how ridiculous the patriot's accusation was. Clearing his throat uncomfortably, Governor Mansfield attempted to shed some light on their visit. "My lord, the fact is that early this morning one of the rebel smugglers was captured."

"Well, this is cause for a celebration, then," Savage intoned. "Thomas, run along and fetch the governor and the colonel a cup for some tea. I am sure they would appreciate something warm after their long ride to Savage Hall to bring us such wonderful news."

Thomas hurried out of the doorway to do as he was bid while Colonel Burch nervously shifted his helmet about in his hands. Thank goodness the governor had come out to Savage Hall to make these wild accusations against Lord Savage. He was glad the job had not been left to him. As on the other night when he had searched the grounds, he felt strangely uncomfortable in Savage's presence. Savage's beautiful wife with her quiet dignity seemed to read his every thought with her fathomless green eyes.

"That will not be necessary, Lord Savage. We did not come out here for refreshments." Governor Mansfield silently berated himself for allowing Beeking to go with the soldiers to instruct them in clearing the belongings from his house. He should never have agreed to allow Beeking to meet them here at Savage Hall. He should have insisted that he ride out with them. Beeking should be the one to state their purpose for being here, the governor thought.

"Of course, you cannot refuse Savage Hall's hospitality." Savage got to his feet and, striding over to the governor, he took him by the elbow and led him to a large overstuffed chair. "Sit down, Governor, and you also, Colonel. You must both tell us all of your news. It is not often that my wife and I have company here at Savage Hall, so I am afraid we cannot allow you to hurry away."

Kellie was as overwhelmed as the other two gentlemen as she watched her husband in action. He put them off of their objective and gave them no alternative but to comply with his wishes as he ushered them to chairs. When Thomas reentered the parlor, Savage made a great fuss of pushing the lemon-colored silk ruffles back from his sleeves to

391

pour their tea himself. He handed both men a fine bone china cup and a small plate of cakes.

As everyone settled back with their tea, Savage took control of the conversation. "So, Governor, you say you caught one of these bandits. I do hope you have set a heavy guard around him. I have had a thought. Perhaps this fellow will be able to lead you to the outlaw known as the Falcon."

Kellie took a deep swallow of her tea to keep herself from gasping at Savage's words.

"Well, Lord Savage, that is why we are here at Savage Hall this afternoon."

"Good, good. I am always happy to help uphold our British laws. My family history dates back to generations of Savage's helping to enforce the will of the Crown. My own father, the earl, will tell King George himself all we speak about this afternoon, for I promise I will pen him a long letter this evening with all of the details."

Kellie marveled at what her husband was about. He was innocently hinting that everything that happened this day would be reported back to the king; she knew the governor had best beware of any accusations made.

Neither Governor Mansfield nor Colonel Burch were in the dark as to Savage's meaning. Men such as this fancy-dressed lord sitting before them held the power to make or break a lesser man with but a single nod in King George's direction.

"Yes, my lord, I see what you mean," Governor Mansfield managed at last. "We will be pleased with all the help you are willing to give us." Even the gold that Beeking had assured the governor he would gain once Kellie Savage was in his hands was not enough of a temptation to make the governor risk his reputation with his peers in London. There was no possible way the dandy in front of him could be the Falcon, and he would not venture repeating the captured patriot's accusation. Beeking would have to go about obtaining this woman in another fashion; he would receive no further help from him!

"So what is it I can do for you two gentlemen?" Savage knew he had them right where he wanted them, and now he drove the point home and slowly twisted the hilt, his silver eyes glinting as he watched the sweat beads appear upon the governor's forehead.

Before Governor Mansfield was forced to reply, another knock sounded on the front door and Elroy Beeking was shown into the parlor. "I see the men are still waiting outside. Good. I thought I would be too late," he announced, taking in with some bewilderment the group having tea.

"Of course you are not too late, Master Beeking. Thomas will bring another cup; we were just having tea." Savage's eyes hardened as they set upon this new visitor. This was the same man who had dared to steal his wife; if not for the fact that at this moment there was more at stake than his own neck, he would without hesitation have jumped to his feet to ensure that a similar threat was never made again.

More pounding came from the front of the house and before Beeking could demand to know what was going on, Savage exclaimed excitedly, "This is surely the most company Savage Hall has had in many a day!"

As soon as he had spoken, a young lieutenant and a soldier barged into the parlor and announced to all that the Falcon had been seen riding through town a short while ago.

Governor Mansfield jumped to his feet with some relief at this news. If the Falcon had been seen in town, there was no need to search Savage Hall.

"Are the men looking for him?" Colonel Burch questioned.

"Yes, sir," the lieutenant replied. "Word will be brought forthwith if the Falcon is captured."

"Colonel, we had best take your men back to town and begin a thorough search," Governor Mansfield declared.

Elroy Beeking's eyes held on Kellie. All the confusion going on around him seemed not to penetrate his single thought to make the woman his own. Once Savage was arrested, he would return to the hall for her and there would be none to stop him.

"Come, Beeking, we are leaving Savage Hall," the governor stated sternly.

"What?" Beeking swung about and faced the governor. "But, the search! What of our plans to make an arrest?"

"Quite so, Beeking, but not here at Savage Hall." Governor Mansfield looked nervously toward Lord Savage and then back to Beeking. "The Falcon has been seen in the township. We will make an arrest as soon as he is captured." He pushed the other man out of the parlor and toward the foyer with the officers following close behind. Savage and Kellie tightly clutched each others hands, knowing that Vern had saved the day. They slowly made their way to the front door.

As the governor opened the door, attempting to get Beeking out of Savage Hall before he insulted Lord Savage, two soldiers pulled their horses to a quick halt before the front of the house.

Colonel Burch approached the men. "Is there word of the Falcon?"

"We found this, sir." One of the soldiers held up a black shirt and a pair of black breeches.

"You found them, you say?" Governor Mansfield stepped down the steps and lightly touched the clothing with a gloved hand. He had seen the Falcon enough times in the past to recognize the black garb. "Where did you find them?"

The soldier looked to Elroy Beeking and then back to the governor. "We found them in Mr. Beeking's wine cellar, sir." The words sounded hollow in the cold afternoon air, as all eyes turned toward Elroy Beeking.

"In my wine cellar? How could you have found those clothes there? How did they get in my wine cellar?" Beeking questioned frantically.

"I say, this is a strange turn of events." The hardness in Savage's eyes now softened and a silver twinkle of pleasure filled them as he looked from the doorway to Elroy Beeking standing in confusion next to the governor.

"We also found this letter, sir." The same soldier held out a piece of paper.

Governor Mansfield quickly scanned the parchment. "Colonel Burch, you will please place Mr. Beeking under arrest!"

"What?" Beeking shouted. "What is the meaning of this? You cannot arrest me! You came here to arrest *him!*" He pointed a boney finger at Savage.

"This letter tells of an arranged meeting between yourself and a patriot spy, Mr. Beeking. In it you are named as the Falcon." Governor Mansfield ignored Beeking's angry words and hoped that Lord Savage would also.

"This is insane!" Beeking declared as a soldier seized him and pulled him toward his horse.

396

"Someone else put those things in my wine cellar!"

Governor Mansfield sighed deeply as the soldiers took a frantic Elroy Beeking away. "I guess we have at last caught our man," he stated as Savage and Kellie watched the happenings taking place on their front lawn.

"Do you think he could be telling the truth, Governor? Do you think those clothes were put in Beeking's house to make it look like he is the Falcon?" Savage said offhandedly.

"This is not a question for us, my lord." He would take the attitude he had earlier planned to take with the lord himself before he came out to Savage Hall. Though he truly doubted Beeking to be the Falcon, he saw this turn of events as a way out of a very ticklish situation. "I will take Beeking and this evidence back to England myself, and he will have time to present his defense." Yes, the idea pleased him well. He would sail on the morrow after having successfully captured the outlaw known throughout the colonies as the Falcon. What greater honor to arrive on his home shores with the Falcon in irons?

"I guess you know best, Governor. My father will be quite pleased with all of your endeavors, as I am sure all of England will be."

When the governor and the soldiers had left Savage Hall, Savage and Kellie fell against each other in relief and happiness.

"It is truly over then?" Kellie laughed between her tears as she leaned against her husband's chest.

Blakely kissed her fully upon the lips. "It is truly over, my love. The Falcon has been seen for the last time. I will be free to give my full attention to my beautiful wife and my child. Beeking and Governor Mansfield will be gone from Charleston, and if all goes well, the Stamp Tax will soon be repealed."

Vern and Marie suddenly bustled in through the front door. "You heard?" Vern asked excitedly. "They arrested Beeking and he and the governor will be setting sail for London on the morning tide!" Vern threw his arms about his cousin and hugged her tightly to him.

After Kellie and Savage explained to the couple the events that had taken place at Savage Hall, Vern told his story.

"It was Marie's idea to hide the note and the Falcon's clothes in Beeking's wine cellar, after she secreted me in her bedchamber." Vern hugged a blushing Marie to his side.

"Oh, Marie, how can we ever thank you?" Kellie exclaimed, feeling some relief at not having to keep the secret of her husband's identity from her friend any longer. Vern had already explained everything to her.

"I will take care of that, cuz," Vern said goodnaturedly. "Marie has consented to be my wife and

I will have a lifetime to thank her."

Amid the congratulations and well wishes, Kellie made her way back to her husband's side. "Everything has turned out so wonderfully. I love you so much, Blakely."

"You are my heart, Kellie Savage. It was fate that we would one day know happiness. I love you beyond mere words, and one day all that we have endured for the name of the cause will bear fruit. This is but the beginning. The people of this land, this land we claim and hold for our children, will know the meaning of the word freedom."

Kellie felt tears sting her eyes as she heard in her husband's voice the depth of the love he felt for her and for the colonies. "My faith is in you, my lord. I do not doubt the truth of your words." The future was their and their children's. They would always stand strong in their love.

Shortly after the governor's return to England, word reached the colonies that the Stamp Act had been repealed. The main force behind the repeal was the English merchants who had presented letters and loud voices before Parliament with threats of riot, rebellion, and bankruptcy if the Stamp Act continued to be enforced. King George himself voted for repeal due vastly to the appeals of the merchants.

399

The colonies experienced a turning point with the defeat of the Stamp Act, which many saw as the catalyst in the fight for American independence. They had held out against British tyranny and won. Their grievances after winning that battle were more easily voiced. Their struggle for liberty was kept alive. There are many unsung heroes and heroines of the American Revolution, people like the Falcon and Kellie, who contributed in the fight to throw off the beastly yoke of tyranny, and won their independence.